Little Hope
By
D. L. Roberts

This is a work of fiction. Names, places, characters and events are either used fictitiously or are the product of the author's imagination. Any resemblance between individuals, living or dead, places, and events is purely coincidental.

ISBN 978-1-4303-1409-7

Book One in the "Little" series by D. L. Roberts
A Little Beagle Guy Publication
Printed by LuLu

For Geneva, Vernon, Gwen, Mitch, Darryl, Scott, Larry, Shirley, Diane, Amanda, Leah, Tana, Micah, D.J., Misty, and Timmy for showing me how wondrous, eccentric, and necessary family truly is.

For Estill, who believes that I can do anything with enough passion for both of us.

For Tina, who made sure I dotted all those Is.

ACKNOWLEDGMENTS

This is my first novel and hopefully not my last. Obviously I owe thanks to all my family and friends and all the unique people I have met along the way who have helped to shape the way I view the world. I come from a long line of storytellers. From walking down the railroad tracks listening to tales of the people who lived up the holler by my Pa, to listening to my Dad describe all the wild details of the different construction jobs he has dealt with, I have become an avid lover of the story in general. My siblings and I, whether telling Bible stories, bedtime stories, or tall tales to get out of trouble, all have inherited the tendency to elaborate, to expand, and yes, even to exaggerate. We come by this naturally. Believe me, if you ever ask my Mom where she got something, you never get a simple answer of "Walmart," there's a story in there somewhere.

I am fortunate to have a husband who was encouraging during the nights when I came home from school and typed on the laptop from ten at night till two in the morning, for which some strange reason is my most creative and productive writing time. He even kept the dogs occupied so that I could put on my MP3 player and drift away unhindered into the world of my book. So for having the time and space to write, I am grateful to Estill.

I am one of the fortunate ones who got past the phrase, "I bet I could write a book." I hope it is up to your liking and that you enjoy reading it as much as I enjoyed writing it.

Packages wrapped in shiny paper
A nightlight and a kiss goodnight
Stars streaking across the horizon
A card and roses after the fight

Ice cream cones and puppy dog kisses
The smell of fresh cut grass at dawn
Teachers, doctors, a policeman next door
Rabbits, eagles, a glimpse of a fawn

Family reunions with chocolate cake
Prayerful voices raised in song
Easter, spring, a newborn baby
Weeks and days that never seem long

Friends and colleagues, a listening ear
Soothing sunsets of crimson and gold
Hugs and caresses, the human touch
Having someone with whom to grow old

Memories and dreams, new expectations
Past achievements and future goals
Life doesn't have to be just jumping hurdles
Instead it can be a companionable stroll

Hope

LITTLE HOPE

PROLOGUE—THE CIRCLE BEGINS

He stood staring at the house, refusing to notice the chill caused by the early morning coolness and the mist that clung to his clothes as the fog hung thick about him. He used his hatred as a blanket. He'd been here for hours, at the edge of the woods, picturing her inside. There was no moon and it was a night so dark the shadows were weighed down to the ground, lying motionless. He had been standing here earlier when a man, her husband, had come out. He had felt the momentary urge to step from the trees as he watched the man load a suitcase into a car. He wanted the man to look his way, to give him a reason to use the knife he held tightly in his hand. But he was cheated out of that release as the man jumped into the car and pulled away without a glance in his direction.

He glanced at his watch and made a decision to move closer. He crept along edges, moving slowly, careful of where he placed his feet, until he found himself standing at the edge of her deck. Bracing himself he held his breath as he placed a foot on the wood of the first step, smiling as the wood held his weight without a whisper of a creak. He moved upward and across to a kitchen window, peering in from the side, the room inside clearly visible from the light left on by her husband. His hand moved toward the window, but he stopped as he noticed the small telltale signs that this window was protected by a security system. He was here on personal business, but he knew that his bosses wouldn't like any trouble that might blow their way. Still, he lingered. He rested his hand on the window listening for a moment, when he thought he heard movement inside. He cursed under his breath and spun around, too quickly, as his leg bumped the porch swing. He almost took a tumble before regaining his balance to jog back to the woods and beyond to his waiting truck.

She had picked up a book, unable to get back to sleep after she had bundled her husband out the door to another conference. She pulled the pillow from her head and raised a hand to smack it into a more comfortable shape, when a chill went up her back. She quietly set the book on her nightstand and tossed the pillow to the side. She leaned forward her ears straining for any noise, which was difficult over the snores coming from the beagle lying on the other side of the bed. "Scout…Scout." She nudged the beagle who opened one eye to blink sleepily at her before he rolled over onto his back and resumed snoring. She told herself that if there had been a sound, Scout would have heard it and been barking in that wild staccato way of his bursting forth with intermittent howling. She told herself this, but the feeling that something was wrong would not go away.

She eased gingerly from bed, not taking time to slip her feet into a pair of Snoopy slippers that were on the floor by her bed. Nor did she think to take the time to pull her gun from the drawer in the nightstand or even to grab the metal baseball bat that leaned again a chest of drawers. Instead she moved barefoot, peering into room after room as she flicked on lights to chase away shadows.

She had begun to feel like an idiot and headed into the kitchen to get a drink. She took a cold can of Dr. Pepper from the fridge and had just raised the can to her lips when a movement outside her window caused her to cough down a swallow as she cautiously moved to the back door. She flipped on the outside lights and scanned the back yard. Nobody was out there, she released a breath she hadn't realized she had been holding, but as her eyes continued their scan, they rested on the porch swing that was ever so gently rocking back and forth. She glanced at the row of wind chimes hanging still and silent from the roof of the deck, and the small windmill that was on the edge of her tomato garden, also still. The porch swing was large and made of a heavy pine. It would take a strong breeze to move the swing, a strong breeze or something else. She knew someone had been outside, and she also knew inside her heart whoever it had been was now gone. The worry that came with this knowledge found a grasp and refused to leave as quickly. She glanced at the spot on the window where her breath had fogged the pane. With half a smile she took her index finger and slowly wrote her name, Hope. She pushed the fear away for a time as she looked at her name written on the glass, and thought back to her mother's explanation of why she had been given it.

Hope was six years old when she developed a very serious illness. It was 1977, and it hadn't been the best year for her. Starting school had not been the wonderful adventure she had been led to believe it would be. The winter was dreadfully cold and gray. Her three older brothers had been locked in the house with nothing to do but invent new ways to torture her. And the cruelest joke of all, her only sister had left home to attend college a thousand miles away. Shortly after New Year's Eve, she got pneumonia. She was lying in a hospital bed, aching with every breath she tried to draw into her lungs, when her Mama lifted her hand and asked, "Hope, have I ever told you how I got my name?"

Something stirred inside of Hope—maybe there was something to live for after all. Then she felt a sense of dread. Hope knew she was dying. This was her final proof. Tears filled her eyes and she sniffled, "No, Mama. I don't think so."

Mama scooted forward and pushed the bangs out of Hope's eyes. "It's quite strange, really, because it happened right here in this hospital, not more than a few feet away. I was the youngest of seven children. Your Grandmamma always felt it was her right alone to choose our names, since she was the one who had to deal with all of the difficulties of having children. She would never give anyone a hint as to what names she was considering. With all six of my brothers and sisters, she had waited until after the birth, looked into the eyes of each one, and chosen the name that seemed to magically form in her heart. She would write the name on a piece of paper, and my father would take it to the nurses so they could write it on the birth certificates."

Hope shifted a little in the pillow, "So Clyde, Bonnie, Agatha, Alfred, Roosevelt, and Sherlock were all names that magically formed in Grandmamma's heart as she looked at her babies?" She squinted as she pictured each of her aunts and uncles.

A smile formed on Mama's lips, "My mother read a lot of mysteries the nearer she got to her due date. I think the books and the drugs pulled the names from her heart."

"I don't remember ever reading your name in a book, Mama."

"No, you wouldn't have. Your Grandmamma was reading a lot of the Bible around the time of my birth, a change in direction for her. She had become somewhat disillusioned with her life and thought she could use a little hope. So she penciled in my name on a piece of paper for Papa to take to the nurses, Heavenly Hope."

"But that's not your name, Mama."

"Well you see, when Papa went to the nurse's station, they had put up a new window between the sick and the nurses. He had to hold the slip of paper up for them to copy the name from. Unfortunately he had his thumb over the H."

"Why didn't they tell the nurses it was wrong when they saw it on your birth certificate, Mama?"

"Little One, there are lots of things that run in this family. We're all proud. We're all honest. We work hard for what we have. We have a sense of humor, and unfortunately we're all stubborn as a mule. There was no way your grandparents were going to admit such a mistake was made, so they pretended they had meant to call me Eavenly Hope. The point is, Little One, you are my Hope, and I know that you are just as stubborn as your Grandmamma and Grandpapa. Be stubborn a little longer. Don't let this illness beat you. Fight it with everything you have."

"Mama, how did I get my name?" Hope's chest still ached, but she pushed it out of her mind for a few moments longer.

"If my mama was right about one thing in her life, she was right about us all needing a little hope. So your father and I agreed to call you Hope, and you know as long as you live you will be our "Little Hope." Remember, hope is the most important thing. Without it people lose their character, their will, their spirit, and eventually everything moral and true. Hope is what keeps us going. Hope is what's important. Don't ever forget that, Little One."

Hope started to get better the very next day. Not even the doctors wanted to argue; everyone agreed that the thing that pulled her through was her Mama, her will—and her hope. To understand Hope's life, one has to understand her Mama. Hope remembered her Mama's words for the rest of her life.   Over the years, however she came to the conclusion that her Mama had left out one characteristic that was in abundance in Hope's family—eccentricity. Many times throughout her life Hope would find herself thanking God that she never inherited that particular trait.

Hope smiled at the memory as she took her hand to wipe the window where she had written her name. She started to walk back to bed when she paused to pick up the phone in the living room. Not even in her subconscious did Hope record the fact that she had picked up the phone before it had rang, nor did she pay any attention to the fact that she knew who was on the other end before a word was spoken. She merely answered, "Yes, Mama?"

CHAPTER 1—GUILT BY ASSOCIATION

Hope knew it was crazy to be driving the seventy-six miles it would take to return home, but her Mama had called with another of her many emergencies. Although Hope was over thirty, her Mama only had to ask and the guilt would literally suffocate Hope into submission. Numerous times she had returned home to look at the weird purple mark on her Pop's hand, take the dog to the vet, talk to the neighbors about the harmful chemicals emanating from their yard, check on a sibling who wisely wasn't answering the phone, and a plethora of other idiotic emergencies that caused her parents to need her on a semi-regular basis.

It never mattered that her three brothers and only sister lived a matter of minutes from her parents. They hadn't inherited the insane guilt gene as she had. Apparently, she had gotten a quintuple dose of it to make up for the rest of her family, for she was currently driving eighty miles an hour at the early hour of 5:00 a.m. because her Mama thought their dog had run away from home, and she wanted help looking for it. This gave her a total of only twelve hours to find the dog and get back home before her husband, Eric, came home and found out she was out doing something crazy for her Mama again. Luckily, he was out of town and hadn't been home to overhear the 4:30 phone exchange over the missing Dachshund, Jaspers. Eric was part owner of a small computer company, who often had to take short commuter flights leaving before dawn only to return later that night exhausted. This morning's meeting was with a firm that was interested in his latest computer program.

As she pulled into her parents' driveway at 6:00 a.m., she noticed that the kitchen light was on. Her father was standing at the front door before she had even got out of the car. "Need help carrying anything in?"

"No, Pop, I didn't bring anything with me. I just came to help look for Jaspers."

Her Pop's eyebrows briefly wrinkled as he scratched the back of his neck. When he shot a quick glance behind him before returning her gaze somewhat guiltily, she knew that Jaspers was not going to be the issue of the day. The sight of the small dog peeping from a window confirmed her suspicions. She sighed heavily as she stepped through the front door, "Jaspers isn't missing is he, Pop?"

Hope couldn't feel any real anger toward her father as she noticed the perpetual smile begin to lift the corners of his mouth. The deep laugh lines had developed from years of constant smiling and working outdoors in the sun, landscaping magnificent creations with his beloved plants. He was tall and thin with a wiry, muscular build from lifting plants and digging holes. His dark chocolate eyes seemed to both plead for forgiveness and laugh in amusement in the same instant. A large calloused hand gently brushed a lock of hair from her eyes. As the smile became fuller, he dropped his hand and simply shrugged. Hope knew that shrug well. Her father was in on whatever Mama was up to, and he seemed to be enjoying it fully, which was usually the case. He had learned a long time ago it was more fun to ride the waves with his wife than drown beneath them while trying to hold her back.

Her Mama came bustling through the kitchen doorway before her father had a chance to answer. "Leave your father alone, Hope. I don't know why you kids always want to pester him before he's had his morning coffee. Come along, Sam. I have your coffee sitting on the table, and I made Hope's favorites for breakfast: biscuits and gravy, pancakes, fried potatoes, scrambled eggs, bacon, and we have a fresh jar of molasses." Hope shook her head as she slowly followed her Mama into the kitchen. Hope had been born two months early and had to be fed every four hours for the first month of her life. She had been a very small child and her Mama had put great effort into "strengthening" her. Being small was no longer a problem for her. She wasn't shaped like a cow, but had curves on her hips and belly that had to be watched closely in order for her to remain curvaceous instead of fat. This breakfast could very well put her over the line, but you just didn't tell Eavenly Hope you didn't want to eat any or all of her food, so instead she tried diversionary tactics. "Okay, Mama, I know the dog isn't missing. Why did you call and have me rush down here so early in the morning?"

Mama turned her attention fully on Hope. "Hope, where's your manners? I know I raised you better than that. Sit down and eat, and then we'll talk." Hope knew she had no choice—you never argued when the topic of manners had been addressed, at least not in this family. One corner of her mouth lifted a little. Hope's face was accustomed to smiling more than any other facial expression. Her deep love for her parents and her innate nature to find joy in life warred against her sleepiness and irritation at the early morning excursion. She stifled her curiosity, knowing that something interesting must be up for her Mama to have told the fib about Jasper's disappearance. In this family, lies were acceptable only in two instances. The first was when it couldn't cause harm, but could only make a situation more pleasant, like when everyone told Aunt Agatha that the bluish tint to her hair was lovely. The second reason had more gray areas, but it was basically acceptable when you had to lie for the greater good. Hope took a bite of crispy bacon and glanced around, thinking that the kitchen might hold some clue to her parents' motives.

The kitchen was one of Hope's favorite rooms in the house. Unlike the living room, bedrooms, and bathrooms, which always had to be kept in a constant state of obsessive tidiness, the kitchen actually had a feeling of being lived in. Fresh herbs grew on the windowsill and a subtle scent of fresh baked pie always seemed to hang in the air. It was a bright room, painted yellow, with an ivy border. Pictures of family and the artwork of Hope's nieces and nephews were tacked up in various locales about the kitchen. The refrigerator and freezer were stocked too full to be considered tidy, and even the shelf containing cookbooks seemed to be well used and cluttered unlike the alphabetized books and videos on the shelves in her parents' library.

The only other room of the house that was not a model for the retired and the anal-retentive was her father's domain, the den. It gave the appearance that the forest had invaded a small part of the house, with books stacked around a once top-of-the-line Lazy Boy recliner, now held together with duct tape. Plants, potting soil, and various forms of plant items were stacked in every available space.

Hope was just getting ready to take the last bite of her eggs when her Mama came over and took Hope's plate from the table and placed it in the sink. Dishwashers didn't get dishes clean enough. "Hope, stop dawdling over your meal. Come here. I want to show you something." Concern flared up for the first time in Hope's mind; never in thirty years had her Mama wanted her to stop eating. She followed closely as Mama led her to the back bedroom. Her concern grew as Mama left the lights off and crept to the window. Her Mama motioned her to the other side of the window. "Our neighbors are drug dealers. Every three days or so they drive off to make a deal and drop off their drugs."

Hope took a deep breath. "Drug dealers, Mama? Come on! You and Pops live in the middle of Mayberry, for Pete's sake! And besides, how would you know what your neighbors are doing? Their house is at least a half mile away."

"That's why I have these." Mama drew a pair of high-powered binoculars from a table near the window. Hope noticed that there were two pairs.

"Mama, why can't you and Pops act like any other normal retired couple? You could be relaxing in Maui or taking a class or something, but no. Instead you take up spying on your neighbors!" Hope turned to leave.

"I can't believe you are so selfish! There are drug dealers living right here, and you don't care. Tomorrow they might approach one of your nieces or nephews and try to get them to try some Mary Jane, some reefer, or some smack. Then would you care?" Mama was talking loudly now.

"Reefer and Mary Jane both refer to Marijuana, Mama." At the lift of her Mama's eyebrows she added, "And no, I haven't ever smoked any; neither will your grandkids. They're too smart. Besides Mama, your neighbors are not drug dealers!" A car started in the distance. At Mama's insistence, Hope walked to the window and picked up the other pair of binoculars. As she peered toward her parent's neighbor's house, she noticed no lights were on. A big burly man stepped out onto the porch. He looked around several times before re-entering the house. After a few moments, he and another man began carrying some packages to the car. Once again looking around, they both got into the car and drove off. Hope glanced over at her Mama recognizing the woman's smug look as she began to gloat. "See, Hope, what kind of person is up at six-thirty in the morning every few days loading the trunk of his car?"

"It could be nothing, Mama," Hope said hesitantly.

"Then why don't they ever use their headlights when they drive off? It's still pretty dark out and this road isn't that easy to navigate even in daylight."

Hope sighed. You couldn't argue with Mama...especially when she had a point.

CHAPTER 2—SUPPORT

"Okay, Mama. You've been up there long enough. Please, come down now. Your shoes are grinding into my shoulders." Hope felt sweat dripping down the back of her neck from the effort it was taking to hold the weight of her Mama on her shoulders. Her Mama might seem quite petite, but when you have a woman standing on you, petite feels entirely like a full sized elephant.

"Give me a couple more minutes. It's hard to see from this window. Hoist me up higher." Eavenly dug her toes into Hope's shoulders in an effort to stand on tiptoe.

"Mama, I'm going to let go! Come down now! If we get caught, I'll get arrested for breaking and entering!" Hope wrinkled her face as her nose began to itch. It was impossible to balance her Mama and scratch at the same time.

"Oh, Hope, you worry too much. We're not breaking and entering. We're just having a look around."

"Mama, there are No Trespassing signs all around this place. They don't allow teachers with criminal tendencies to continue teaching, and pleading insanity won't work because you're the one who's insane!"

A heel roughly grazed Hope's ear, "Oops, sorry about that, Honey. Are you okay?"

Hope grimaced. She knew full well that her Mama had kicked her on purpose. "Mama, I swear if you don't come down now, I'll let go!"

"Oh, hush, Hope. You wouldn't believe the horrible things they have in this house!" Another toe pointed deep into her shoulder and Hope almost lost her balance as her Mama shifted her weight.

Curiosity got the better of her. "What is it, Mama? Do you see any drugs?"

"No, but there's a pile of laundry that must be at least two weeks old, and there's a banana peel and a half filled container of milk sitting out on the counter spoiling." This was finally too much. Hope dropped her hands and let go. Eavenly quickly grabbed the windowsill and started kicking at the wall to keep from falling.

"Hope Angel Rhineholdt, you help me down this instant or...eiyah, " Eavenly stopped mid-sentence as she lost her grip with her left hand and found herself hanging from her right.

"You're only about two feet from the ground Mama. Go ahead and drop." Hope smothered a giggle, "And I've been married for five years, Mama. If you're going to try to scare me, it's Hope Angel Rhineholdt Jamison." Hope jerked around quickly as she heard a twig snap behind her. Sam Rhineholdt seemed to be having trouble deciding whether a glare or a smile would be more appropriate as he quickly took in the situation. Eavenly glanced down as she too had heard the snapping sound.

"Sam, look at what your disgraceful daughter has done to me! Come and get me down from here!" Hope almost started to laugh at the sight of her father trying to gingerly lower her Mama from the windowsill while he got kicked and smacked by his wife who was too afraid to let go. With a final tug by Sam, both of Hope's parents found themselves slung to the ground. At this point, Hope could no longer contain the laughter from erupting, but she quickly stifled her amusement at the sound of a car approaching from the road. Hope's parents must have also heard the sound, for when she looked back to the spot on the ground where they had fallen, they were no longer there. A flash out of the corner of her eye confirmed that the couple was running into the section of trees that bordered a corner of their land. She was surprised at the speed the two were able to generate and wondered briefly if fright or a healthy exercise regiment and vitamins were the most likely source of her parents' energy. Hope started to follow them when a car door slammed behind her and a deep male voice called out, "Excuse me, ma'am. Could we help you?"

Hope closed her eyes and said a short prayer before she turned to face the owner of the voice. If this was to be her last moment on earth, she prayed that on her tombstone there would be a note of the fact that her parents' insanity and cowardly desertion were chief contributors to her short life. Hope smiled at the angry-looking gentleman moving toward her. Hope had become accustomed to being noticed at an early age. She had always been attractive, but not what anyone would call a classic beauty. It was something more difficult to explain that caused people to pause for a second or even third glance as they passed her on the street. Her hazel eyes, with a golden star pattern surrounded by a darker brown and green were quite normal, but when she looked at you they seemed to see more, to sparkle brighter, to shine from an inner source rather than merely reflect the light. Her smile was too crooked to be used in an ad by any orthodontist, the right corner of her mouth always rose higher causing a small cluster of dimples on one side, and her teeth though white and straight were not the perfection found from caps or braces. However, the smile beckoned to any who saw it and often people found it impossible to not return a smile of their own, feeling a little happier from the brief exchange. She knew that she was caught.

Although he looked angry, the man moving toward her appeared to be an average type of guy. His blond hair was cut short in the latest style, and his muscular build was enclosed in casual Dockers and a Tommy Hilfiger shirt. His companion, on the other hand, could easily have been awarded a role in the latest Stephen King film. Although he wasn't grotesque in any way, his height was intimidating. He was well over six feet tall. He, too, had blond hair stylishly cut, but his bulging muscle mass was not as casually concealed in his clothing. It was the scar that zigzagged across one cheek that first shook Hope's reserve, but it was the unmasked menace in his eyes that had her stumbling for a plausible reason to be standing in their yard.

"Hi…my name's Hope." She cocked her head to the side, in what she knew to be a cute, endearing manner. She purposefully aimed all the charm she could muster in the direction of the two angry gentlemen. "Your neighbors, the Rhineholdts, are my parents. You wouldn't by any chance have seen a small daschund around here anywhere, have you?"

Both men seemed to deflate as they smiled, "No Ma'am. Would you like for us to help you look for it?" Hope felt the rush of relief. She was used to men offering to help her with problems. Now that she was on familiar ground, her heart lightened and her sense of humor returned. Luckily, she wasn't the only one who was gullible enough to fall for her Mama's story.

CHAPTER 3—SEARCHING FOR ANSWERS

Hope returned to her parents' kitchen after spending two and half hours with their neighbors, Bob and Jake Smith, looking for Jaspers—who wasn't lost. She was feeling very irritable due to the fact that she had spent a good part of that time walking in circles through the woods including briars and bushes, and climbing steep inclines which were infested with mites, chiggers, fleas, ticks, and unreasonably hungry mosquitoes. She hadn't realized that the two men would have been so dedicated to searching for her lost dog. She had originally had no intention of spending such an arduous time trying to make them believe her small lie. Maybe, she had thought to herself, that was how God had decided to punish her for trespassing and lying to the men. During the hike back to her parents' house, Hope had grown more irritable and frustrated that her Mama had placed her in another bad situation. She fumed as she pictured Mama rushing up to her begging her forgiveness as she opened the kitchen door.

She was hot, sweaty, and her shirt had a tiny tear. Her already red face was inadequate to express her anger as she walked into the kitchen to find her Mama baking a cake and her father sitting at the table reading the newspaper while drinking coffee. Mama only briefly glanced at her before returning to her cake. Hope felt her pulse beating in the side of her neck. They didn't appear to be the least bit concerned, or guilty, and Mama was definitely not begging her forgiveness.

"Are you insane!? Leaving me alone like that with two drug dealers? I could have been killed, or raped, or sold on the white slave market. I'm your own flesh and blood, and you left me!" Hope really didn't believe she had been in any danger, because she didn't believe the Smiths were really drug dealers, but she wanted her parents to feel at least a little guilt for the situations they had gotten her into so far today, especially since it was only nine o'clock in the morning.

"Oh hush, Hope. You didn't think they were drug dealers in the first place, and Honey, you're a little plump to sell for much on the slave market. Besides, your father and I watched you through the binoculars until you started home. What were you doing roaming around with those men all over the place, anyway?" Hope's Mama returned to placing cherries in the center of the pineapples she had lining the bottom of the cake pan.

"I told them you had lost Jaspers, and that I was at their house looking for him." Hope filled a glass full of ice from the door of the refrigerator and held the cool glass to her face.

"Tsk, did you really think that they would fall for that? I mean who in their right mind would be out at six-thirty in the morning in order to look for a dog. You've given us away. They know for sure that we're on to them now. Really, Hope, you should have come up with a better lie than that." Eavenly turned from her cake to see Hope leaving the kitchen and heading in the direction of her car. "Well, what poor manners! Can you believe she just walked out on me like that, Sam?"

"Huh…What?" Sam looked up from his newspaper with a look of consternation.

"Never mind, Dear. Just go back to your paper." Eavenly returned to the cake she was baking for Hope—pineapple upside-down cake was Hope's favorite—and so she didn't see the wide smile that had spread across Sam's face, but she didn't need to see it after forty years of marriage to know it was there.

"Since you think all of this is so funny, why don't you drive down to the Dairy Queen and have her come back home. You know she'll eat an entire banana split and ruin her lunch if you don't hurry." Eavenly sighed as she heard the kitchen door click behind her husband.

She knew she was right about where Sam would find Hope, as she had been right about so many other things in her long life. Her intuition was stronger and more accurate than the average person's. It bordered on the psychic if one believed in that kind of thing. Her

Mama had it, her aunts and uncles had it, and her children had it, especially Hope. And for that reason Eavenly knew this would not be the end of their interaction with their suspicious new neighbors. Something bad was going to happen, something very bad, unless she did something to stop it.

Eavenly crossed over to the counter to pick up the cordless phone. She dialed the number she had memorized for the county sheriff's office. The other line was picked up immediately.

"County sheriff's office, can I help you?" Justine Wells, the sheriff's secretary, had a grating voice with the ability to send shivers up and down Eavenly's spine.

"I need to talk to the sheriff." Eavenly spoke quickly in order to keep the conversation with Justine as short as possible.

"I'm sorry, the sheriff isn't available at this time. Is there a crime you would like to report? Would you like to talk to…"

Eavenly cut her off sternly, "This is Eavenly Rhineholdt, and I want to talk to the sheriff right now!"

"Oh, I'm sorry Mrs. Rhineholdt. I didn't recognize your voice. I'll patch you through to the sheriff's car. He's on his way to Lincoln Holler to check on some alleged cows blocking the road."

It was only a few moments before the sheriff's voice came on the phone. "What do you need, Mama? I'm kinda busy."

"Now is that any way to talk to your Mama, Mike? I want you to come for lunch today. I have something important to talk to you about, and you better show up." Eavenly turned the phone off.

Fifteen miles away, Mike glanced down at the radio in his hand and grimaced at the sound of the phone disconnecting. He took a long breath and smiled to himself as he muttered, "Don't count on it, Mama. You don't just boss the sheriff around."

Justine beeped him on the radio again, "I'm patching Mrs. Rhineholdt through again, Mike."

"Don't do that…" Mike was too late. He heard his Mama's voice crackle across the radio.

"And Mike, if for some reason you decide not to listen to your Mama, I'll just have to keep myself busy by telling your wife, Kathy, about that wild trip you took to Vegas the week before your wedding, when you were supposed to be out fishing with the boys."

"But, Mama, I was fishing with the boys!"

"Who do you think Kathy will believe?" The radio went dead again as Eavenly once again hung up.

Mike glanced at his watch. He was going to have to rearrange his schedule in order to make it to Mama's for lunch. The anger began to rise in his throat at the thought of three of his deputies and Justine listening to his conversation with his Mama on the police wire. It was humiliating for anyone to hear how his Mama bossed him around. It was no consolation that everyone else in town would bow to her wishes even more quickly than he had.

"Damn, Mama. Why couldn't you have just bothered Hope?" He swerved the wheel quickly to avoid ramming the cruiser into one of ten cows blocking the road. He stepped out of the car glaring at the cows.

"Move... yaw... yaw." He screamed and waved his hands at the congregation of bovines. They continued to moo and chew the grass at the sides of the road.

Mike removed his hat and scratched his head. Somehow he felt this, too, was a problem that should be blamed on his mama. "Damn Mama and damn these cows!" Mike pulled his gun from its holster and fired, reloading twice even though the cows had scampered off before the first magazine had been emptied. He turned to go back to his car when he heard a loud splat and felt his foot sinking into something soft. As he glanced down, he once again felt the anger that had been only slightly released by the firing of his gun. "Shit, Mama!" he said, and indeed it was.

CHAPTER 4—LITTLE SISTER

D r. Kate Burns tiredly wiped a lock of blonde hair out of her face as she turned the corner in her shiny blue Mercedes. She had just conducted a difficult operation on one of her young patients who had managed to run his four-wheeler through a plate-glass window. Thanks to Kate's skill, he would pull through fine, and the scar where a large piece of glass had been imbedded into his chest, nicking his heart, would be minimal. Kate felt that ice cream to celebrate was in order. Thanks to a very active metabolism, Kate could eat anything she wanted without gaining an ounce of weight, and thus far her non-health conscious diet had not affected her cholesterol or anything else negatively.

As she pulled into the Dairy Queen, she noticed her sister Hope's Jeep in the parking lot and pulled along side it. Through the Jeep's window she recognized her sister's familiar silky auburn hair that seemed cutely styled, even though she knew it probably hadn't been anything but finger combed this morning. Hope was drumming her fingers on the steering wheel. Kate, knowing her sister's concern with weight, guessed that Hope was deciding whether or not she should go inside the Dairy Queen. Kate walked around her car and leaned against the passenger side as she smiled down at her younger sister. Surprised hazel eyes met her gaze, and Kate noticed that the normal accompanying smile was missing. "So Hope, you want to tell me what Mama's done so early in the morning to make you look so agitated, or should I order us both a double banana split first?" Kate knew that Hope would have a difficult time turning down her favorite ice cream dessert.

"That woman drives me crazy sometimes!" Hope's lower lip trembled in agitation. "She woke me up at 4:30. I drove down here barely avoiding a traffic ticket. She stepped on me and kicked me in the ear. She's spying on her neighbors, who probably think I'm crazy. I spent hours climbing around in the weeds looking for Jaspers who wasn't even lost; and if Eric hears about this, I'll be divorced for sure!" Hope had been in many plays, both in high school and college, and she was using every ounce of the dramatic skill she possessed to share her frustration with her sister, anticipating the reassurance she knew Kate would give.

Kate readjusted her purse on her shoulder and leaned in toward Hope, "Come on, let's go in and get an ice cream. It will be my treat." Sympathetic blue eyes looked into hazel ones.

Hope looked up at her sister and smiled, "Extra chocolate syrup and cherries, right?"

"Of course."

A stranger watching the two women walking towards the door of the Dairy Queen would have found it difficult to discern a family resemblance between the blue-eyed goddess who walked with natural grace and the dark, full-figured, smiling young woman who seemed to exude energy. However, the expressions on their faces were identical as Sam pulled into the parking lot. Kate put her arm around Hope's shoulder as Sam walked up to them. "Daddy, I don't care what Mama told you when she sent you here. Hope and I are both going to go into Dairy Queen and consume a huge banana split each."

Sam scratched his head as he took in the firm stance of Kate and the slouching shoulders of Hope. The smile so much like his youngest daughter's spread across his face, "Extra chocolate syrup and cherries?"

Some of the protective tension left Kate's shoulders as she nodded suspiciously at her father.

Sam held the door open for his daughters. "Sounds good. I'll treat—but I think it best if we don't mention this to your Mama." The smiles the three exchanged were identical in intent.

Kate led the group and turned back toward Hope. "So, did I hear you say Mama kicked you this morning?"

Hope nodded. "I was holding her up to see through the neighbor's window, and she kicked my ear."

Kate suppressed a giggle. "Well, I believe that deserves extra whipped cream and nuts then, doesn't it?"

Sam seemed to perk up. "She fell on me and knocked me to the ground after Hope left her hanging."

Kate's forehead furrowed. "Well, I guess we'll get you extra whipped cream and nuts, too. Why don't you both tell me what's going on after we eat."

With piles of ice cream happily settled in their stomachs, the three felt more at ease as Kate leaned forward. "So what's going on?"

Hope sighed, "Mama and Pop seem to think that their neighbors are drug dealers."

Sam interrupted, "That's not entirely true. Your Mama thinks that they are drug dealers." Both Hope and Kate looked at their father in surprise at this show of dissent, but the surprise turned into consternation with his next words. "I personally think they're international jewel thieves…and I have proof."

Hope turned wide eyes to her father, "What's your proof?"

Sam looked smug as he pulled out his wallet and removed three shiny green gems. I found these this morning by their front steps before I came around back and saw you dropping your mama from a window."

Kate picked up the three gems and looked at them closely. "Pop, I hate to tell you this, but these aren't emeralds."

Sam frowned, "What are they then?"

Kate hesitated, "I'm not sure, but I think I know someone who could find out. I'll take them to Scott at the lab and see if anyone there has any idea."

CHAPTER 5—FOOD FOR THOUGHT

Hope reached under the table to loosen the button on her jeans while keeping an eye on her Mama to make sure she didn't notice. She had only managed to eat half of the fried chicken, mashed potatoes, soup beans, greens, and fresh-sliced tomatoes that had been piled onto her plate, but she felt that it was going to take a miracle to finish the rest. Kate smiled knowingly at Hope as she reached for another spoonful of mashed potatoes. Her amazing metabolism had already burned away the huge banana split.

Hope had already listened to her brother grumbling about cows and his new boots for the first part of the meal and was waiting for him to somehow find a way to blame everything on her. She and Mike had a somewhat strained relationship ever since she had moved away from home. Mike talked around a huge bite of chicken and reached for another leg as he glanced accusingly over at his youngest sister, "So Hope, what's this I hear about drug smugglers and you dragging Mama and Pops down to the neighbors snooping around?" He had wanted no part of Mama's investigation of the next-door neighbors and had been irritable during most of lunch. "Can't you ever visit without causing a commotion? How would it have looked if I had to arrest my own sister and parents for trespassing?"

Mama reached across the table with a wooden spoon and rapped Mike hard on the knuckles. "Where do you think you are, talking with your mouth full like that? Let me tell you something, Michael Daniel Rhineholdt. The day you try to arrest me or your little sister will be the day your father will find another use for his belt besides trying to hold up his pants. We should have spanked you more as a kid. Then maybe you wouldn't have grown up to be so hardheaded."

"Sorry, Mama." Mike rubbed his knuckles and looked grumpily at Mama. The events of the morning, first with Mama making him sound foolish on the radio, then the cows, and the fact that his brand new boots were ruined, had made him more impatient than normal. "I just get worried sometimes, you know. You and Dad aren't exactly that young anymore, and you shouldn't let Hope drag you into these things all of the time."

How anyone could believe she was the instigator of her parents' crazy schemes was beyond Hope's understanding. The fact that her brothers blamed her for her sense of responsibility to her parents was one of the major reasons Hope had moved seventy-six miles from home. Her brothers believed if everyone just ignored her parents then most problems would just disappear. This was a theory that Hope agreed with in principle, but she had not yet been able to find the backbone to refuse her parents anything. Maybe it was because she was a Cancer and felt the need to nurture and take care of her parents. Or maybe it was just because her Mama managed to make Hope feel so guilty she always caved to her wishes.

Kate noticed the sudden slump to Hope's shoulders and the lack of sparkle in her eye. She glared at Mike. "You know as well as I do that Hope isn't the one who starts these things. Mama would have you running over there right now peeking in windows if she hadn't felt it was more important for you to keep the township safe from crazed cows. Thank God, we all have jobs. Has it escaped your keen cop sense of observation that the only time Mama goes off on one of her hair-brained schemes is when Hope is on vacation from teaching? This past Christmas, it was the fake Santa with a criminal record getting information from kids so that he could break into homes during the holidays. Last summer, it was crazy Mr. Harris who was stealing supplies from the school and selling them back at a profit. If Hope ever starts working at a job with less predictable days off, you would find yourself dealing with a real crime wave, so just back off, Mike. Besides, if you believe anyone could stand up to Mama's manipulation, especially a sympathetic sap like Hope, you're crazy."

Everyone's eyes darted straight to Mama. It wasn't everyday someone said she was manipulative and that she had hair-brained ideas, and for that person to be one of her own children sitting at a table full of Mama's food was unheard of in the history of this family. Eavenly looked at Kate with an expression Hope was shocked to see. Was that admiration she saw on her mother's face? Could what Kate have said been true? Now that she thought about it, it did seem that most of her vacations were spent with one crazy event after another, whereas she never seemed to have the same problems during the school year. She started to say something when Mama rose from her seat. Mama smiled at everyone, and the tension in the room seemed to evaporate. "For dessert I made pineapple upside down cake. I'll be back in just a second. Mike, apologize to your sister. You seem to have made her lose her appetite. I've never seen her eat such a piddly amount before. Kate, don't be absurd. I never plan things around Hope's vacations, that's just when things seem to have happened in the past. Now, if you think you have room for cake with all the ice cream most of you ate, we'll begin dessert."

Mike quirked an apologetic smile in Hope's direction as Mama went into the kitchen for the cake. "Sorry, Hope. I know none of this is your fault. I haven't been having such a great a day so far, but I shouldn't be taking it out on you. Those new neighbors of Mama's were in the station the first week they moved in asking about trespassing laws, police patrols, and neighborhood security. They didn't seem like the friendly type. Hell, they might decide to sue or press charges if they find out you guys were snooping around their house. I reckon Mama's really stepped in it this time."

Sam's eyes widened. "By the smell of your boots sitting by the door as we walked in, I would say that you've stepped in something, too, Son."

Mike blushed, embarrassed for the third time that day. "There was a problem with some cows. I was craving something a little stronger than ice cream myself after Mama embarrassed me on the radio again this morning."

"Yeah, how does she know about the ice cream anyway, Dad? She always seems to know exactly what we've been up to. She always has. What gives? Does she have spies throughout the county or what?" Kate nudged her father lovingly.

"Well, as for ice cream, it isn't too hard to figure out that Hope is going to be at the nearest ice cream stand as soon as she gets upset. She's done the same thing since she was old enough to ride her bike into town. As for the rest, you know that she just knows things, always has. Hell, she knew I was going to marry her before I ever had the nerve to ask her out, and she knew if you were all going to be boys or girls long before ultrasounds could give that information. She just knows things."

Hope shifted uncomfortably as she listened to her father ramble. Kate laughed, "That's silly Dad! She can't just know stuff."

Mike grumbled, "Bull! She knew about me going to Las Vegas before my wedding. Heck, all I did was go to a few shows."

Sam looked at his son shocked, "I thought you were out fishing with the boys."

Mama walked back into the room at that moment. "Fishing, heck, I didn't know that's what they called it. Maybe that's what he was doing when he was pushing those dollars into those girls panties." She set the cake on the table. "Cake anyone?" She glanced around the table at her family. Mike looked a little green around the mouth. Kate's hand covered what looked suspiciously like a smile. Sam looked decidedly embarrassed and seemed to be avoiding looking at any of the females present. The use of the word panties at the kitchen table was one of the few things he never expected to hear from his wife, much less in connection with dollar bills being tucked inside. Hope handed her plate to Mama, "I'll have a slice." She smiled as she took a huge bite, her appetite fully restored. For once, it wasn't her life Mama was messing with. It was Mike's. Besides, Hope couldn't pass on Mama's pineapple upside down cake.

Later, as Hope drove past her parents' new neighbors' home, followed closely by Mike, she was feeling decidedly better. Ice cream and cake had a way of doing that to her. She noticed the two men who had helped her look for the not-lost daschund this morning sitting on their front porch. She smiled and waved even though she doubted that they could see her from the distance their house was from the road. However, they did notice that it was a police car that was following Hope. A certain amount of concern followed this realization as the memory of Hope's arrival on their property occurred this morning around the same time they had lost three rocks that they had still been unable to locate. And since there weren't any other houses in that direction, they could also see that the police car was coming from the Rhineholdts'. They could see it and wonder why the Rhineholdts would be talking to the police.

CHAPTER 6—HOME

Hope's tires squealed as she pulled into her driveway. No blue BMW in the drive meant that Eric hadn't made it home from the airport yet. She rushed in the door and ran into the kitchen before the assortment of bags and containers could fall out of her hands. She took a second in her rush to thank God that Kroger had a deli department. Hope had picked up a baked chicken and an assortment of other vegetables and side dishes that would give Eric the feel of a nice home cooked meal. She handed her beagle, named Scout after the character in the Harper Lee novel, a cheeseburger she had picked up from McDonald's. Eric didn't feel that they should feed the dog human food. However, Hope had a hard time looking into his brown puppy dog eyes without caving in. She felt pathetic that even the dog could manipulate her, but, hey, what was she to do?

Hope had just finished transferring all of the food into a variety of Furio plates and pans, shoved the Kroger containers into the trash can, and sprinkled some flour on the counter so that the kitchen looked cooked in when she heard footsteps in the hall. She quickly grabbed into the drawer for a weapon. "Stand back or I'll let you have it!" She screamed as a masculine shape came around the corner.

Eric stopped the act of drying his damp hair with a towel and glanced at the spatula in her hand. He leered at her with a wicked grin, "What were you going to do with that, spank me?" He moved closer to her and enveloped her in a hug and affectionate kiss. "Anytime you want to let me have it, I'll definitely take it."

Hope shoved at his broad shoulders. He looked younger than thirty-five with his black hair damply tussled and his blue eyes laughing. Hope removed herself from his embrace. "Where did you come from? Your car wasn't parked in the driveway!"

Eric frowned at her. "Not exactly your warmest welcome, Honey. The car wouldn't start so I had it towed to the shop and took a cab home from the airport." He glanced around at the food. "Wow, you work fast."

Hope felt as if she could actually feel her head growing warmer from the speed of which the wheels were turning in her head. "You didn't look in the oven and fridge when you came in, did you?"

"Nope, you know how long flights make me feel. I went straight to the shower. Why?"

"Oh, that's where the food was. I started cooking earlier, but I ran out of tarragon and had to run across to the store for some more. Everything is ready if you're hungry." Hope glanced down and saw Scout eating the remainder of the cheeseburger. She grabbed Eric and gave him what she hoped was a long enough kiss to allow the beagle enough time to wolf down the evidence.

Eric smiled. "Wow, a home-cooked dinner and what a kiss. You've got to be the best wife in the world."

Hope sighed and silently thanked God for allowing Eric to be so gullible. "Yeah, you're the lucky one. Why don't you go pick out a movie, and I'll bring our dinner into the living room so we can eat while you relax."

The living room looked like several different people had decorated it. One wall was completely covered with bookshelves. The shelves contained an array of books ranging from several of Hope's old books she had read as a child to current interests. *The Canterbury Tales*, sat perched between Grisham's *The Chamber* and a well-worn volume of *The Cove*. Steven King and J.K. Rowling were shelved next to *Don Quixote*. One section of books focused on famous artists and another section was filled with various computer manuals. Several snow globes and music boxes decorated small openings amidst the books. One shelf contained a stack of board games. The center of the shelves held a hundred-gallon aquarium with several brightly colored salt-water fish swimming laconically along. A stone fireplace took up one corner of the living room. An entertainment system made of cherry housed not only a large television, sound system, VCR, and DVD player, but several different video game systems, which had cords draped around controllers in a haphazard fashion.

Picture frames were on every available wall space. Several copies of famous prints were tastefully framed and hung about, but most pictures were of family members and different places that they had vacationed, taken by Eric, whose hobby was photography. Mama always complained at the cluttered, messy look of Hope's house. Although it was very clean, shoes were often lying around wherever they had been discarded, Scout's dog toys were strewn from room to room lying about waiting to be stepped on, one corner was stacked high with old vinyl albums, and newspapers were stacked two feet high waiting to be placed in the recycling bin.

Eric and Hope had met at a basketball game in college. They were each surprised to discover the wide array of interests of the other: camping, going to plays, watching stand-up comedians, a love of movies and literature, and dancing. Hope knew that she was in love with Eric from the first moment they met, but she was convinced that he was the one for her after everyone in her family decided they liked him, which was a first. Mike couldn't even dig up a speeding ticket on him when he ran a background check. Eric didn't stand a chance once Hope had made up her mind. They were married one week after their graduation. Hope had earned both her Bachelor's degree and her Master's in a hectic three years in order to graduate when Eric did. Her wedding present to him had been the house and the car.

It was during their honeymoon in the Bahamas that Hope first told Eric of her financial situation. Basically, due to the shrewd investments of a great-great grandfather in businesses like Coca-Cola, ATT, General Electric, and Ford Motors, no one in Hope's family would ever have to work for a living, though they all chose to. Those closest to her great-great grandfather said it was almost as if he could somehow predict what businesses would succeed and which would fail. The family shared a yacht and a few vacation homes spread in several choice vacation spots. Mama had instilled a good work ethic in all of her children, and all five of them, like their aunts and uncles before them, chose jobs in which they could give back a little of their blessings to the community.

Hope had chosen to teach in one of the most destitute high schools in the state. She worked with some of the more "challenging" students in what was lovingly dubbed the "rabbit hole" because of the warm and nurturing environment of her classroom. It was stocked with books, many of which she gave the children to keep, and plenty of couches and chairs for reading purposes. Not wanting to induce jealousy in other teachers, she claimed she had found a generous benefactor and then made contributions to the school in the fake benefactor's name. Annually, she contributed over twice the amount she earned to purchase supplies for not only her classroom, but also for the school, especially the out-of-date library and English department. She was motivated not only by concern for the kids but also by respect for her fellow teachers who managed to do a grueling job with low salaries and very rare recognition.

Hope carried dinner into the living room and wasn't surprised that out of their immense video collection of over three hundred DVDs that Eric had opted for *Jaws* again, but how anyone could watch the same movie once or twice a week was something even a movie buff like Hope couldn't understand.

After dinner, Eric fell asleep on the couch watching the video. Jet lag had finally caught up with him. Hope draped a blanket over him, turned the security system on, and carried a book she had started earlier to bed.

Hours later, Hope awoke from sleep with a start. She sat up and jumped as the book she had been reading thumped on the floor. She glanced at the clock and saw that it was two a.m. Hope listened to the quiet, trying to discern what exactly had awakened her. Scout was asleep beside her, with his head on Eric's pillow, snoring loudly. No sounds came from the rest of the house. Hope got up feeling a real urgency that something was very wrong. She checked on Eric who was still sleeping contentedly on the couch. When the phone rang, Hope grabbed it hurriedly.

"Hello?" Hope's breath caught in her throat.

Kate's voice was calm as it relayed the events of the night to Hope. Kate was always able to keep calm in any event.

"I'm on my way." Hope set the phone on the hook as Eric sat up on the couch.

"Honey, what's wrong?" Eric moved to cradle Hope in his arms, sensing her distress.

"Mama and Pop's house is on fire."

CHAPTER 7—FIRE

Eavenly and Sam had gone to bed early after the day's long events—both sound asleep by nine. The shrill piercing wails of several smoke alarms going off at the same time jolted them awake, as smoke grew thick in the air. Sam crawled to the door with Jasper in one hand and Eavenly close behind. He felt the door and was relieved to note its coolness before pulling it open. Both hurried to the front door stopping only to grab Eavenly's purse, which contained her cell phone, and a couple of jackets from the hall closet.

Once they were outside, they could see the flames leaping through the air circling around the sides and roof of the garage. A breeze fanned the flames and the smoke circled as it wisped heavenward. The garage was attached to the large two-story home, and the flames had already begun to move toward the wall that connected them. Sam could see smoke continue to blow into the open upstairs window immediately over the garage where moments earlier he and Eavenly were sleeping. Sam handed Eavenly the dog as she quickly called 911. He then hurried to the garden hose and started spraying water on the quickly spreading flames.

Within minutes, they could hear sirens as the fire trucks made their way down the road. Sam had paid to have a fire hydrant installed at the end of their driveway. It took only minutes for the trucks to start pumping water onto the hungry flames. One fireman separated from the group and ran over to Eavenly, quickly searching through her purse. After finding the car keys, he ran into the garage backing out both cars and moving them a distance from the flames. If either gas tank had exploded, the house would have become a fiery skeleton. Mike pulled into the driveway closely followed by Kate. He had called his sister the moment he had heard the news on the dispatch. They both rushed to where their parents were standing and watched as the firemen worked to get the blaze under control. Finally, almost an hour after the fire alarms had awakened the Rhineholdts, the fire was extinguished. The fireman who had moved the cars from the garage walked over to the group, a look of serious concern on his face as he handed the keys back to Eavenly. "You guys okay?"

Sam nodded, keeping an arm around his wife's shoulders. "What about the house? How much damage was done?"

The fireman glanced at the smoking garage and then looked back to Sam. "The garage and everything in it's ruined. The rest of the house seems to be okay except for the smoke and soot. It will have to be aired out and most of the items inside will have to be cleaned." He ran a hand through his hair as the fire chief started toward them.

"Luke, what the hell were you thinking getting into those cars like that? You're lucky they didn't blow up with you inside. I never saw such a foolish thing."

Luke glared back at the chief, "I know it was dangerous. I also knew I had time. If I hadn't moved them, the whole house would have been lost."

Another fireman approached the group carrying a few soggy items. "Chief, we found what we believe to have started the fire. We found the remains of a couple of gas cans, some oily cloths, and a couple of cigarette butts lying beside the garage."

The Rhineholdts all glanced at each other in surprise.

Luke fingered the materials before glancing up. "Chief, we're going to have to label this one an arson."

The other fireman stiffened. "Whoa, Luke, don't jump the gun here. We don't have any evidence that points to anything but an accidental fire."

Luke grimaced, "Chief, you remember I told you I liked to start fires as a child?"

The chief nodded at Luke. "Yeah, I remember. That's the reason you said you joined up."

Luke glanced over at Sam and Eavenly. "These are my parents, and this was my house. It has more fire safety features then any other house in town. Pops put a smoke detector in every room of the house, and ever since I was six, he's locked up things like gas for the lawn mower and any other dangerous chemicals in that shed over there." Luke pointed to a small shed sitting a few yards from a greenhouse. Both were a hundred yards from the house.

The chief looked over at Sam. "It's been a long time since Luke was six. Did you start leaving gas cans in the garage?"

Sam looked offended. "I have grandkids to think about. I've always locked things like that away. There weren't any gas cans in the garage."

The chief nodded, "We had a small field that caught fire a few weeks ago. We figured it was a couple of kids playing around and things got out of hand. Maybe they've progressed to something a little more dangerous."

Mama stepped forward. "I doubt kids are responsible for this. I have a feeling…"

Mama's words were interrupted as a shape flew toward her from the driveway yelling loudly, "Mama, Pops, are you okay? Oh my God, what happened?"

Mama moved forward putting her arms around Hope. "It's okay, Dear. We had a small fire, but everything's going to be okay. You know all the important stuff is locked up in a fire-proof safe, and your dad, Jaspers, and I are just fine." Eric caught up with his wife giving Sam a sympathetic pat on the back.

The chief nodded as he started to move away. "You guys have had a difficult night. Mike, Luke, I'd like to talk to both of you first thing in the morning. Mr. and Mrs. Rhineholdt, I'm sorry about the fire. My men will make sure everything is under control before they leave. For now, I would suggest you both go home with one of your kids and get some rest."

Mike, Luke, and Kate started to shift nervously on their feet. Hope was too busy hugging Mama and looking at the still smoking garage to notice their stares, but Eric wasn't. He had been a member of the family long enough to know how the story was going to end, so he decided to save them all time. "Mama, Pops, why don't you guys come home and stay with us. We have plenty of room, and Scout and Jaspers get along well enough that they'll have a fine time."

Sam beamed at his son-in-law. "Thanks, Eric. That's a fine offer, isn't it, Evy?" He glanced up to see his wife, daughter, and dog already heading toward Hope's Jeep Grand Cherokee and started to follow.

Eric glanced over at his sister-in-law and brother-in-laws who were all looking relieved. "I guess we'll talk to you guys tomorrow."

Kate quickly hugged Eric and patted him on the back. "You're a good one, Eric. Hope's lucky she found you. Tom would be in a snit if I showed up with my parents in tow for who knows how long. I'll call tomorrow and hire an agency to begin cleaning the house and rebuilding the garage."

Eric nervously scanned the faces of his brother-in-laws. "What do you mean for who knows how long?"

Mike stepped forward, "Kate's teasing, Eric. It won't be more than a week, maybe two."

Eric frowned as the others began walking to their respective cars. He liked Hope's parents. He knew that within a week Hope's father would have the yard looking amazing and everything in the house that needed fixing would be fixed. Sam was a lot handier about repairs than he was. He also knew that it wouldn't take a week of Eavenly rearranging their house to drive Hope crazy. He was startled from his thoughts by the honking of a horn. Mama had one hand through the window on the horn, one holding Jasper, and her exasperation was aimed entirely at him, "What are you dawdling for? Do you think I want to be standing out here in nothing but my gown and a coat all night so that the whole county will have time to come take pictures? What's wrong with you boy? Hurry up!"

Eric sighed as he realized his estimation might have been wrong. It might take less than a week for craziness to settle into his normally peaceful home. A cough seemed to come from the woods near the house. Eric glanced at the woods but didn't see anyone nearby. He thought the firemen must have been checking to make sure no stray sparks had made it to the woods. The horn honked again, and he hurried to the SUV without glancing back at the woods. If he had, he may have noticed the two shadows that suddenly detached themselves from the others and started moving deeper into the woods.

CHAPTER 8—MORNING

Hope awakened to the blaring screams of Marilyn Manson. She sat up straight in the bed looking around dazedly. She turned to Eric who was lying, now awake, beside her. "What the hell is that?" she croaked.

Eric listened for a second, and the volume of the music became discernibly lower. "Sounds like your mom is trying to figure out how to work our stereo." He leaned over to give Hope a kiss, but she raised her hand and pushed his face away. She flopped back into a fetal position and mumbled from her pillow, "Not until we've brushed our teeth. Damn Mama, couldn't you have put on some classical music?"

Eric and Hope were once again startled as their bedroom door was thrown open, and Mama entered, angrily waving a CD case. "Have you listened to these lyrics? This guy is mental! How could you listen to such trash?"

Eric glanced confusedly from the CD case in Mama's hand to her angry face. "I like the music. I don't really pay any attention to the lyrics."

Mama huffed, "Buying things like this just makes these loonies more accessible to children." She turned and started for the door. "Hurry up and get out of bed. Breakfast will be ready in twenty minutes."

Hope called to her before she left the room. "Mama, in the future it would be a really good idea to knock on the door before you come into our room. Eric and I could have been lying in here naked or something!"

Mama looked back over her shoulder and laughed. "I doubt that—not with your dad and me staying in the house. You're the most wary child I could ever have had. Get up and come eat breakfast." With that she bounced out the door.

Eric inhaled deeply, "What's that smell?"

Hope tried to burrow deeper into her blanket. "Just guessing, I would say enough biscuits and bacon to feed an army. Don't you have to leave for work soon?" Hope squinted at the clock, but the numbers were too fuzzy to read without her contacts.

"That's the good thing about being part owner. I can call in when I need to. I figured I would stay home today and help your parents get settled. The guys and Kelly can handle anything that comes up for a few days."

Hope rolled over and gave Eric a kiss on the cheek. "Have I ever told you that I'm crazy about you?"

Eric laughed, "Yeah, but I know you just want me for my body. Let go, I need to take a shower before your Mama comes back to check on us." Eric walked into the master bath. Soon, water could be heard running, but not loudly enough to drown out his baritone rendition of *I'm Too Sexy*.

Hope pulled his pillow over her head and snuggled back down into the bed. A few minutes later her eyes snapped open as she felt something crawl across her foot. She sat up throwing the blanket off of herself to find her dad smiling at her from the foot of the bed. Tickling Hope on the feet had always been one of her father's favorite strategies for waking her up in the morning. "About time to get up isn't it, Little Girl? After you get dressed, I want you to come out back. I found something I want to show you."

Hope sighed as she watched her father walk from the room. She got up and grabbed some shorts and a top, just as Eric came from the bathroom smelling of Old Spice and Irish Spring soap. He leaned toward her smiling. "I've brushed now."

Hope grumbled, "Yeah, but I haven't."

"I don't mind." Eric grabbed her and pulled her close giving her a kiss and a hug before letting her go. He winked at her as he walked to the closet.

Hope walked into the shower beginning to feel slightly more awake as the hot water sprayed over her body. She noticed a slightly smoky smell as she began to wash her hair, and the events of the night before came rushing back to her. Hope was really worried about her parents. It seems they were getting involved in something dangerous.

She pulled on her clothes and after noticing the bedroom was now empty, she followed her nose to the kitchen. Eric and her father sat at identical plates stacked high with pancakes. Plates filled with biscuits, bacon, and gravy were strewn across the table, along with a serving pitcher of homemade maple syrup, still hot from the stove. Eric smiled up at Hope and pulled out a chair for her. "Guess what I found out, Honey? Not all pancakes come from mixes. Your Mama says these are something called 'made from scratch pancakes.' You wouldn't know anything about them though, would you?"

Hope glared at Eric. Mornings were not the best time for her to be teased. "Laugh it up, Goofball, but don't get used to it, because I'm not getting up an hour early just to make you breakfast. I know how to make pancakes—I just don't. I told you before we were married—I don't do breakfast."

Mama turned from the stove eyeballing Hope. "Hope, what in the world are you wearing? Those clothes look like rejects from the Salvation Army."

Hope looked down at her ragged jean cutoffs and her faded Scooby-Doo T-shirt. Though not something she would wear to school, both were clean and comfortable. "Don't start with me Mama. You and Dad aren't exactly the statement of fashion wearing Eric's and my sweats."

Hope's sweats were baggy on her petite mother and a good foot-and-a-half too long. The cuffs and sleeves had both been rolled up several times. "We look this way out of necessity. I assume you dress the way you do out of choice."

Eric winked at Mama. "It's okay, Mama. I think she looks kind of cute, myself."

Hope glanced over at her husband, her eyes full of love. The conversation swayed to more peaceful topics, and the food quickly disappeared. Sam got up from the table and took Hope's hand. "I was out looking at your plants this morning, and I found something I want to show you," he said as he led Hope into the back yard. He walked toward a tree several yards from the house and then hunkered down. Hope came up to his side as he pointed to a small hole in the ground filled with wiggling fur. "It's a rabbit's nest. Looks like there's four or five little ones in there."

Hope started to reach toward the baby rabbits, but Sam gently took her hand. "You don't want to touch them or their mama won't take care of them anymore. I just wanted to show you so that Eric could maybe not mow around this area until they leave." As he stood up, they both noticed Scout walk over to see what they were doing. The beagle looked down into the hole and sniffed before wandering over to the tree and hiking his leg. He then went over to the shade and promptly went to sleep. Sam grinned over at Hope, "I don't know how you've done it, but somehow you've convinced that dog that he isn't a dog."

Hope smiled at her father. "Keep it down, Dad. It would break his heart to find out he isn't human."

Eric came up to both of them. "Hey, Sam. While you're here, I was wondering if maybe you could help me out with a project. I was wanting to build an arbor with a swing in the middle of it for Hope, but I'm not really sure where to start."

Sam seemed to grow taller at the thought of a project. "You want to cover the arbor in flowers, and you want a long swing like on most front porches?" At Eric's nod, Sam's smiled widely. "Well, you and I could do something like that in just a day or two."

Eric patted his father-in-law on the back as everyone started walking back toward the house. "I'm glad to hear you say that. I thought maybe we could go shopping and you could pick out some lumber and plants for me, while Mama Rhineholdt bought some new clothes. You guys can't run around in sweatpants the whole time you're here."

Eavenly was standing a few feet away on the back porch and had heard Eric's suggestion. "Eric, that's a wonderful idea! I'll just go get my purse and things."

Eric leaned over to Hope as Sam followed his wife inside. "I figure that will give you at least two or three hours if you want to go back to sleep."

Hope smiled up at Eric. "You know, if we were in the army, you would have won a purple heart for this. My parents are nightmares to go shopping with."

Eric walked into the house calling over his shoulder, "Love and war, it's all about how you protect your loved ones."

Hope turned to call for Scout. No matter how human he acted, she didn't trust him to stay out alone with a bunch of baby rabbits. Last summer he had scared a chipmunk to death trying to get the thing to chase him. Besides, it wouldn't be long before Jaspers came in search of Scout, and she had no doubts that Jaspers would find the bunnies interesting.

Just as Hope and Scout entered the kitchen, she heard the doorbell ring. Walking into the living room, she threw the door open wide. Standing on the front step was a tall, handsome man in his late thirties. His hair was a little too long in back. He was muscular, and even though it was summer, he was wearing black slacks and a long-sleeved black shirt. His smile was disarming as he looked down at Hope. She began to smile in return until she opened the storm door and the odor of tequila hit her full force. The man was obviously the source of the smell. Hope glanced to her driveway noticing the shiny black Porsche sitting empty behind her Jeep. Images rushed back to Hope from high school. She once again saw the bloody forehead and slashed throat of her best friend Amy who had been hit by a drunk driver. She had spent three days waiting in the hospital for Amy to recover, but she had died from her injuries on the fourth day.

Before the man had a chance to react, Hope had pulled her arm back and swung with a hard punch that knocked the air out of him as it landed squarely in his stomach. Hope turned and walked back into the house. As Eavenly, Sam, and Eric were coming down the hallway, ready to go on their shopping trip. Eric looked over at her tight mouth and still fisted hands. "Honey, who was at the door?"

Hope ignored everyone's concerned looks and went into the bathroom to splash some water on her face.

Sam, Eric, and Eavenly all walked out onto the front porch to find the man gasping and dry heaving over the porch's side railing. He turned as he heard the storm door shut behind them. His smile was weak, and he looked very pale in spite of his tan.

Eavenly rushed forward, Sam at her side. Sam took the man by the arm to help him walk inside. "What in the world happened to you, Ty?"

"Hope seems to have been working on her right hook. If she had been that good in school, none of us would have had to worry about her, Pops." Ty grimaced as his stomach clenched in pain. He wouldn't be surprised if his kid sister hadn't left a few deep bruises. This was going to be harder than he had thought.

CHAPTER 9—STAY ALERT

Hope ignored the confused voices belonging to her parents, brother, and husband, which were emanating from the living room. She slipped out the kitchen door accompanied by both Scout and Jaspers. She began to run toward the thick expanse of forest that lay on her property and several acres beyond. After ten minutes, she began sweating and feeling the burn in her chest; she slowed her pace to a moderate jog. She entered the wooded area and continued to jog along a barely visible path, which led her through a tangle of foliage where she leapt over several obstacles including fallen trees and a small stream.

She found herself in a part of the wood that was dark and cool even though somewhere above the trees overhead a warm sun was shining down. She bent over, kneading a calf muscle, regretting not having warmed up before her spontaneous run. She continued to knead the sore muscle, and as her breathing slowed, she became more aware of her surroundings. Hope loved the scent of the woods. The combination of pine, cedar, and leaves refueled her spirit. She also loved to sit under a tree quietly watching whatever wildlife decided to wander into her view and listening to the gentle chirping of the birds. Hope realized that the woods, however, were especially quiet today. In fact, she couldn't hear any birds singing at all.

She turned quickly looking down the path she had just traveled as she heard a stick snapping somewhere behind her. She noticed that both Scout and Jaspers had lagged a long way behind and were busy sniffing around the foot of a pine tree. She felt more than saw the shadow that fell on her shoulders from behind. Hope realized she should have been paying more attention to her surroundings as she steadied herself to face her attacker. A smile spread across her face as she felt the familiar surge of adrenaline that was all part of this game she often came to the woods to play.

The muscular man lunged at approximately the same instant Hope turned. Without thinking, Hope twisted, using surprise and a quick hip-toss that sent him sprawling. Hope took a defensive stance as she eyed her opponent now lying unmoving on the ground. A furrow of concern creased the smooth skin of her brow. She dropped her hands and walked quickly forward, kneeling to gently shake his shoulder. In mere seconds, Hope, unsure of how it had happened, found herself on her back with the man's body covering hers in a way that prevented her from moving. She swallowed and her eyes widened as she felt the cold edge of a very sharp knife pressed against her neck. Tears began to fall quickly from her eyes and her shoulders began to shake with her sobs.

Hope watched as the man's dark brown eyes crinkled. He ran a hand through the short gray hair that was styled in a short military buzz and quickly closed the knife, putting it inside his pocket. "Ah…hell," he muttered as he stood and offered Hope his hand. "I didn't mean to hurt you, Doll. You okay?"

Hope smiled as she took his hand. "Fine," she said as she shifted her weight and used her body as leverage to pull the man down in a flip so that once again he was on the ground and she was the one standing. Hope laughed as she mimicked his earlier actions and leaned towards him with the offer of a hand. Laughing, she teased, "I win, Joe!"

Joe Salinger laughed back at her as he took her hand and pulled himself to his feet. "Doll, that crying shit would never work in a real attack. You cheated."

Hope turned and continued to follow the path through the woods. "I'll concede a tie." She tossed back over her shoulder.

Joe smiled as he knelt to scratch Scout's head. Both dogs had hurried back to their master when they heard her cry out, but sensing no real danger to Hope they had both sat by and watched the tussle. "Your master cheats, Scout, but she's getting better." Joe chuckled as he and the dogs followed Hope further into the woods.

CHAPTER 10—JOE

If Colonel Joseph Salinger was to sustain a cut, he would undoubtedly bleed red, white, and blue. He had served his country faithfully in many of its conflicts, both those the general public were aware of and those they weren't. A marksman of unequalled caliber, he could blend into any environment, and survive for months with nothing more than his knife and wit.

Five years earlier, Joseph's wife, Maggie, had died a long painful death as one of the many victims of cancer. Joseph had spent more time by his wife's side during those last, painful months than he had in the thirty years they were married. It was after her death that guilt fully hit him. As he was going through her belongings, he discovered for the first time an array of interests and hobbies he had not been part of. He had loved his wife dearly but had not really shared much of her rich life with her, nor had he shared in the lives of his three children, now adults. Watching them ensconced in grief at the funeral, he paused to wonder if his own passing would wreak such sorrow, or if they would grieve as they would for a familiar figure they had known but with whom they had not been close.

He had wanted to reach out to his children at that time, to hold them and comfort them, but he was unsure of how to reach them through their grief. Maggie had always been the one to wipe away tears and dispense hugs.

He had soon found himself too often tracing the rim of a half empty glass of whiskey as if in doing so he could trace his life to the point where he had lost sight of himself. He retired from the Marines with the purpose of finding out who he was beyond the uniform, the gun, and the blood he had so often spilled onto the earth.

After two years, he was closer to becoming an alcoholic than he was to finding the elusive part of himself for which he was searching. He had decided to start afresh and sold everything, purchasing a house a few miles from Hope's home, separated by the acres of forest which lay in between.

On the second day in his new home, Joe began to jog through the woods, a morning ritual he had began in the service and had never allowed to lapse. His mind had started to wander to the dark spot dedicated to his grief over his wife. He was so focused inwardly that he had not noticed the woman half in and sticking half out of a hollow log, until he had tripped over her legs and fell head first into a thicket of briars.

He brushed himself off and stood to find the top end of the body pulling a beagle pup out of the log. The young woman quickly jumped up at the sight of him and rushed forward, the puppy wrapped firmly in one arm. She started to brush off a few twigs he had missed and seemed to be trying to assess the damage, "Gee, I'm sorry, mister. Scout got stuck plumb at the other end of that old log. Are you okay?"

As Joe looked into the warm hazel eyes with the quirky smile plastered beneath, he felt something stir inside. Warmth seemed to spread through his veins. Being an accurate analyst, he quickly tried to decipher the specifics of the feeling. The woman before him was definitely attractive, though younger than he normally liked, and that smile both sweet and mischievous at the same time could definitely be a turn on. She held the puppy and herself in an innocent way that made him feel the need to protect her, and the sparkle in her eye reminded him of a time when he was twelve and friends would come to the door asking him if he wanted to play. He didn't believe in love at first sight, and now that he had time to think about it, he really wasn't attracted in that way, but there was something about her.

As a giggle erupted from her lips, it dawned on him that this woman was so full of life that it seemed to shimmer in a halo around her. He realized he had found what he had needed. He had found someone to show him about the part of life that was about enjoying searching for your dog in the woods without fear that a stranger would be anything besides a potential friend. He needed to learn about the part of life where the blood coursed through your veins with the feeling of pleasant expectancy.

Joe held out his hand toward the woman in a stiff attempt at a handshake. "Hi, my name's Joe."

Another giggle erupted, as she looked him up and down, "Well hello there, G.I. Joe. My name's Hope, and this is Scout."

Joe looked down at his clothes and remembered that he had pulled on an old pair of sweats, boldly informing everyone that he was "Property of the U.S. Marines," combined with a pair of combat boots. He began to laugh himself, a little rusty at first, then more fully. "Hope," he thought to himself, "what a perfect name."

CHAPTER 11—SOLACE

A log cabin, secluded in the woods, had been included when Hope and Eric had purchased their house. Eric had not been interested in the cabin, and though he knew Hope used it as a getaway, he himself never used it. Though he was an only child, the time he had spent with Hope had made it easy to understand why she felt such a need for a private place. They very rarely could enjoy a peaceful night at home without the phone ringing and some long conversation with a Rhineholdt family member ensuing. It seemed that the phone intentionally would peel into the silence if Hope was cooking, sleeping, or bathing. If they took the phone off the hook, and turned off their cell phones, it would not be long before someone was at the door checking on their well-being. This great bounty of love and protectiveness was reassuring to Hope at all of the bleak moments in her life, so she bore it well, never wishing to hurt the feelings of others.

However, she spent such a great amount of time at school, with her family, at church, at neighborhood events, and charity functions, often being the center of attention, that her natural energy seemed to ebb. Hope automatically turned up a notch in the presence of others, so once a week or so, she would go to the cabin for solitude and time to recharge.

Hope as a child had often longed for a tree house like the one her brothers had shared, but she never was allowed one, and only managed to sneak into her brothers' once, so she loved the one-room cabin the moment she laid eyes on it. She spent thousands of dollars having it renovated to include electricity, running water, a bathroom, and small kitchenette. One wall was covered with bookshelves. A record player sat in one corner with old forty-fives lying in piles on the floor. Most of the living space was occupied with two large, extremely comfortable couches and one coffee table, all strategically placed so that she could read by the light of the windows or comfortably watch a fire burning in the fireplace. Trees were removed to create a small grassy clearing, a hammock hung between two nearby trees. A few weeks after Hope had first met Joe Salinger, she had come upon him lying in that hammock, one of her books lying across his chest. He had jumped guiltily to his feet and apologized. Hope's first reaction had been an immediate feeling of anger that her private sanctuary had been invaded, but she had always been highly intuitive about the feelings of others, and there was something so sad and hopeless about Joe that instead of displaying her anger, she found herself waving off his apology and inviting him to use the cabin any time he wished. She understood the almost sedative quality of the cabin secluded in the woods, and felt that Joe was a man who needed peace brought into his life and a sense that this was her responsibility found footing in her soul.

They began meeting weekly at the cabin and the friendship had grown. They found they enjoyed many of the same books and had similar taste in music. Hope had yet to beat Joe in a game of chess, but she was not an easy opponent to beat. Hope cherished this new friendship and kept it secret, except for the sad discussions she had with Eric about Joe's painful past. Joe was the first person that was a part of her life that her family knew nothing about, and Hope felt the fact that it was a secret only made the friendship dearer. She was sure that her family would find this gruff and sweet man lacking in qualities they deemed necessary in any of her friends. The fact that he had such little to do with his adult children's lives would be reason enough to cause Mama to dislike him instantly, and changing Mama's opinion was a chore.

It was the cabin where Hope led Joe on the morning she had punched her brother in the stomach. He could tell immediately that something was wrong.

"So are you going to talk to me about it or is it a secret?" Joe attempted an unconcerned tone.

"What are you talking about?" Hope's voice was much more defensive than Joe had heard before.

"Come on…you're never this quiet. You haven't said two sentences to me since you flipped me back there in the woods." Joe brushed his hand through his short hair, as was his habit.

Hope bit down on her bottom lip. "I punched my brother in the stomach this morning."

"What did Mike do to make you mad enough to hit him?" Joe knew a lot about Hope's family, even though they had never heard of Joe. She often shared stories of her family's deep love and delightful wackiness. He had met Eric on the rare occasions when he had accepted one of many invitations to dinner, and he had understood from the phone calls from Hope's family that often interrupted the meal and from the gentle bantering on Hope's end of the conversation that her irritation at the constant demands for her time was always deeply laced with familiarity and jest.

"It wasn't Mike—it was Ty." Hope flopped down on one of the couches.

"Ty? I thought Ty was the one you got along with the best."

"I did until he showed up at my house drunk this morning, driving his new car."

Joe sat down beside Hope. He knew of Hope's aversion to anyone drinking and driving, but sensed more was going on here. Hope, as far as he knew, had never hit anyone before. "Is there more?"

Hope sighed. Her worry was almost palpable as she looked into his eyes. "When I opened the door and saw Ty standing there, I had one of my feelings. I felt that somehow Ty's being here is going to cause pain to someone I love."

Joe knew enough about Hope's "feelings" to know why she was worried. Hope sometimes got a strong feeling that something would happen…and then it always did. He tried to reassure her. "Maybe it's just that you were angry because he was drunk."

A tear fell from Hope's eye as she slowly shook her head. "There's more…there's death. Someone's going to die."

Joe stared out the window, allowing time for Hope's words to sink in. He was not a superstitious man, but he believed that his young friend at times had an insight that was uncanny, almost psychic. The fact that she had a premonition of pain and death was not something he took lightly. Hope had been in a few close scrapes in the past, and Joe had done everything he was capable of to ensure she was as safe as possible. He had started giving her self-defense training after a student, under the influence of drugs, had shoved her into a locker bruising her ribs. Later that afternoon, a gun had been located in the student's locker. The student had not been one of Hope's, but Joe had begun to worry about her safety. Images of Columbine had flashed through his head. Eric had quickly agreed that self-defense training was a good idea.

He turned back and walked over to the couch, plopping down beside Hope. "Why are you so sure that this isn't just stress over the fact that you're upset with your brother for drinking?"

Hope raised her head. Joe noticed that her irises appeared almost black instead of their normal sparkling hazel. He glanced around to see if something was casting a shadow over Hope. He turned back to her at the sound of her anguished whisper.

"Joe, I know this sounds strange, but I don't think something bad is going to happen. I don't *think* that someone is going to die. Somehow I *know* it. That's crazy isn't it?"

Joe put an arm around Hope and gave her a fatherly squeeze. "You're not crazy, kid. In the bush, I've seen men develop an uncanny sixth sense. Some people are more attuned then others. I guess God made them that way, so it must be for a purpose, right?" He felt Hope's shoulders rise in a shrug and continued to hold her. Again he glanced toward the window. A sad smile appeared on his face. "Don't worry, Hope. I won't let anything happen to you or your family. I have a few connections yet. We'll find out what's going on." He felt Hope's breath on the side of his neck, as she let out a sigh of relief. Joe's smile faltered. The irony, he thought, was that the person who had finally enabled him to come to terms with a life away from the violence and isolation of his past was going to somehow pull him back into danger because of their friendship. Joe had found a surrogate daughter in Hope, and she had taught him what responsibility came with such emotions. The angles of his face appeared to sharpen and become more severe. Joe had killed in the past for his country, and he knew that if he had to—he would kill again—for Hope.

CHAPTER 12—EXPLANATION NOT NECESSARY

Eric sat on the back porch sipping a cappuccino, waiting for Hope's return. Her parents and brother Ty had left over an hour before to take care of the shopping items Eric had suggested earlier that morning. Eric eyed the wooded area behind the house with concern. As well as he knew Hope, the idea of her ever physically hitting someone was absurd. The fact that she had punched Ty this morning was deeply unsettling. He knew that Hope had probably spent the majority of the time she had been gone talking to Joe. A smile lifted the corner of his mouth at the thought of what a change her friendship had wrought in the man.

A less confident person might have felt jealousy at the friendship his wife shared with another man, especially if he had grown up with as many stepmothers and stepfathers as Eric had, all a result of both his parents' infidelity and promiscuity. Eric, however, had known from the moment he met Hope that her loyalty and commitment could not be shaken. He trusted her completely and believed in his heart that the two of them were soul mates, destined to be together for eternity. It was this faith in Hope that allowed him to never question her reasons for feeling such a need to help Joe with the obvious pain he had been carrying, although at first he did question the motives of the man she had befriended.

Being a computer wiz came in handy. Within a half hour of Hope's telling him of the strange new neighbor to whom she had decided to allow free access to their cabin, Eric had run a check on Joe

Salinger. After confirming that he was a retired US marine, it took him two more hours to read through the files he found on the man, many marked confidential and buried in mainframes belonging to the government that Eric had skillfully hacked into.

The man's record was impeccable. He had won every medal the government awarded, some multiple times. Eric also read the obituary for Joe's wife and noticed that his phone records indicated that Joe didn't have very many contacts, even with his own children. He had decided that Joe seemed like an okay guy. A few dinners with Joe and he had come to care about the older man himself. After the incident with the student who had attacked Hope at school, he was delighted that Joe was teaching Hope self-defense. He knew he would not stand a chance in getting Hope to switch schools or quit teaching, and when he suggested her need to be more careful, she had become defensive. Joe had supported Eric and suggested the training, at which point Eric had decided that he really liked the man.

A movement out of the corner of his eye caught Eric's attention. Scout and Jaspers came running up to him with Hope following closely behind. He handed her the mug of chamomile tea he had made for her, which was luckily still warm. She smiled as she took a sip and sat down next to him. They sat quietly watching the dogs playing in the yard while Eric gently massaged the muscles in Hope's neck with his free hand. Hope leaned her head against his shoulder and inhaled the heady scent of his soap and aftershave. "I'm an idiot. I don't know what came over me hitting Ty like that. I bet Mama is steaming. I'll never live this down."

Eric took Hope's mug, placing it along with his own on the wicker table beside them. He grasped her hand and softly rubbed his thumb in a circular motion against her soft palm. He used his left hand to raise Hope's chin so that she was looking him in the eyes. "Actually Pops seemed more distressed. Both your Mama and Ty, after the initial shock, acted like your punching him was the most natural greeting in the world. It was even your Mama's idea to go ahead with the shopping to give you some time to cool off. What's going on Hope?"

Hope's front teeth gently chewed on her lower lip as she considered Eric's words. Instead of being reassuring, the fact that her Mama wasn't ready to tear into her made her wonder if perhaps her mother had the same ominous feelings she herself had at the arrival of Ty. She stopped nibbling at her lip and looked into the concerned eyes of her husband. "Eric...I think something bad is going to happen, and I'm scared."

"Ty scared you? Honey, that's silly. Or maybe you're just nervous because of the fire at your parents' home."

"No, I think maybe it has something to do with the drug dealers."

Hope realized her slip the instant the words were out of her mouth. She hadn't wanted to inform Eric of her Mama's latest harebrained adventure. Eric's puzzlement was quickly followed by bewilderment and a mixture of hurt and anger.

"What drug dealers, exactly, are we talking about here, Hope?" His voice, though still soft and regular, had a new edge to it.

"Umm... that's right. I forgot to tell you about that. Well you see, yesterday while you were in Saint Louis, I went down to check on Mama and Pops..."

Eric's features stiffened to resemble granite as Hope relayed the rest of her day. From inside the house, Eric heard a door shut and the voices of Hope's parents and brother. Eavenly came out on the porch and smiled brightly at the tense couple. "Hurry up and come inside. I've got a surprise for you two." She reentered the house in a flurry of color, her new clothes leaning towards the flamboyant.

Hope started toward the door and was surprised when Eric grabbed her by the wrist. "Hope, she better have brought us a new DVD or lunch from McDonalds, because if her surprise has anything to do with drugs, her neighbors, or the fire at her house, your Mama and I are going to have a long discussion about involving you in such stupid activities."

Hope visibly swallowed. The smile she plastered on her face appeared to take great effort. "Oh Eric, I'm sure it's nothing. I mean...Mama hardly ever has days like she did yesterday. I bet she bought a roast for dinner. I'm sure this feeling I had doesn't have anything to do with Mama and her drug dealers. We'll just have to keep our eye on Ty." Hope swallowed the lump of guilt forming in her throat. On one hand, she didn't want Eric worrying about her and being irritated with her family; on the other, something inside her told her he probably had every reason to worry; and that made her want to hide in his arms until Christmas. She forced a smile on her face she hoped appeared reassuring.

Eric walked through the door into the kitchen, Hope slowly following. Before she passed the threshold of the door, she glanced back at the dogs still playing nearby in the yard, mumbling to herself, "Mama, please have brought a roast…or a pie would work nicely…heck, I'll settle for a bologna sandwich. Just don't mention anything to upset Eric." Hope closed her eyes and stepped into the house.

CHAPTER 13—IT'S ALL RELATIVE

Hope's eyes had not accustomed themselves to the dimness of the kitchen after the brightness of being outside, so she did not see Eric as he suddenly stopped in front of her. She almost tumbled to the floor as she ran into his back and tripped over his leg. Eric quickly grabbed her before she could fall, but Hope noticed that his eyes never left the direction of the living room. As she peered in the same direction her mouth fell open at the sight of a lady with silver-blue tinted hair, wearing black spandex and a string of lustrous pearls hanging low against a dark purple t-shirt that had a hand pointing to the left with the phrase "I'm with Stupid." Hope's gaze couldn't help but follow the finger to gape at the man standing beside the small woman. He was clad in a pair of faded overalls, a plaid jacket, and a silk tie with a picture of Rudolph, nose brightly lit with a small red bulb.

"Aunt Agatha? Uncle Bob? Where did you come from?" Hope took in her mother's disapproving look and made an effort to stop gaping.

Her uncle gave a deep belly laugh as her aunt cackled and replied, "Bob and I just got back from eating lunch at the Four Bells. We thought we would test out their gotta-wear-a-tie-and-jacket-to-be-allowed-to-eat-in-their-fine-establishment malarkey. It was a great time, Hope. You should have been there. I thought the Maitre'de was going to die of apoplexy."

Hope covered her mouth to keep the smirk from being evident. Opposing the laws of high society was a favorite pastime of her eccentric aunt and uncle. Somehow, they never realized the fact that the priceless pearls, which her aunt was never without, and the fact that the couple arrived everywhere they went in a Rolls Royce, never more than a year old, would influence most establishments to overlook their natural kookiness. They had recently had to resort to driving a great distance to even get a rise out of anyone since every hotel and restaurant in a sixty mile radius of their home was willing to humor them for the sake of future business.

Hope's Aunt Agatha rushed forward, engulfing Hope in a hug. Hope smiled and returned the hug. Her aunt's customary scent of vanilla, real vanilla dabbed on the wrists and behind the ears, brought back warm memories of her childhood. As children, Hope and her brothers had spent many hours listening to Agatha's tall tales. There had always been something inherently comforting about the smell of vanilla, the comfortable pillow of Agatha's ample bosom, and the lilting quality of her voice as she made up stories full of giants, witches, dragons, goblins, trolls, and tax collectors. Hope, being the smallest though not youngest, was often the one who won the prized seat in Agatha's lap, but her aunt always enveloped everyone in so much love and attention that none of the children ever felt slighted and each one felt as if he or she must truly be Agatha's favorite.

"Seems like I got here in the knick of time, Hope. You're nothing but skin and bones. I guess I'll have to whip up a nice home-cooked meal to put some meat on you. Your husband could use some fattening up, also."

Hope and Ty exchanged a nervous smile as they noticed the sudden straightening and stiffening of Mama's shoulders. Bob and Sam both took a small, hesitant step toward the hallway. The battles over the best meatloaf, creamiest mashed potatoes, and hottest chili had been going on as long as anyone could remember. Although the two had never come to blows, there was one occasion when both were discovered covered in flour, and rumors of a food fight had quickly spread throughout the family.

"Hope just had a home-cooked meal at my house yesterday, and who do you think cooked her breakfast this morning?" Eavenly's hair appeared to bristle slightly.

Hope took Eric by the arm and tried to nudge him closer to the hall.

"Humph. Pancakes with imitation flavoring I suppose?" Agatha volleyed the opening challenge.

"*What*, exactly, is wrong with my maple syrup?" Eavenly leaned forward on the tips of her toes.

"Eavenly, every *decent* cook in the country knows that you need to add a touch of vanilla, and besides your syrup is always too thin to even stay on top of the pancakes." Agatha leaned back crossing her arms with a raised eyebrow waving another challenge.

Hope, remembering the flour incident, glanced around her state-of-the-art-kitchen with gleaming chrome and spotless counters. She stepped between the two sisters, facing her aunt, nervous about the fact that this left her blind to her Mama standing directly behind her. "Aunt Agatha, you never did tell me what brings you to town. I don't think you have been to our house before, have you? Why don't you let me show you around? I'm sure that Eric and Dad would be happy to show Bob the backyard where they're going to build me a nice arbor. Ty, why don't you carry in what you guys got shopping? I'm sure Mama can show you where to put everything."

"Oh! I forgot the ice cream is still in the car along with the roast. Hurry up, Ty, before it melts!" Eavenly rushed out of the kitchen. Ty gave Hope a quick grin and a wink before he turned and followed. Hope knew that Ty was aware of her purposeful distraction and that he was both impressed and found the situation humorous at the same time. They had always been able to communicate large amounts of thoughts and feelings with a minimum of words, often with just a look. Agatha grabbed Hope's arm and started pulling her toward the hallway.

"I want the grand tour, Hope. Don't leave anything out!" Agatha was perpetually curious and loved snooping around other people's homes. Hope watched as Agatha pulled out books, opened drawers, read the labels of everything in the medicine cabinet, and felt the texture of her clean towels. They had just entered the master bedroom when Agatha plopped down on the bed, bobbing up and down to test its springiness.

"From the looks of that handsome husband of yours, I would lay down even odds that this bed sees enough action to warrant a new mattress before too long."

"Aunt Agatha!" Hope's face bloomed with color. She took a step back in shock.

Aunt Agatha smiled cheekily, "Well, it's the truth. Where have you been keeping the poor boy? None of us have seen him since your wedding. He's not been to a single family reunion. Oh, well, that will all change tomorrow."

"Wh…. what will change tomorrow?" Hope stammered.

"Well, the moment we ran into Eavenly and Sam and heard about the fire, I knew they needed some cheering up, so I made some calls while we finished up shopping. Everyone's coming here to brighten things up a little bit for your mama and dad."

Hope sat down on the bed, "*Everyone's* coming *here*?"

"Well, not everyone…just family. Show me the rest of the house." Agatha left the room heading down the hall.

Hope shook her head in bewilderment. Family get togethers often took on the feel of small military encampments…with lots of food. And tomorrow her family would be camped out at her house. She let out a heavy sigh. Eric poked his head into the room. "Hope, I think you might need to come help your Mama put away the groceries. She bought enough food to feed an army."

Hope forced a smile as she followed Eric, beneath her breath muttering, "We're going to need it."

CHAPTER 14—UNDER SIEGE

Eric awoke to the sound of voices and hammering coming from their backyard. He squinted at the clock's red confirmation that it was only 5:37 a.m. and stretched as he walked to the window, pulling back the curtain to look outside. He paused as he took in the commotion in the backyard, rubbing his eyes vigorously before looking again. Allowing the curtain to fall back into place, he walked over to Hope's side of the bed, gently shaking her shoulder. "Hope...Hope wake up."

"Wha...What?" Hope pulled the blanket tighter and snuggled farther into her pillow as Eric sat beside her on the bed continuing to try to rouse her.

"Hope, there are a lot of strange people in our back yard."

"Uhmmm."

"Uncle Bob seems to be showing some of them where to set up what looks like the parts of a Ferris wheel."

"Uh-huh."

"Some other men seem to be roping off parts of the yard, and they're filling the swimming pool with dozens of inflatable objects. Hope, there's a flatbed truck in our back yard stacked with wooden picnic tables, and I swear I saw a dunking booth. Hope?" Eric leaned forward gently raising the lid of one eye to stare into the sleepy hazel gaze of his wife. Hope had just opened the other eye when Mama and Aunt Agatha suddenly slung the door open. Hope jumped up so suddenly that Eric accidentally poked her in the eye into which he had been peering.

Hope, with one hand covering her injured eye, managed to glare with the other. "Damn, Mama!"

Mama ignored Hope's cry and walked toward Eric, who was starting to examine Hope's eye, sticking a forkful of pancakes in his face, "Here taste this."

Eric quickly opened his mouth and swallowed the sticky concoction before it wound up covering his face. As he swallowed, Agatha rushed forward with a similar forkful, "Now taste this." Both women eyed him as he swallowed the second sample.

Mama placed one hand on her hip and glared at her son-in-law. "Which one is better?"

Hope, having been abruptly awakened from her sleep three mornings in a row, could not take any more. She stood up on the bed, glaring down at her mama and aunt and pointing at the door. "GET…*OUT!*" The words were strongly enunciated through clenched teeth.

The two sisters glanced quickly at each other before heading toward the door. Agatha leaned toward Mama as they left the room, shutting the door, speaking just loudly enough for her voice to carry back to the room. "Eavenly, you saw how he was hovering over her. I bet they were just getting ready to do it. You and Sam are going to have to buy stock in the Mattress Warehouse for those two."

"Oh, stop being ridiculous, Agatha. I know you're just trying to change the subject. It was obvious from Eric's expression that he thought your pancake syrup was too sweet. It almost made him choke."

"I ought to choke you, Eavenly, for telling such a lie. We'll go back inside and ask him."

As the two opened the bedroom door again, a pillow flew past their heads missing by inches. The first was quickly followed by a second. The sisters shut the door quickly before Hope had a chance to reload.

Agatha looked over at Eavenly, a commiserating look on her face, "Shameful, a daughter treating her own mother in such a way. I always said that you and Sam spoiled that one too much."

"Don't tell me how to raise my kids, Agatha. Your Josh and Justine turned out to be lawyers! What kind of parenting is that?"

"You didn't seem to mind their choice of professions when you hired them to have that statue removed from the park near your house!"

"Well, how would you like to take your grandkids to the swings only to find yourself eye to thigh with that huge bronze…" Both voices disappeared as the two headed back to the kitchen.

In the bedroom, Hope still stood on the bed, her eyes now alert and fully awake. Eric put his arms around her and pulled her back down to the bed. "Hope, there are a ton of strange people messing up our backyard."

Hope nodded resolutely, her voice waxing dramatic, "Eric, that's the family. I can't protect you any longer. Run…flee to Maui. Take me with you. We'll live on a deserted island without any phones, airports, or homing pigeons."

"Honey…" Eric gently kissed her on the forehead. "They're your family."

"Exactly! Let's leave now before it's too late. We can't even leave a hint as to where we're heading—they would find me somehow. Probably have a school of trained sharks circle the island until they caught me and drug me back."

Eric kissed her again before setting her back on the bed and then turned to the shower. "Honey, I met your family at the wedding, remember? I *like* your family."

Hope sighed as she looked at the door and muttered to herself, "I'm sure the people on the Titanic liked boats, too." She flung herself back onto her pillows.

CHAPTER 15—HOPE LOST

Eric stood between Luke and Ty eyeing the activity that was taking place in his back yard. "How many people do you think this is?"

Ty took a sip of his beer and shrugged, "Hundred, hundred and fifty maybe."

Luke grinned, "You should see it when everyone comes."

"This isn't everyone?" Eric gulped. "There were only maybe half this many people at our wedding."

"Yeah, Hope ticked a lot of people off by limiting the invitations like that. They put her in both the dunking booth and the pie in the face contest at the next reunion. Good thing you weren't there. They would have gotten you, too, for conspiracy."

Eric glanced over at the dunking booth, which currently had a bald-headed man who looked an awful lot like Hope's dad egging people on to try and hit him; thus far he had remained dry. "Every time you guys have one of these things has been when I was out of town, or when the two of us have been on vacation."

"And how do you, being your own boss and all, decide when to go on these out of town trips?" Ty and Luke shared a smirk.

"I usually check with Hope and we discuss a good time, when it won't be an inconvenience." Eric felt a frown as he remembered the times he had juggled the trips due to some request or need of Hope's, often during a time when she decided she could take a mini-vacation to visit some family member. Comprehension began to dawn on him as the brothers continued to smile knowingly at him.

"Hope was just trying to protect you, Man. The first two years that Kate's husband, Tom, attended…they terrified the poor guy. Look over there at him—fifteen years of these things, and he's still almost too afraid to leave her side."

Eric gulped as he looked around the crowd for Hope. "What did they do to him?"

"It's not like they *did* anything to him. It's just that everyone wanted to get a chance to meet him. The poor guy had to participate in every event. He was run ragged. And then to top if off, they tried to make him one of the judges of the bake-off." Ty shivered.

"That's a bad thing?" Eric thought he had heard Hope arguing over something to do with a bake-off this morning.

Ty looked at him in surprise, "You've met Mama and Agatha, right?" Eric nodded. "Well, they're pussycats compared to Aunt Bonnie and Aunt Sherlock. Sherlock's the oldest, you know?" Eric hadn't. "Well, she always lords the fact that she's older and wiser over everyone else's head. If she was ever to win the bake-off, we would have real problems."

Eric nodded as if this all made perfect sense, "So she's never won?"

Luke glanced around before leaning in closer to Eric, "She can't."

"You mean the contest is rigged?!" Eric said a little too loudly.

Ty jabbed him in the ribs, "Hey, Man! Be careful. You want to get us all killed? Of course it's rigged. There are always five judges. One is always Uncle Roosevelt or Clyde; they think it's a good thing for Sherlock to lose, to keep her modest. Then Pops and his brother Zack are always judges."

"Your dad's brother comes to these things?"

Luke nodded his head toward the dunking booth, "This is a *family* event, which pretty much means if you are in somebody's family, you're welcome to come. Family isn't only the people that you share blood with. I think Uncle Zack was in charge of putting flyers in all of your neighbor's mailboxes inviting them—you know, doing a little PR to keep noise complaints low. That's him over there in the booth. You ought to get him to tell you some of his war stories sometime. The man is a killer storyteller." Ty nodded his head in agreement. The brothers shared a large smile as they looked at Eric.

Mike and his wife, Kathy, walked over to the group. Mike removed his arm from his wife's shoulder and glanced around. "Have you guys seen Hope?"

Luke laughed. "Looking to get some practice in before the race, Bro?"

Ty gestured toward the Ferris wheel, "You checked the wheel? You know how she digs that thing."

"I already checked." Mike answered. "Besides, she would have old Eric with her if she was just riding rides. I can't find her anywhere."

Eric moved to stand beside Kathy, "So what did they do to you the first year you came to one of these things."

Kathy smiled brightly, "Nothing. It's only the guys they give a hard time to. If you're a female, you just bring a baked dish; and if it's good enough, you're an instant hit."

Mike nodded. "Only problem is Kathy can't cook. Can you, Babe?"

Kathy put her arm around her husband's waist and squeezed, seeming to not take offense. "That's why they invented restaurants. Anyway, that's how I know your Mama really likes me." She turned back to Eric. "Every time we come to one of these things, Mike's Mama bakes something, changing the recipe just enough so no one will know it's hers, and puts my name on it. The woman loves me."

Mike looked more closely at Eric, "How long has it been since you've seen Hope?"

Eric shrugged, "Forty-five minutes, maybe an hour."

Concern wrinkled Mike's brow. "That's odd. With your being Hope's husband, these people are going to be all over you like white on rice. I can't believe she left you by yourself on your first real family get together."

Luke laughed, "I can't believe you just used a line like 'white on rice'."

Eric frowned. Now that he thought about it, Hope was so polite that she never left him at any event for more than ten or fifteen minutes, and she always made sure he knew where she was. He started toward the house to look for her, but was stopped by a couple of Hope's second cousins. A man who stood a good foot taller was pumping his hand vigorously. "So you're Hope's husband. I haven't seen her in months, and I want to give my favorite cuz a hug. Where is she hiding herself anyway?"

"That's what I would like to know," Eric thought to himself.

CHAPTER 16—INTO THE WOODS

Hope had struggled with whether or not to invite Joe to the family get together. She was sure that Uncle Zack would have put a flyer in his mailbox this morning along with the other neighbors, but she didn't know if Joe would show up without a personal invitation from her. When he hadn't answered his phone, she had decided to walk down to the cabin to see if he was there. Her ingrained politeness had won out over her desire to keep this small part of her life separate from her family. She had not noticed when a man had detached himself from the line to ride the spin-a-whirl and ducked into the woods behind her. She first became aware of his presence as she neared the cabin. She could make out the window and clearing a few feet ahead. Normally, she would have heard the heavy footsteps following behind her earlier if she had not been so focused on inviting Joe to meet her family.

Thinking it was Joe planning another sneak attack, she whirled with a smile on her face. The smile wilted as a blur of motion swung toward her, and the log the man was holding tightly in his grip connected with her head. A yelp from her mouth was the only sound as darkness encompassed her, and she fell unconscious to the ground.

Hope grimaced with the intense pain as she tried to make out the features of the figure hovering over her. The sun streaming through the leaves into her eyes contrasting with the natural dimness of the woods made it impossible until he leaned within inches of her face, gently dabbing at the blood on her temple with a handkerchief. "Hope, you okay?" Joe felt a pain of empathy so intense he flinched as he helped her to a sitting position.

"You're getting a little too realistic for me, Joe. You almost took my head off this time." Hope tried to stand.

"Hope, don't be ridiculous. I didn't do this. I was in the cabin when I heard you cry out. When I came to investigate, I found you lying here knocked out. Are you okay?"

"I guess so..." Hope fought back the wave of nausea that overcame her. "Joe, if you didn't attack me, who did?"

Joe felt a tightening in his chest. "I don't know, Hope. I don't know." He then heard the sound of running footsteps a little distance farther into the forest. Joe's first impulse was to run after the sound, hatred of Hope's attacker reviving a bloodlust he had tried to forget. It took only a glance at Hope's pallid, distraught features to realize that he could no more leave her in this condition to chase her attacker than he could sprout wings to fly. The knot on her head was already beginning to swell, and Joe had seen enough injuries to detect the slightly unfocused stare that was not a comforting sign with a head injury.

Joe knelt, lifting Hope into his arms. He headed toward the cabin, being careful not to cause her any more pain. Hope looked around groggily in the direction Joe was taking her, and childhood instincts quickly kicked in, "Joe, take me home, please...to my family." Joe nodded and gently shifted her weight as he started the longer trek back to Hope's house. As he drew near, the sounds of a large group of people laughing met his ears. He glanced down at Hope and could tell by the sudden gnawing of her lower lip that she had heard the sounds, too. Hope smiled wanly up at Joe, "I forgot about the party. Joe, I hate to ask you to lie...but do you think we could tell them....tell them...maybe you could tell them I fell in the woods? If they hear that someone attacked me, we'll have a hundred of my relatives out in mass ready to jump on the first stranger they run into. Tell Eric and my brothers, but not the whole crowd." Joe grew more concerned at Hope's seeming inability to focus and simply nodded down at her reassuringly as he stepped out of the woods bordering Hope's property.

He almost ran into a worried Eric, who had himself, after looking everywhere else, been on his way to the cabin.

"Oh, Christ!" Eric's face turned white at the image of his wife lying crumpled in Joe's arms, a large red knot on her head, seeping blood. He reached to take her from Joe's arms, hands shaking so badly that Joe merely nodded his head in response, "It's okay. I've got her. Lead the way."

Eric swallowed hard still unmoving, "Wh-what happened?"

Joe took a step encouraging Eric to start moving. He leaned closer with a lowered voice as he eyed the crowd that had just seemed to notice them standing at the edge of the woods and had begun to move quickly towards them. "Bastard attacked her in the woods. She doesn't want to alarm anyone, said to say she fell."

Eric suddenly felt as if his stomach had dropped into his shoes as a soft moan came from Hope's lips. He was grateful at the sudden appearance of Mike and Kate at his side. Kate quickly took in the situation and began to deliver instructions in an authoritative voice. "Okay, take her into the house, and let's take a look at that cut." She glanced around the yard and yelled to her husband, Tom, who was on the far end of the yard and had just started jogging toward them, "Tom! Run to the car and get my bag." The group, led by a confident Kate, began its way to the house but was immediately stopped by a mass of Rhineholdts' relatives, all asking questions and trying to get a glimpse at what was wrong with Hope.

Hope peered around dazedly, a feeling of claustrophobia overwhelming her with the blur of faces swarming in and out of her line of vision. Her stomach threatened to revolt at the jolting motion Joe was making as he tried to sidestep her various family members, and she noticed Eric was becoming frustrated as he tried to edge them all forward through the crowd, pleading with everyone to just move out of the way.

Hope noticed a sudden shift in the crowd as a path began to be cleared through the anxious group. People began to move quickly out of the way, and although Hope couldn't see the force working behind the people, she instinctively knew that Mama was making her way to them. Relief coursed through her body as she fought back the waves of blackness that remained on the edge of her uncertain grasp on consciousness.

"Mama's here," Hope thought, for the first time in years with the childhood certainty that somehow Mama would make everything all right.

CHAPTER 17—HEADACHES

"This may sting a little." Kate warned as she dabbed antiseptic on Hope's forehead, cleaning the wound.

"Damn! That hurts a lot!" Hope growled and tried to move her sister's hand away.

"Hope, stop being such a baby and let me get a good look at this. I can't even tell if you need stitches or not." Kate, as gently as possible, continued to dab at the gash. The room was empty except for the two of them and a concerned Eavenly. After Kate had pronounced that Hope was in no real danger from her wound, Sam had been put in charge of crowd control. Though worried about his youngest daughter, he had remained outside encouraging the others to return to the festivities. Eric, Ty, Luke, and Mike had quickly found out from Joe that Hope had been attacked in the woods. The five of them had sectioned off areas near where Joe had found Hope and had started a quick search in hope of, in Luke's words, "Finding the bastard and beating the ever-living shit out of him."

Kate continued to dab a minute more before pulling clean bandages from her bag. "Well, it doesn't look like you're going to need stitches, and with the speed with which you usually heal, I doubt you'll even have a scar." She pulled a small light from her bag and had Hope follow it in several directions with her eyes. "I don't think you have a concussion—must be thanks to that thick head of yours. I think you were disoriented and in a bit of shock more than anything."

Eavenly leaned in closer patting Hope on her head, her eyes on Kate so that she didn't see Hope biting her lip at the pain she was unintentionally causing. "You sure she's okay? There sure seemed to be a lot of blood, if you ask me."

"Head wounds have a tendency to do that. You know Hope, she's always getting hurt, but she'll be okay." Kate and Eavenly shared a smile. "Remember the time she jumped off the house with the sheet thinking it would work as a parachute?"

Eavenly clucked her tongue. "We were just lucky that she had the sheet. She was always thinking she was some kind of superhero or another."

"I wish you would stop talking about me as if I wasn't here." Hope felt embarrassed at the memory of some of her less logical, youthful antics. If she didn't put a quick stop to it, the conversation between her, Mama, and Kate would likely spread to the rest of the family, and they would spend the rest of the day telling stories of Hope's oddball antics. Hope never could understand why her family was always so interested in her life when it was probably the most ordinary out of anyone in the family. Unfortunately, her family had enough fodder to keep the conversation going for several days. So she had been an imaginative child! So she was a little danger prone! It wasn't like she was always getting arrested for things like naked demonstrations protesting chemical plants like her uncle Roosevelt.

Eavenly and Kate's attention returned to Hope as Eavenly sat beside her looking sternly into her eyes, "Now, why don't you tell us what in the world you were doing to get hit in the head? What were you doing in those woods alone, anyway?"

"I was just taking a short cut to invite our neighbor, Joe, the guy that carried me here, to the party. I have no idea why some wacko hit me in the head!" At the disbelieving look exchanged between Kate and Mama, Hope suddenly wished she had just let them talk about her as if she wasn't there. At least then, they wouldn't be able to make her feel guilty for getting attacked.

At that moment in the woods, Joe was hunched down on one leg eyeballing a footprint he had found near the stream a few yards from where he had found Hope. The tread was a common Nike brand that would be next to impossible to trace. Joe ran a hand through his hair in frustration. The odds of them catching up with Hope's attacker were slim to none. Joe sensed more than really heard someone coming up behind him. He quickly stood and moved to hide himself behind some bushes. Ty was coming up the path, following the same trail that Joe had been following. There was something about the way that Ty moved through the forest that was achingly familiar to Joe.

For what reason he didn't know, Joe decided to stay where he was behind the bushes as he watched Ty kneel beside the footprint Joe had been examining. Ty glanced around before pulling out a very small camera. He placed a quarter beside the imprint and quickly took a picture. He then took out what looked like a wallet-sized computer. He attached a cord from the computer to the camera and punched some buttons. He waited a minute before returning both to his pants pocket and glancing around once again; then he returned to tracing the attacker's trail through the forest. Joe came out from behind the bush, a very puzzled look on his face as he stared after Hope's brother—the same brother she had punched because of a feeling of danger.

Hope stared at the twins, Mike's sons, standing before her. She tried to hide her smile and match their very serious countenances. The two eight year olds stood stiffly holding a huge super-soaker each. Their black hair was tussled and sweaty from their hours of playing outside. Tommy, the younger of the two by three minutes, had a pink smear from cotton candy across his face, while Timmy had what was definitely the yellow signature of a ball park frank covered with way too much French's mustard, his usual choice. She struggled to keep from giggling at two of her favorite troublemakers. "Okay, tell me what you're supposed to be doing again?"

Tommy sighed from the effort of having to explain something multiple times to a grown up. "Granpops said that Timmy and I were supposed to stand outside your door and guard you from 'sturbances. He said that if anybody 'sturbed you, we were 'lowed to soak 'em"

"'Cept Grandmamma," Timmy interrupted.

Tommy nodded seriously, "Course 'cept Grandmamma." His head wrinkled as he thought, "and Eric…we like Eric."

"And probably Mom and Dad," Timmy interrupted again.

Tommy frowned as he thought about it. "Yeah, we'd probably be in trouble if we soaked Mom and Dad, 'less Grandmamma said it was okay."

Hope couldn't keep the smile from forming at the very clear logic of the children. Even at their age, they realized that very few people would stand up to Mama. Her smile widened as the door was gently opened and Kate's daughter, Leslie, walked in, all of her five-year-old concentration on the glass of water she carried in her hands. Timmy and Tommy gently moved out of their younger cousin's way. Hope took the glass from her small fingers and laughed as Leslie took a tape of *The Little Mermaid* from beneath one of her arms.

Tommy took the tape from Leslie and moved to put the tape in Hope's VCR, explaining as he went, "Aunt Kate thought you should stay in here and rest for a little while, and she thought Leslie would be good company for you while Timmy and I guarded you." As he moved toward the door, Timmy quickly helped Leslie climb up on Hope's bed, both boys showing a deference that was reserved for this young cousin alone. Both boys turned and saluted before heading out the door and closing it behind them.

Hope felt eyes watching her and turned to peer into the concerned blue eyes of her niece. Leslie raised her hand to point at Hope's forehead, now neatly bandaged. Hope lifted her own fingers to touch the white padding, "This? Don't worry about this. Your old Aunt Hope just tripped in the woods and got a little boo-boo. Lucky for me, your Mama was around to kiss it and make it all better, huh?" Blue eyes peered into hazel a moment longer before Leslie turned her full attention to the opening credits of *The Little Mermaid.*

Hope felt a small pang of pain that was more closely connected to her heart than it was to her newest injury as she cuddled up to Leslie to watch the video. Six months ago, Tom and Leslie had gone to the hospital to pick up Kate. While waiting outside in the hallway, a young man high on something ran down the hall toward them. He had somehow gotten hold of a scalpel, and it flashed menacingly in his hand. Before he had gotten within fifteen feet of Tom and Leslie, Mike and one of his deputies, having earlier brought the man to the emergency room for treatment, rounded the corner. Mike got to him first. As Mike grabbed the man by the arm, his first thought to keep the man from moving closer to his niece, the man swung with the scalpel and stabbed him in the stomach. As Mike's grasp was transferred to his wound, Dave, his deputy, quickly tackled the man and wrenched the scalpel from him. Mike was bleeding badly and a pool of blood was already surrounding him by the time Kate and a few nurses got to him. Mike recovered and the man, after a speedy trial, was sent to jail. Leslie hadn't said a word since that day.

Kate and Tom had gone to several of the leading psychologists, and all seemed to agree that Leslie would talk again, when she was ready to. Hope's family tried to follow the doctors' suggestions and treat her as normally as possible, speaking to her as if they expected at any instant she would reply. Hope loved all of her nieces and nephews and was constantly teased by her family about not having children of her own. Since the stabbing incident, Leslie and Hope had come to form a special bond. Hope often was the one who understood what Leslie needed while others where baffled by her silence. Leslie followed her aunt around whenever they were in the same house together like a small puppy.

As Hope sat next to her young niece thinking about the cause of Leslie's self-induced silence, her parents' flame-eaten home, and reflecting on the dull throbbing in her head, she felt a burning in her stomach and the throbbing grew worse. Hope had not experienced the sensation very often, but she could easily recognize the gnawing anger that had risen inside of her for the people who had so cold-heartedly caused her family pain. Hope was a very optimistic person. People often smiled as they teased her about her need to always find the glass half full, even when it was three quarters empty. Hope knew that her greatest strength and strongest flaw was her strong feelings for the people whom she loved. For them she was a positive, caring individual…and for them she would do almost anything.

CHAPTER 18—WE'VE MET BEFORE

Hope's attacker leaped into the pick-up truck and Kyle Murdock pushed the gas pedal to the floor with his heavy work boot, which was caked in concrete. He glanced over nervously at the dark haired man sitting beside him, lightly panting after his mad dash to the truck. Kyle's gaze returned to the road as he worked his tongue around the words he wanted to speak. He always spoke carefully when dealing with Rob. He was less than thrilled that the men who had hired him had paired him up with this hardened character.

He had already begun to have serious doubts about the men he was working for when the news that the Rhineholdts had been inside of the house he had set on fire reached him. He had been told that the house was empty and that the family had left on vacation. He had gone to school with the Rhineholdt brothers and did not want to ever run into them if they learned that it was he who had endangered their parents. He would have ended his dealings with these guys the day after the fire if he had not been so afraid of how they would react to his resignation. The two blond Mr. Smiths seemed to be the type of men you were either with…or you were dead.

The hiring of Rob only confirmed his suspicions. After Sandy left him and he lost his job because of his bad temper, he knew that the only hope of keeping his boys with him was the money the men offered for setting the fire. He glanced nervously in Rob's direction again as he stopped at a red light. He was deeply regretting getting involved, more so every minute.

Rob, however, was at that moment feeling a great deal of satisfaction as he replayed in his mind the image of the log he had carried in his hand and how it had connected with Hope's head. Rob had grown up in the same town as the Rhineholdts; and if the town were to have a black sheep in it, all would definitely agree it was him. Throughout his life Rob had always been jealous of the Rhineholdt children. They seemed to glow with all their wealth and good fortune, while he had lived in a shack with his drunken, abusive father and uncaring mother. It was Mike who had arrested Rob ten years ago for the murder of his parents.

A few months earlier, he had finally sucked up enough nerve to ask Hope to their prom, only to have her smirk in his face as she told him no. It wasn't enough for the Rhineholdts that she had turned him down. They had enjoyed tormenting him when he followed Hope home one day to give her a chance to reconsider only to be caught by Mike and Ty. The two of them ordered him off their property as if he was some mangy cur. Then they threatened him if he bothered Hope any more. Well, he had bothered Hope today, and if that guy hadn't come running through the woods when he had, Rob would have done more than hit her on the head with a log. He smiled as he remembered the feel of her skin as he had stroked the side of her face moments before being forced to flee back to the truck.

Rob had escaped from prison six years ago while being transferred to one of his court appeals. He was sure that the Rhineholdts had been extra careful during the first months of his escape, but by now they had probably forgotten all about him. A grimace crossed his face at the thought of being forgotten. During the four years he had been in prison, and the years since, he had not gone a day without remembering Hope and Mike with all of the hatred he could feel. He promised himself that soon it would be impossible for the Rhineholdts to ever forget him again, especially Hope and Mike. A smile spread across his face, which thanks to funding from his new-found friends and plastic surgery a few months ago, was much different from the face the Rhineholdts remembered. Maybe fortune had finally come his way. What were the chances of those men hiring him because of his connections in the Rhineholdt's town to do some illegal odds and ends and suddenly deciding to *pay* him to get rid of the very people he hated the most. Yes, he decided, fortune was finally on his side, even if he did have to work with Kyle the coward.

Kyle had finally worked up the courage to speak, "Did you find the stuff?"

Rob returned his look with one that was filled with equal parts of condescension and loathing. "No…" he mocked Kyle's tone of voice, "I didn't find the stuff. You know how tiny those things are?"

Kyle gulped, "So what happened?"

"I gave her a little warning."

"The Smiths wanted you to bring back the stuff."

Rob smirked, "That what you think? That why they had us set fire to the house where they thought it might be? So we could go in later and sift through the ashes and look for something so small it would take us months to find it? The Smiths want the Rhineholdts out of the picture before they can mess with their plans. They don't care about the stuff, as long as no one else knows about it. The Smiths wouldn't have even noticed they were missing any of it if they didn't have the exact amount to fit onto the design on those purses. You have to admit that's a great way to smuggle the stuff past cops. They know we couldn't find it anyway. Today was just a little reinforcement."

Kyle felt his sweat start to bead on his forehead. "What is that stuff anyway?"

"I don't know." Rob was getting tired of the conversation. He was thinking of accidents that could befall his "pal" Kyle. He always preferred working alone.

"Aren't you curious?" Kyle's voice shook.

"No. The Rhineholdt chick was, and look where that got her." Rob once again recalled the image of Hope crumpling to the ground, and his lips turned up at the memory.

Kyle was silent for several moments as he maneuvered the car onto the interstate, nervously checking his rear view mirror. He glanced over at the smile on Rob's face and felt as if ice water had been poured into his veins. "What did you do to her?"

Rob's smile widened as he slumped in the seat getting comfortable for the ride back to town. He glanced over at Kyle, a glint of something akin to anticipation in his eyes, "Not nearly as much as I plan to."

Chapter 19—DISCORD

Luke, Joe, Ty, Mike, and Eric had regrouped in the clearing near the cabin. Eric looked wearily at each of them, "So did you guys find anything?" He looked around the group as everyone gave a negative reply.

Luke stepped forward and put a comforting hand on Eric's shoulder. "She'll be okay. This was just probably some idiot who saw the fliers and thought he had an opportunity to lift a few valuables from some of us. I don't think he'll be back."

Mike nodded, "I'm sure Luke's right. Let's go back and check on Hope. I'm sure she's probably ready to hop right back onto the old carousal at this very moment."

Eric started to follow his brother-in-law with slumped shoulders when he noticed that Joe wasn't following. He turned back to his friend, "Joe, aren't you coming?"

"Crowds aren't my thing, Eric. Tell Hope I'll come by and check on her in a few days." Joe gave Eric's shoulder a reassuring squeeze before he turned and headed back to his own property.

Eric turned and jogged to catch up with the others. He wanted to see that Hope was really okay with his own eyes.

Eric felt relief as he walked into the bedroom to find Hope watching a video with Leslie, who seemed to be enjoying herself. He crossed to the bed and leaned down to gently kiss the white bandage covering the majority of Hope's forehead. "You okay?"

"The good thing about having a skilled doctor for a sister is that she can give you the most fabulous drugs. It aches a little when I touch it, but that's about it." Hope smiled up at him reassuringly.

Eric's concerned eyes remained on Hope before turning to Leslie, "Hey, kiddo. Why don't I take over babysitting for a while and you can return to playing outside. It looked like everyone was getting ready for some kind of race."

Hope started to jump up, but Eric gently pushed her back to the bed, "The race?! Eric let me up. I gotta get out there before they get started."

Eric waited until he heard the door softly click closed behind Leslie before responding, "Hope, someone just attacked you. Don't you think we have more to deal with than some family reunion event?"

Hope's eyes widened, "Did you guys catch him?"

"Hope, we didn't find anybody. Don't you think we should report this to the police?" Eric's forehead wrinkled with concern.

"Mike and a couple of his deputies are here. They are the police," Hope answered matter-of-factly. "Eric, I'm not going to let some guy make me live my life in fear. Family and friends surround me, and if I hadn't been distracted, I would have probably been able to take this guy down instead of being hit on the head. I *always* compete in the race. Come on, Honey, I'm okay—it will be fun."

Eric, though still worried, couldn't stand the thought of disappointing Hope on top of the attack she had already dealt with today. "Okay, let's go and do this race thing, but if you start to feel the least bit dizzy or anything, you're going to come right back in here and lie down, deal?"

Hope smiled as she flung her arms around his neck and hugged him. "Deal, Honey. You go ahead and go out back. I'm going to wash some of this blood out of my hair and change shirts. I'll be out in a minute."

Hope went into the bathroom and took a washcloth from the shelf. She took in her pale appearance and grimaced at the bandage across her head.

Joe was looking in his bathroom mirror, worry shimmering behind the lids of his eyes. After he had splashed some water on his face and run a hand through his damp hair, he went into the living room. He hesitated before picking up the phone. Hope's attack in the woods just didn't make any sense. It sure wasn't a matter of theft like Luke wanted to think. He had a strange feeling that this was something much more. His hand hesitated over the phone cradle. He knew how protective of her family Hope was, and he didn't want to do anything to jeopardize their friendship, but the memory of Hope's dazed look as blood trickled down her forehead made his decision for him. He quickly punched in the number before he could change his mind.

"Stevens here." A commanding voice briskly answered on the other end of the line.

"Mac…it's Joe. I need you to find some background on someone for me." Joe heard some movement in the background as his old friend searched for a pad and pen.

"Okay, give it to me." Mac didn't ask Joe what he needed the information for—they had served together, and Joe had saved Mac's life on three different occasions.

"The name's Ty Rhineholdt. It might be nothing, but I want you to find out all you can." Joe sighed picturing Hope's reaction if she ever found out he had run a background check on one of her brothers.

"No problem, Joe. I'll get back with you as soon as I find anything." There was a pause, "…and Joe, it's good to hear your voice. It's been a long time."

"Yeah, I know, Mac. Let's get together for a beer soon, okay?" Joe smiled as he hung up the phone. It felt good to talk to his old friend. He had broken off most contact with his service pals after Maggie's death. The smile faded as today's events resurfaced in his mind. He thought of another old friend he hadn't been around, not since the darkest days when he struggled with his own guilt and despair. Joe went upstairs to the spare bedroom. He opened the closet to pull out an old army footlocker. He took his keys from his pocket and unlocked it for the first time in five years. Inside, he moved the boxes of medals and some other gear until he found the wooden box he was searching for. As he opened it and looked at the 1911 Model Colt .45 inside, his smile was bittersweet. "Hello, friend."

Hope was gently drying off her face with a hand towel. When she removed the towel and looked into the mirror, her eyes met another pair besides her own. A small yelp came out of her throat before she realized it was only Mike standing behind her. "Don't sneak up on me like that. You nearly gave me a heart attack."

Mike's serious expression did not change as he stared at his little sister. "Hope, the man who attacked you. Do you know who it was?"

Hope's eyes widened in consternation, "Are you crazy? I already told you that I don't know who it was. Did you think I was keeping his identity a secret?"

Hope started to brush by him but Mike put his hand on her shoulder. "I know you don't know the guy, what I'm asking you is…" Mike took a breath, "do you *know* him. Could you sense him?"

Mike took a step back at the flash of anger in Hope's eyes. Mike was the only individual who had ever seen such anger and darkness in Hope's expression before, and he hated that he was the one to cause her to feel so angry once again. Hope moved closer to him, her eyes glaring into his. Her words were short and clipped as if each one was being torn from her clenched teeth. "You and I have had this conversation. I will not have it again." She started to walk past him but stopped at his next words.

"What about the fire, what if it was connected? What about if he comes after you again? They know where you live." He appealed to her weak spot, "You and Eric could both get hurt. You could…"

His words were cut short as Hope interrupted him. "I couldn't…I won't" They stood staring at each other for several long moments, both refusing to back down, when they heard a scream from outside. The door was suddenly thrown open and the twins raced inside to stand behind Hope and Mike. A very angry looking, orange-covered Aunt Agatha entered the room right behind them. "Those….Those…" She wiped at the kool-aid dripping from her face as she sputtered angrily, "Those…*heathens* squirted me. I came to check on Hope, and they refused to let me inside. Then they had the audacity to *squirt* me!"

Eavenly appeared in the doorway behind her older sister and quickly hid the smile that had spread across her face, as she took in the scene…Agatha whirled to face her. "Eavenly, your grandsons just

sprayed me with orange kool-aid. What are you going to do about it?"
Agatha almost seemed to quiver with her anger.

Eavenly placed a placating hand on Agatha's shoulder and
started to lead her out the door. "Agatha, I'm shocked. Come with me,
and we'll get you a change of clothes. I would offer you some of mine,
but they would be way too small." She looked back over her shoulder at
the twins, "I'll take care of the boys. Don't you worry." Eavenly
continued the conversation as she led her older sister down the hall.

Mike turned to look at his two sons who were still standing
behind him, "Well, boys, you've done it now. What do you have to say
for yourselves?"

The twins looked at each other nervously before Tommy
swallowed and started to reply, "Granpops said not to let Aunt Hope be
'sturbed..." His words trailed off.

Timmy took up the explanation. "She looked definitely like a
'sturber' to us, didn't she, Tommy?" The other twin nodded in
agreement.

Mike frowned as he took a squirt gun from Tommy, "I know
your Mom told you not to fill these things with Kool-Aid."

Tommy shook his head vigorously. "Uh-uh...she said not to fill
them with grape juice. She never said anything about kool-aid." Timmy
nodded his head in agreement.

Both looked frightened as Eavenly once again appeared in the
doorway. Staring down at the boys, she said sternly, "Well, I said I
would take care of you two and that's what I'm going to do." She bent
and quickly hugged both boys, handing each a twenty-dollar bill in turn.
"Well, that takes care of you. Now you boys run outside and get your
Granpops to give you some ice cream."

Both boys marveled at the money then looked at their
Grandmamma before rushing towards the door. Eavenly stopped them
just before they dashed out, "It would be a good idea for you two to stay
away from Agatha for the rest of the day, I think." Both boys looked at
her with a look of admonishment, as if to say that they weren't stupid
enough to do such a thing as go around Agatha for a while.

Mike called after them as they ran from the room. "And no
more Kool-Aid!"

Hope giggled, "That leaves a lot of liquids, you know? Maybe you should have just taken the guns away."

Eavenly smiled as she looked Hope up and down. "Well, you're already looking better. You better hurry up if you want to race this year." She looked down at the carpet, "If those stains don't come up, I'll pay to have this place re-carpeted. It was worth it…did you see the look on Agatha's face? I wish I had a camera."

Hope and Mike eyeballed each other as Eavenly left the room. Mike was the first to break the silence. "Truce?"

Hope nodded, "Truce, but only because I don't want Josh and Justine to have a chance of winning."

Both grimaced at the thought of their two least favorite cousins ever getting bragging rights by winning any of the contests. Since Mike and Hope usually worked as a team in the contest, they would be better off letting the matter of Hope's attacker drop for a while, but Mike promised himself this wasn't the last conversation he was going to have with Hope about it.

CHAPTER 20—COMPETITION IS EVERYTHING

Eric looked at the wide array of flags, ropes, and strange obstacles spread across his backyard once more before leaning down to Hope, who was sitting on the ground stretching. "What did you say this thing was again?"

Even the clean, white bandage on her head paled in comparison to the sparkle of Hope's smile as she squinted against the glare of the sun to look up at her husband, "It started out as the usual reunion kind of games, back before I was born. You know, horseshoes, potato-sack-races, that sort of thing. But at some point somebody, probably Aunt Sherlock, decided to make it more interesting by breaking the contest up into a competition among branches of the family, and offering a trophy."

Mike walked over in time to catch the end of Hope's words and placed a hand on Eric's shoulder to point out various sections of the back yard and continue the explanation. "The reunion contest is broken up into seven smaller contests. Each contest is worth twenty points for first place, fifteen points for second place, and ten points for third. There's always a baking contest, which you've already heard about. Mama *always* places in the top three, usually the top two. Then there's the horseshoe contest, Pops is our ringer there. There's the relay for the kids under twelve: egg in a spoon, three-legged race, anything else that might wear down some of their energy. The twins help us out quite a bit there. Then there's the shake and spin contest. The contestants drink a milkshake, spin for three minutes on the spin-a-whirl and repeat until all, except one, gets sick. Ty with his army training is usually pretty good there. We have a jeopardy contest—Kate and Hope usually smoke them there. There's a game of bullshit, which we're all pretty good at, I have to say, and finally there's a little surprise event, survivor style, that no one knows exactly what it is except for the group that sets it up.

"You automatically get second place points for that part of the contest just for setting it up. The setup difficulty level has almost become its own contest. This year was Sherlock's group's turn and let me tell you, those guys are creative. The other catch is they tell you how many people can compete and you enter that one blind, hoping you do okay. Hope and I are always in the survivor contest, and we *always* come in first."

"Except for when Hope missed that year." Luke had walked over and decided to contribute. "Even superman, Mike, needs his trusty side-kick. So, I just heard, this year the number stands at four. I figure, Mike, Hope, myself, and what about you Eric? You up to it?"

"Actually, I thought Eric should play bullshit." Hope interrupted.

Luke and Mike looked doubtfully at each other. Usually, in-laws didn't try to compete against the family in bullshit, but Hope's instincts were always accurate.

"You sure that's not the knot on your head talking?" Mike was still hesitant.

Hope stood up from her stretching and shared a conspiratorial smile with Eric. "If Eric feels up to playing, I say he's our man."

Mike shrugged. "Okay, with me then. I guess we'll get Ty to join us in the survivor event, and we're good to go. Who has first watch on Eric?"

"Watch me? Why!" Eric was startled.

Luke nodded to the group of people standing near Hope's Uncle Roosevelt—all eyes were on Eric. "They sense a weakness since Hope was hurt this morning. I figure they're either going to pester you in order to distract Hope, or pester you in order to make you concerned enough to ask Hope to quit. So one of us is going to be around to help pester them back."

Eric felt frustrated. "I assure you I can take care of myself."

Hope hugged Eric before smiling up at him. "Honey, you're a tough guy, we all know that…but this is my family."

Eric suddenly became aware of the sound of Agatha and Eavenly's voices as they approached the group. Eavenly's voice easily carried loudly enough to be heard clearly. "I already told you Agatha that Hope will not let Eric be a judge in the bake off. Your asking will not change her mind."

Eric swallowed as he quickly turned back to the group of smiling siblings. "Okay, so let's hurry up and decide, people! Who has first watch?"

A voice that was unrecognizable to Eric wafted from behind his right ear. "I would be honored to take first watch." Sherlock smiled at the nervous looks the Rhineholdt brothers quickly exchanged. "You have a problem with that, boys?"

"N…n…no, Ma'am," both muttered in unison, before wandering quickly off.

Hope quickly hugged her aunt. "Thanks!" She turned to Eric, "Believe me, you're in good hands." She hugged her Aunt Sherlock and winked before trotting off after her brothers, looking so much like the young tag-a-long-sister she once was.

Eric was sure that he had never met the regal woman now standing before him. He was positive that he would have remembered meeting a woman whose eyes were identical to his wife's. His thoughts were broken by the intervention of Agatha's voice as he felt her hand clench his shoulder.

"Eric, would you please tell your mother-in-law that you would enjoy helping judge the bake-off!" Agatha smirked at Eavenly, "It was obvious from the way you enjoyed *my* pancakes that you would be a fair judge—for a change!"

Eavenly immediately began arguing with Agatha once again over pancake recipes, but both women stopped immediately as the very cool voice of their oldest sister, Sherlock, calmly interrupted. "I'm so sorry Agatha, but Eric has already promised to help me locate a shady location from which to watch the activities. I'm sure *everyone* will understand that he is otherwise occupied."

Eric found himself dumbstruck as he watched both women become speechless, before simply nodding in agreement and heading back to the table laden with baked goods. He eyed Sherlock with new admiration, "How did you do that?"

Sherlock laughed and Eric was mesmerized as he discovered that not only did Sherlock have identical eyes to Hope's, but the smile that accompanied her laughter was the same one Hope had used to capture his heart.

Sherlock leaned in conspiratorially to Eric, "I'll tell you what, let's get a nice glass of lemonade and we'll talk about it. I've been waiting a few years to talk to my favorite niece's husband." Then she winked. "Don't worry, no one will bother us while we talk. You might find this difficult to believe, but for some reason the others find me a little intimidating." Sherlock cackled in a way that reminded Eric of drunken witches sipping cheap wine from a cauldron. She winked and again shot him that amazing smile, "You don't have to worry though. I'm sure any man that Hope has picked for a husband will have enough gumption in him to not be intimidated by a fragile old lady like myself." Eric knew immediately that he was going to like Hope's aunt.

CHAPTER 21—QUIRKS

Eric leaned back in his chair and took a sip of lemonade, mentally comparing the refreshing tartness to that of the lady sitting beside him. He smiled as he decided that Hope's Aunt Sherlock was definitely the more tart of the two. They had pulled chairs beneath a tree, close enough to see the events as the contests got under way, but far enough away from the family mass for their conversation to go unheard.

"Watch this…" Sherlock leaned in toward Eric conspiratorially before yelling across the yard to a short, pot-bellied man, who had sweat pouring down his head as he visually lined up his horseshoe with the stake. "Alfred, pull up your pants, for Pete's sake! Your moon is brighter than the sun, and we don't want to blind the neighbors."

The horseshoe flew from Alfred's hand to land six feet from the metal pole he was aiming at, as he quickly grabbed his pants to jerk them up, even though his tucked in shirt had kept anything other than pink pinstripes from being seen. Sherlock chuckled and slapped her knee with her hand as she turned back to Eric. "He falls for that one every time. His trunks fell down at the lake one summer when he was about five, and ever since then it's a reflex for him to pull up his pants every five seconds. He wore a belt so tight for a few months that Mama thought he was going to do serious damage to his insides and confiscated it." Her chuckle lowered an octave and the deep throaty laugh, along with the mischievous twinkle in her eyes, enticed Eric to lean in closer to the older woman.

"Tell me, Aunt Sherlock, you don't seem that bad. Why is it that everyone is so scared of you?"

"Why, because I choose for them to be, young man. Why else?" Sherlock patted him on the knee. "Believe me, if I had wanted you to be, you would have been afraid to come within five yards of me."

Eric looked around at the clan of laughing and smiling faces before turning back to Sherlock. "But why would you want everyone to be afraid of you?"

A serious look passed across Sherlock's face for the first time, "I find people somewhat…" She paused as if searching for the exact right word before sincerely stating, "…*draining*. And such a large family, with such intense emotions, well, I find if I don't at times distance myself from the ones I love the most, that I am particularly drained. I'm sure being married to Hope, that you know what I'm talking about."

Eric frowned as he tried to follow Sherlock's explanation, "I never find Hope draining." His eyes left Sherlock's for a moment while he scanned the crowd to find Hope cheering on the twins as they ran with spoons laden with eggs. He noticed that Hope had positioned herself in front of a still very angry looking Agatha and smiled as he returned his attention to Sherlock. "On the contrary, I find Hope invigorating."

"I was referring to Hope feeling drained…not yourself." She leaned closer, looking into his eyes, and for a moment Eric imagined a brief rustle inside his mind as if his thoughts and emotions were shirts being slid to the side in a closet, each one examined ever so briefly. "Hmm…interesting."

"What's interesting?" Eric was puzzled.

Sherlock's attention wavered as her eyes returned to the crowd. They hesitated as they connected with Hope's own stare before traveling past to the pie table. Eric thought that he had been forgotten until he suddenly found himself once again the center of attention. "Do you know why I never win the bake off?"

Eric swallowed, stalling as he wondered briefly if somehow Sherlock had found out about the contest being rigged and had decided to pump him for information, but Sherlock answered her own question as if she hadn't expected an answer from Eric. "I always lose because a long time ago I decided I could put a lot of energy into baking, which I *can* do, but find no real enjoyment in, or I could pick up a dessert at Kroger, stick it in one of my dishes, and enjoy the time I saved in whatever fashion I want."

Another chuckle, "Usually, I spend that time watching Agatha and Eavenly drive each other crazy, instead of me. But they are both proud women who want to be the best. Proud people, who forge ahead alone, because somehow that makes their accomplishments more of an accomplishment, I guess. Hope's proud like that, Eric, but I think you might be the person who can help her find out that leaning on someone doesn't necessarily mean that you're weak." Sherlock stood and glanced down at Eric's perplexed expression. "Oh, and besides, I've always known that the contest was rigged." She walked towards the horseshoe area laughing loudly enough to draw a good number of stares in her direction.

"Well, huh." He muttered. His eyes were pulled by a loud explosion of laughing and cheering at the tilt-a-whirl where one of Hope's cousins was in the process of being violently sick into a trash can, while Ty, who was also a little green around the gills, waved his arms triumphantly in the air. "Weird." Eric decided that maybe Hope really hadn't been exaggerating about her family.

He was startled from his thoughts and jumped as a strong hand thumped him on the back. He turned to the smiling faces of his father-in-law and Zack, whom he now knew to be Sam's brother.

Eric extended his hand to Zack, "It's a pleasure to meet you, Sir. Ty and Luke told me you have some quite amazing stories to tell about the war."

Eric wasn't expecting the thunderous explosion of Zack's response, "What, you think I was put on this planet to *entertain* you, boy? You think I spent four years of my life living through hell, wondering if I would survive one more day, so that I could come to a reunion and have a *story* for you?! Are you some kind of sick freak, son? Well, are you?" Zack paused a full minute watching the struggle on Eric's face before he burst out laughing. "We got you good, didn't we, Eric? Boy, the expression on your face! I gotta go tell Ty and Mike." Zack wandered off toward the crowd, laughing loudly.

Sam handed Eric a Pepsi as he sat in the chair exited by Sherlock. "How you doing, Eric? Having a good time?"

Eric thought a moment before answering. "I'm having an…okay time." Eric was feeling slightly shell-shocked and decided to forget about the encounter with Zack. "Aunt Sherlock…she said some stuff I didn't quite get just now."

"Hmm." Sam took a sip of his Coke. "You like horseshoes?"

Eric was puzzled by the change of subject, but didn't want to offend Hope's father, "I've never been very good at it, myself. I guess I should practice more. How did you do in the horseshoe contest?"

Sam smiled, "We won. It's all in the arc of your throw. I could teach you sometime, if you like."

Eric smiled. "That's nice of you, Sam. I'd like that. Did Eavenly win the bake-off?"

"Yep, it was close…but she brought in her secret weapon." Eric's eyebrows rose quizzically as Sam answered the question he saw there, "Rum cake…a few bites of it and the judges are in what you would call a more *lightheaded* frame of mind."

"You mean *lighthearted*?" Eric questioned.

"No, Son, I mean lightheaded." Sam momentarily placed his cold soda can against his forehead. "I have to admit, a few more bites of that cake and I wouldn't have been able to pick the pole out of the middle to aim at." Sam's expression became serious, "So, what did Sherlock say to make you look so confused?"

"I'm not sure." Eric thought of how to best explain his odd experience with Hope's aunt. "I mean, everyone's scared of her, but then she's really nice to me and Hope's face just lit up when she came around. Then when she's sitting here talking to me, she went off on some tangent about being drained, and how Hope's drained. What did she mean by that? Is there something wrong with Hope that I don't know about?"

Sam took a drink of soda, and Eric watched Sam's Adam's-apple bob as he drained the can. He paused long enough to crush it in his hand, in a way that made Eric believe that he wasn't even aware he was doing it, before once again becoming focused on the conversation. "I wouldn't worry too much about Sherlock. She was probably just trying to get a rise out of you. Sherlock can be intimidating."

Eric frowned as he noticed that Sam couldn't quite meet his eyes as he said this. "No, I don't think she was trying to intimidate me. Actually, I think she was being pretty friendly. I think she was trying to tell me something about Hope."

Sam nodded, "Let's go see how Hope's doing. The survivor contest will be starting soon. We've won the cook-off, horseshoe, and shake-n-spin contests, but the twins seemed to be distracted by Aunt Agatha and lost the potato-sack-race and egg relay. Looks like it's your turn to give us a hand. Let's see your skill at bullshit."

Eric was puzzled until he remembered that Sam was talking about competing in the card game. He followed Sam to a table set up under a blue-and-white- striped tarp. An hour later, he felt awful as he came in second to Hope's cousin, Lester. He just couldn't seem to concentrate on the card game. Hope had the same trouble during the trivia contest as her thoughts wandered to the mysterious attacker in the woods. So the Rhineholdt's found themselves tied with Agatha's family for first place. Everything would come down to the survivor contest, which as promised seemed to be quite a remarkable challenge.

Eric found himself sitting beside Kate as everyone gathered around to view the final contest of the family reunion. He couldn't believe how extreme the final contest was as he listened to the layout of an obstacle course that would not only challenge each team's strength, but also ingenuity and dexterity. The beginning of the course involved Hope and her cousin Justine being soundly tied up and waiting for the signal to attempt to untie themselves before they could tag the next member in the relay.

Kate smiled broadly as she leaned over to Eric conspiratorially. "Don't worry—this first part will be a breeze. Hope was tied up all the time as a kid. There isn't a knot out there that can hold her. Plus, Ty was the one who tied Justine's knots, and he was an Eagle Scout."

Eric cleared his throat, "Do I even want to know why Hope would have been tied up as a kid?"

Kate laughed, "She was the youngest sister of three older brothers. That's the reason for a lot of what happened to Hope as a child." Their attention was quickly returned to the competition as Sherlock blew the whistle that began the contest. Hope quickly began her efforts on the ropes by scooting her hands under her butt and then under her legs until they were in front of her instead of tied behind her back.

Kate again leaned toward Eric, "It also helps that she's double-jointed." She paused as she looked at his face, "Oh, yeah. You would have known that."

"Of course he would know that, the man's a sex maniac, probably twists her into the shape of a pretzel." Eric didn't have to turn around to identify the owner of the loud, brash comment as Aunt Agatha.

Kate's elbow gently slammed into his ribs. "Ignore her, she's trying to get a rise out of you and to distract Hope from the contest. She thinks she needs to talk about sex all the time in order to keep her gift for writing those trashy romance novels of hers." An image of a book his secretary was reading last week popped into Eric's head. He was sure the author's first name was Agatha. His mouth dropped open in astonishment and Kate smiled apologetically, before they returned their attention to Hope and Justine. Hope had managed to untie the ropes around her legs and was now using her teeth to work on the ones around her hands, whereas Justine was still trying to untie her legs.

Hope untied her hands and tagged Ty who started running across the yard to an obstacle course reminiscent of the ones he had trained on during basic training in the army. Justine had tagged Josh, who was now doing his best to close the head start between himself and Ty. Ty finished the course first, handing off to Luke, who had to climb a pole and remove a flag from the top, which he dropped down to Mike. The flag had a key attached to it. The key opened a suitcase enclosing an anagram that had something to do with computers. Mike struggled and the gap began to close as he found a new reason for resenting technology. James was opening his suitcase when Mike finally figured out that the answer was "Pentium processor." He handed off a key that had been given to him when he got the correct answer to Hope for the final leg of the contest.

Hope ran to the pool and quickly dove in keeping her eyes on the small box that was locked on the bottom of the pool in the deep end. The first one to open the box, remove the contents and swim to the top would be the winner of the contest.

Hope welcomed the silence as the water muffled the screams and shouts of her family as they cheered above. Calmness enveloped her as she stretched forward, her strokes strong and confident. Hope loved the water. She had learned to swim before she could walk. It was the one sport that Mama approved of, due to the lack of physical contact like so many other sports; however, Mama had never been present the times that the boys had thrown Hope into the pool and wrestled her to the bottom. Hope felt her muscles as they smoothly pushed her through the water.

She reveled in the feel of the buoyancy the water naturally provided. She sometimes felt that in water, as in nature, a closeness could be found to God that was cleansing, as if all worries and concerns were being washed away. It was the same feeling she remembered from when she had risen after her baptism, breaking through the barrier from the water to once again return to the earth, after—the feeling that all weight had been lifted from her soul and the feeling of cleanness that reached far inside her—a feeling that there was a connection, as life-giving as the very essence of hydration the water itself possessed.

It was as she entered her normal state of relaxation and allowed all of the worries and stress of the contest and her life to ease away, as the sting of the wound on her head was forgotten, that the image came to her. Again she was in the woods, but this time she saw past the log that was swinging towards her, past the arms, into the eyes of her attacker, and beyond. As Hope recognized her attacker, she gasped in surprise and fear, but instead of air she deeply inhaled the taste of chlorinated water as it filled her throat, her nose, and her mouth, choking her. Panic engulfed her as she tried to cough and swim to the top, the ache from the wound on her head exploding into a bright, searing, engulfing pain, as once again she left her surroundings to enter the unconscious darkness beyond thought, beyond reaction, beyond any instinct for survival.

The quiet was deafening as the group gathered around the pool, collectively realized that below the tranquil water, Hope was drowning. Mike felt panic burst forth in his chest, as he feared that his life-long quest to protect his kid sister would somehow end with everyone who loved her standing helplessly around as the life left her body. All of this went through his mind in a brief instant before adrenaline kicked in, propelling his body forward over the edge and into the pool to his sister. He heard splashes and knew that Ty and Luke were right behind him. They quickly grabbed her limp body and pulled her to the surface, over the side, and into the hands of Kate who for the second time in a matter of hours, found herself administering her medical expertise to her kid sister. She forced the panic from her throat as she gulped in huge breaths of air, which she forcefully transferred past Hope's cold lips.

Tears of relief formed in her eyes as Hope coughed, water removing its icy hold from her lungs. Hope looked into the worried eyes of her sister, trying her hardest to remember how she had suddenly come to be lying beside the pool with her entire family surrounding her. She looked around, noticing Agatha and her cousins on the fringe of the crowd. She suddenly remembered her parents, the fire, the reunion, and the contest. "Did we win?" She croaked as Kate helped her to stand. That was the last thought from her watery struggle that Hope was able to remember.

CHAPTER 22—WINNING ISN'T EVERYTHING

First place was given to the Rhineholdts since it was obvious to all present, except for Agatha, Justine and Josh, that Hope would have won if not for the fact that she had blacked out and almost drowned before she could open the box. The near drowning dampened everyone's spirits and soon afterwards food began to be boxed up, rides were taken down and loaded onto trucks, picnic tables stacked and hauled away, and once again, Eric and Hope's backyard looked as it did before the family invasion. Though the backyard was empty, the house was not. Hope had been sent to bed, while Agatha and Eavenly worked relatively peacefully together cooking both chicken n' dumplings and homemade vegetable soup. Sam, Ty, and Uncle Bob stared at the television as baseball players ran around the diamond on the screen.

In the bedroom, Eric stood with his back to the window. His attention was on Hope. Her skin was pale. Barely discernable was the stark, new, white bandage that Kate had applied before she had left. Hope had been sleeping the sleep of the exhausted, where no noise or movement seemed to penetrate into the peaceful void that allowed the body and the spirit to recharge. She had just experienced a very long day, following other very long days. Knowing all of this, Eric felt there was something else, something more that lurked below the surface. Something that possibly Sherlock knew about, and everyone else seemed to be denying. He sat on the side of the bed and brushed Hope's hair back away from her bandage, yet she did not stir. Looking at her kind face softened by the magic of sleep, he felt foolish thinking that there was anything that she could be keeping from him.

Eric stretched out beside Hope. The need to be close to her was overwhelming. Careful not to wake her, he put his arms around her, pulling her closer to his body. Hope moved without waking, snuggling deeper into his embrace, resting her head on his chest. Eric lay like this a long time, quietly listening to the steady rhythm of her breathing. Gradually, the long day and nerve-wracking threats to Hope's well being reeked their havoc on Eric's body, and he succumbed to an exhausted sleep beside his wife.

The first hint of a disturbance was more a shadow than a sound, but Hope thought that was strange, because how was it possible that she had heard the shadow that woke her? She forced her breathing to remain even and mentally tried to force the stiffness of fear traveling down her spine to go away. Again, the shadow moved against the wall, but this time Hope could tell that the source was coming from outside of her bedroom.

Her muscles relaxed as she slowly slid from beneath her blanket. She grabbed the huge Maglite flashlight from her nightstand. Her hand gripped the cold metal and she felt reassured by the weight of the eighteen-inch barrel. She could imagine the impact it would make if the need arose for it to make contact with someone's skull. She moved slowly toward the window, the place she believed to be the source of the shadow. She hesitated for a moment thinking of other options—calling the police, running from the room, getting Eric's Smith and Wesson .38—but the window seemed to have a power over her, dragging her ever closer to it, against her will.

She saw that her hand was shaking as she touched the curtain, hesitating a moment before leaning forward, peering out the glass into the inky darkness, confused about the shadow that had somehow appeared without a hint of light. Menacing eyes peered back at her through the window, piercing with their unmasked hatred. A hand shot forward, and suddenly the window had disappeared. There was no longer a barrier to keep the hand from circling her neck, choking her, and locking her scream deep inside the pit of her stomach.

Hope clawed at the air, fighting the grasp around her neck, confused to find herself in her bed with the late beams of daylight streaming through her window. Eric was sleeping soundly beside her and the window was still firmly in place. It had been a dream, a strange, dark nightmare that had left her shaken. She still felt the cold touch of fear that had traveled up her spine as she remembered the hatred and menace of the unknown attacker in her dream.

The door opened, making Hope jump, as Mama and Aunt Agatha popped their heads around to peer at Hope. "Good, you're awake. We made you dinner. You'll feel better after you've had something to eat."

Hope wasn't sure if even Mama's comfort food could remove the chill that had enveloped her.

CHAPTER 23—SMOTHERED

After a plate of chicken n' dumplings and a piping hot bowl of vegetable soup, Hope was feeling considerably warmer and her nightmare was quickly becoming a shadow of a memory. Eric was on his third bowl of soup, "This is really good soup, ladies. In fact, this is the best soup I've ever eaten."

Both Eavenly and Agatha beamed as they set a plate of warm oatmeal raisin and a plate of chocolate chip cookies on the table. Eavenly sat down next to Hope nibbling on a cookie, her eyes observant. Agatha took a seat on the other side of the table, unusually solemn as she topped off Bob's bowl of soup. Eavenly glanced over at Sam who had barely touched his plate of chicken n' dumplings, before placing a couple of warm cookies on both his and Hope's plates. Her attention returned to her daughter. "How are you feeling, Sweetie? Want another bowl of soup?"

"No, thanks. I'm full." Hope wiped her mouth with her napkin.

Eavenly leaned forward. "Your head okay? Do you need me to get you one of those pills Kate left you?"

"No, I'm okay."

"Want me to fix you a nice cup of tea? We don't want you to catch a cold after nearly drowning like that."

Hope pushed her chair back and glared at Mama. "Look, I'm fine. I don't need you hovering over me, okay?" She walked out of the kitchen without another word.

Eric was shocked at Hope's attitude. She wasn't the type to snap at anyone and was the most patient person he had ever met. He felt uncomfortable as he saw a hurt look pass across Eavenly's face. "I'm sorry about that, Mama Rhineholdt. I'm sure Hope didn't mean to sound so snippy."

Eavenly nodded, "I'm sure she's just feeling under the weather still. You know…first the attack in the woods, and then with almost drowning. Anyone would be a little snippy after that."

Agatha looked at Bob in shock, before returning her gaze to Eavenly. "Hope was attacked in the woods?"

Ty walked into the kitchen and let out a whoop as he eyed the food on the table. He quickly stuffed a cookie in his mouth, talking around it, "Boy, those chicken n' dumplings look great. Hand me a plate."

Agatha interrupted, "Eavenly, you didn't answer me."

Eavenly ignored Agatha and swatted at Ty's hand. "Don't talk with your mouth full…and say please. I raised you better than that."

Ty struggled with swallowing the cookie in his mouth as quickly as possible before choking out, "Please?"

Agatha at this point stood up, her voice raised, "Damn, it! Would somebody please tell me what the hell is going on here?"

Ty, having missed the first part of the conversation, tried to appease Agatha, "You see Aunt Agatha, Mama gets pretty angry when she thinks any of us are using poor manners."

Eric walked out of the kitchen as he heard Sam jump in trying to shine some light on the confusing conversation and calm everyone down. He was momentarily puzzled when he didn't find Hope in the bedroom, but he soon heard the sound of running water and followed it to the master bath, where he found her.

If anyone had any doubt about the wealth at Hope's personal disposal, it would only take a visit to the master bathroom to be convinced. Hope had a weakness for long, hot baths. The bathroom was opulent by any standard. The floor was heated. The marble countertops were covered with exotic lotions, bubble baths, and soaps. The shower contained sixteen sprays that massaged as it cleaned. The fixtures were made of brass and the towels made of the softest fabrics available. There was an industrial size water heater that assured water would be consistently hot. A television and VCR/DVD combo in one corner of the huge dressing area was easily viewed from the centerpiece of the bathroom, and the sunken tub had every spa feature available. Beneath a thick layer of jasmine-scented bubbles, Eric found his wife sitting with a look upon her face as if she had just found out that the dog was dead.

Eric sat on the side of the tub and lathered up a washcloth with plumeria-scented soap. He then began to gently wash Hope's back. He could feel her muscles begin to relax as the tension started to leave her body. Hope leaned back against the tub, tilting her head so that she could look into his eyes. "I was a bitch, huh?"

Eric's hand paused. "I would never say that about you. I don't think you have it in you. Are you okay, Hope?"

A long sigh whispered past her lips. "I'm not sure."

Eric wasn't sure how to respond. It was not like Hope to be pessimistic. Even in her darkest moments, she would always focus on the brighter side. Before he could think of a reassuring comment, Hope continued as if guessing his thoughts, "I'll be okay. I'll tell Mom that her cookies are obviously better than Aunt Agatha's, and she'll forget all about me being grumpy. I guess I'm just tired. It's nothing to worry about Eric—really."

Eric wasn't sure if it was the acoustics of the bathroom or the effects of the day, but Hope's words had a hollow ring, as if she herself didn't believe what she was saying.

CHAPTER 24—STOLEN POTENTIAL

The house was unusually quiet. Hope stood in the kitchen looking out the window watching Eric, Uncle Bob, and Pops as they cut, hammered, and stained boards for her arbor and swing. Ty had driven Mama and Aunt Agatha the seventy miles home, to look around and to meet with the cleaners about what she wanted done with the fire and smoke-damaged items around the house. Both activities were the type to eat away at the day.

Hope had finally been allowed to sleep in and had just gotten out of bed, long after everyone else had begun the day. Eric had been in to check on her, to make sure her head was feeling better, and to let her know that everyone planned on being busy the whole day. He had also suggested that she spend the day relaxing and watching videos or reading a book. Hope felt guilty that he was so concerned over her injuries, and she had a feeling that everyone else was trying to give her some space due to her irritability the day before.

She was feeling guilty enough over her earlier grumpiness to drive down and help Mama sort through the mess with Ty when she decided to first eat a bowl of cereal. After opening several cabinets in search of first, a bowl, then cereal, and finally a spoon, only to discover that every item in her kitchen had been rearranged to better suit Mama, she was swayed to change her mind and to spend a little more time alone.

Hope was feeling out of sorts as she dug into a bowl of Cocoa Rice Crispies, her spoon circling the bowl in order to expedite the process of turning her milk chocolaty. After only a few bites, she set her bowl in the sink, forgetting to place it in the dishwasher, and wandered into the living room. She gazed at her video collection without really seeing it. She felt as though there was something she should be remembering, but whatever it was kept eluding her. The more she tried to remember, the more a dull ache attempted to become a terrible headache.

She pulled a video from the shelf aimlessly before replacing it. She glanced at the books on her bookshelves and although she had the latest novels by James Patterson and Clive Cussler on her nightstand, she didn't really feel like reading. She wandered back into the kitchen thinking she would reorganize her cabinets, but the fruitlessness of that effort kept her from beginning, at least until Mama returned to her own home. Hope finally decided a trip to the video store to pick up a couple of new releases might do the trick to cheer her up.

Hope still felt jumpy as she drove to the video store. She noticed a black pickup with two men in it following a few cars behind her, which looked identical to one she had seen earlier as she had pulled out of her driveway. She mentally kicked herself for being paranoid. She pulled into the parking lot of the video store and noticed that instead of following her, the truck drove past and went on down the street.

Hope was beginning to feel better when she walked into the store and saw that one of her students, Jimmy, was working behind the counter. His young face immediately broke into a wide smile as he saw Hope. "Hey, teach. What's up? You thinking of spending a nice day like this locked up inside watching a movie?"

Hope returned Jimmy's smile, "Somehow, I don't think the owners would appreciate you trying to convince the customers to avoid movies, Jimmy…no matter how pretty a day it is." Hope actually knew for a fact that the owner wouldn't really mind too much, because Hope was the owner of this particular video store. Jimmy wasn't aware of that piece of information.

The manager had agreed to keep Hope's involvement, and her ownership, a secret. Her family also had influence in the law firm where she had mentioned a job opening that Jimmy's mom might be interested in applying for—a job that involved benefits, flexible hours, and a large enough salary for Jimmy, his mother, and young brother to be able to move into a better home in a safer neighborhood. She had been hired and trained as a secretary, despite the fact that she hadn't met the usual employment requirements. The lawyers had at first been doubtful, but Jimmy's mom was a hard worker and fast learner, and she had kept the job on her own merit.

Jimmy did not seem to be the same person now that he was when he had been a freshman in Hope's class and she had caught him trying to steal her purse from her desk drawer. Hope had checked into his file and found a disturbing record of the use and distribution of drugs, poor grades, disrespect of teachers and students alike, and violence. At fourteen, Jimmy had already been assigned a social worker and a parole officer. He was one step away from a life of desolation and a waste of the intelligence Hope saw lurking behind the anger she saw in his eyes.

The fact that he was failing and could hardly read had landed him in Hope's English class. That first year had been an ongoing battle of wills. Everyday in class a struggle ensued as Hope demanded more from Jimmy than he had ever been asked to do. She openly challenged him to prove his intelligence and ability. Jimmy, never one to back down from a fight, never missed Hope's class, even though he skipped all others except for wood shop and gym.

Hope decided to make Jimmy one of her causes and enjoyed the look of surprise on his face as he wound up with her as a teacher for sophomore English. By the end of that year, their battles had ended in a cautious truce. Jimmy was reading on level, with a C in English, and Hope's classroom was furnished with some beautiful handmade bookshelves.

During his junior year, Jimmy began showing up to Hope's classroom, where he again was a student, before and after school, giving her a hand with anything that needed doing. Jimmy had a reputation for being a tough character from his earlier years, and word quickly spread that Hope was not a teacher that anyone should mess with, unless they wanted to discuss the problem after school with Jimmy.

It was on one after-school occasion when the conversation had turned to part-time work. Jimmy had begun to open up to Hope, and she knew what a hard home life he had and the need for spare money. It was then that she had came up with the job positions for both Jimmy and his mother.

Now as Hope looked at the man Jimmy had turned into, she couldn't help but feel a certain level of pride. Jimmy had taken correspondence courses and attended summer school in order to make up for lost time and graduated in May with the rest of his class. Although, due to his early problems settling down, he wasn't in the top ten percent of his class, he had somehow been able to earn a rare scholarship that paid for not only tuition, but also food and housing, from an anonymous foundation, also owned by the Rhineholdts.

Hope couldn't conceal the look of pride that spread across her face as she looked at Jimmy. "You ready to start college in a couple of months, Sport?"

Jimmy beamed as he stopped sorting returned videos and leaned across the counter towards Hope. His expression quickly changed as he got his first close up look at Hope's face. "Damn, teach. What happened to your head?"

Hope heard the anger that underscored the concern in Jimmy's voice. "It's not a big deal Jimmy. The bandage makes it look worse than it is."

Jimmy didn't look convinced. "I don't know teach...that don't look like no accident to me."

"Doesn't look like any." Hope corrected reflexively.

Jimmy nodded without correcting himself. "Looks to me like someone whacked you upside the head." He leaned in closer and lowered his voice. "You tell me who did it, Teach, and I'll take care of it. Me and a couple of my friends will take care of it pronto."

Hope put her hand consolingly on his shoulder, "You mean, 'A couple of friends and *I* have no reason to get into trouble over something that doesn't involve me, because *I* don't want to throw away all the hard work my English teacher has spent on me by going to jail.' Right?"

Jimmy grinned sheepishly. "You know me, Teach. I don't even jay walk anymore."

"So how are your mama and Jamal?" Hope decided to change the subject.

Jimmy's smile widened to it's fullest at the mention of his six-year-old brother. "Moms is doing great! She started dating a guy who finally treats her with the respect she deserves. You know what I mean?" He continued at Hope's nod. "And Jamal finished out the year with perfect attendance. And he made the honor roll! That little dude has it all together. He thinks school is tight and his teacher told Moms that he's one of the smartest kids she has ever taught, no lie. That boy is goin' to be all right."

"How could he not be, when he has a great big brother like you?"

"Well, you know teach…I woulda probably been a drop out or somethin' if you hadn't always been on my case." Jimmy's voice became gruff as he tried to keep his emotions out of his voice.

"Thanks." Hope blushed at the obvious gratitude felt by Jimmy. "So what have you got in new that's good?"

"Seen Terminator Six? It's pretty good." Jimmy opened up the DVD drawer and started flipping through titles.

"Actually, I think I would like something with a little less action."

"You want something funny or you want a good drama?"

Hope peered over the counter trying to decide on a category. "Hmm…I'm not sure, probably comedy. I need something to cheer me up."

Jimmy glanced up from the drawer studying her for a moment, "Well then, I've got the latest Harry Potter and a new Disney movie, too. Those kinds of movies usually cheer you up, right?"

"Those would be perfect, Jimmy." Hope was always surprised at how insightful Jimmy was about her personality traits.

Jimmy put the videos in a bag and handed them to her across the counter. The manager had told Jimmy that Hope was a special customer who received free movie rentals. Hope was glad for this excuse for two reasons. She didn't want to suffer through the white lie of paying for a video that she technically already owned, and also she had worried that Jimmy might have been too tempted to give her videos for free, and she didn't want to contribute to a backslide in his moral development. She reached across the counter and brushed a hand against his braids, knowing that no matter how much he complained, he had always liked the attention. "So, I'll be back in a few more times before you're off to become the big man on campus, but I heard you plan on still working here part-time once classes start, too."

"Yeah, things are finally workin' out right for me. That scholarship pays for all the big stuff, and then the manager says we'll work out my schedule around classes so that I can have some spending money, too."

"I'm proud of you, Jimmy. You've turned into a man I'm proud to know." Hope turned and walked to the door, knowing that she had embarrassed Jimmy, but also knowing that her words still meant a tremendous amount to him.

She lightly swung the bag as she started toward her Jeep. She was already feeling better, and although she had seen both movies when they came out at the theater, she was looking forward to watching them again once she got home. She opened her purse, digging around past her checkbook, cell phone, and a large pack of Big Red gum searching for her keys. She had just come to the decision that she had probably left them on the counter in the video store and turned around to go back and get them when she came face to face with her assailant from the woods. Her breath froze in her throat as the sun glinted off the blade of the very sharp knife the man was holding, and the fact that he was only a couple of steps away from her was frightening. It was obvious from his stance that he had been about to stab her from behind.

Reflexes and training kicked in, and she found herself automatically redistributing her weight so that she was evenly balanced on the balls of her feet. She was set and ready to dodge or kick as the situation demanded, keeping her eyes on the knife blade.

She glanced up at her attacker's face, reminding herself of Joe's instructions on how to predict the attack based on the movement of the attacker's head. When she found herself gazing into the eyes of her attacker, she felt as if once again she was in the pool drowning. Suddenly she remembered what had been hovering on the edge of her thoughts, just out of her reach. She *knew* her attacker! Though the face did not resemble the teenage boy she had known, and his body was larger and more muscular, the eyes and the evil they held within them were enough for Hope to know Rob Stinner in any disguise. Suddenly, she felt as if she couldn't breathe, old fears and memories shutting down the logical side of her brain that was signaling her how to fight back, how to flee, how to win.

Memories of Rob's parents' funeral, his arrest, and even worse the images of their actual murders began to seep past the barriers she had so painstakingly built and touched her deep inside, filling her with nausea. She was overcome by the horror, no longer seeing the Rob before her, but the one of her past. She was unaware of the beating of sneakers on pavement or the shouts from a voice that should have been familiar.

She was frozen as the knife sliced the very air, searing it as it swung in an arc and rammed deep into flesh. Blood seeped from the stomach wound, the knife locating vital organs, slicing cleanly through, before twisting and shredding with its serrated edge as it was pulled away. Rob smiled as he wiped blood from the blade onto his hand. Screams from other customers in the parking lot forced him to turn and run. The black truck that had been following Hope earlier squealed around the corner, stopped only long enough for him to jump inside, and rushed away before the door was once again closed.

Hope looked at the blood, *knowing* it was a mortal wound. Tears filled her eyes as she looked down at her hands, still clutching her purse. She hadn't fought back. She had not swung, or kicked, or delivered one blow. She fell to her knees pulling Jimmy's head onto her lap, her tears dripping onto his face nearly as quickly as blood seeped from his body.

Jimmy grasped her hand and gasped for breath, his eyes older than his years. "Teach…Teach…w…w…woulda' happened anyway." The voice she had thought held so much promise, moments earlier became a whisper, "It's…okay." Then silence.

Hope wiped her tears from his face. "No." She answered. She sat holding his still body as life left him, as the sirens screamed in the distance, as gloved hands pulled her away. "No." She cried, knowing that the medics didn't understand her, but she still tried to explain, "No…it can never again be okay!"

CHAPTER 25—HOPE'S NOT HERE

Eavenly Rhineholdt looked as if a small breeze would blow her over, if it were not for the supportive arm of Ty as they walked into the hospital's main entrance. Agatha for once in her life was speechless, as two television news crews rushed towards them.

"Are you related to Hope Rhineholdt?" A tall man, who would have been handsome if not for an obnoxious air of arrogance, shoved a microphone towards Eavenly's face.

"I'm her mother. Now please excuse me, I want to see about my daughter." Eavenly, used to being obeyed, calmly started to once again proceed forward.

The microphone was shoved in front of her as the lights from the camera momentarily blinded her. "What was her involvement with the deceased? Is it true he was her student?"

The other reporter jumped in, "Were they having an affair?"

Not to be outdone, the first reporter shoved forward, "The deceased had a known drug involvement in his past. Is Hope Rhineholdt involved in drugs?" The look of arrogance left his face as Eavenly's hand made contact with a loud smack. She and Ty quickly made their way past the cameras and down the hallway, but not before the reporter recovered and turned to his cameraman, "Did you get that?" At the cameraman's nod, he smiled maliciously, calling to Eavenly's back. "That was a mistake lady—I have it on tape. I'll see you in court!"

Agatha calmly searched through her purse, triumphantly pulling out a business card and handing it to him. "Here, contact my son." She aimed a smug smile over her shoulder as she walked away, "And when we go to court…I promise you'll lose." The reporter looked down at the card and then stood in bewilderment as she bustled quickly along catching up with her sister.

"The nerve of that man! Don't worry, Eavenly. Josh and Justine will take care of him. I wish I had given him a good smack myself." Agatha's steps faltered for a moment as if contemplating going back to hit the reporter, but changed her mind as her concern for her favorite niece overrode the thought. "What did Sam say about Hope again, when he called?"

Eavenly sighed as she repeated the information that she had already repeated numerous times on the ride to the hospital. "He said that she hadn't been cut or anything, but the doctors suspect that she's in shock or something." As she turned the corner and caught sight of Eric, Sam, and Bob sitting in the waiting room, her steps sped up and she virtually jumped into Sam's embrace. "Where is she? How is she?"

It was Eric who answered, looking older and more tired than any of them had ever seen him. "She's in a room resting. After she talked to the police, they gave her a sedative. The doctors won't let any of us go in to see her. They claim she asked not to be seen by anybody."

Eavenly looked thunderstruck as she pulled away from Sam. "Well, she was upset and not thinking straight. Surely, they don't believe she wouldn't want to see her family after the ordeal she's been through?" The silence that followed was answer enough to declare that Sam and Eric had already tried to see Hope. Eavenly pulled Eric close, tightly hugging him, "Don't you worry, Son. It's all a misunderstanding. That girl of mine couldn't last five minutes without wanting you near her." She patted him on the shoulder as she pulled away. "Let me find a doctor, and I'll get this all straightened out."

Eavenly was stricken, a light blush of angry color spreading across her face. "What do you *mean* I can't see my daughter? I'm her mother! She'll want to see me."

Dr. Hyder was not swayed. "I'm sorry, Ma'am, but she requested not to be disturbed by anyone. The only people who have been allowed to see her since she was brought in have been the police."

"Well, how is she? You can at least tell me that." Eavenly was becoming more agitated by the minute.

"Besides the wound on her head, which she apparently acquired yesterday, she isn't suffering from any physical ailment, but she does seem to be showing evidence of some form of post-traumatic stress. I'm sorry, but that's all I can tell you."

Eavenly glared at the doctor's retreating back. "Won't let anyone but the police in, huh? Well, we'll just see about that." Eavenly flipped open her cell phone with such force it almost snapped the hinges. She angrily punched in speed dial number three and tapped her foot while she waited for an answer.

Mike's voice was tense as he answered, "Hello?"

"How far away are you from the hospital?" Sam had called the others as soon as he had told Eavenly that their youngest daughter was in the hospital after being once again attacked.

"I'm about fifteen minutes away. Luke and Kate are following right behind me."

"Do you have your uniform on?"

Mike was puzzled, "No, I wasn't on duty when you called…why?"

"Do you have a uniform in the car?" Eavenly's voice was short and clipped.

"Yeah, I have a clean one in the trunk."

"Put it on before you come in to the hospital. I need you to talk some sense into your sister." She paused for a moment. "And if a reporter starts shouting insults about Hope when you walk in, see if there isn't some legal way to give him a flesh wound."

Mike quietly opened the door of Hope's room, unsurprised by the civility the doctors had awarded to a man in uniform. He walked over to the bed and quietly dragged a chair up to its side. Any other member of the family might have walked back out of the hospital room as they first glanced at the woman lying there.

She lay quietly staring at the ceiling, her hazel eyes somber and almost black in the dimness of the room. Without a hint of a smile, and with the look of weariness that surrounded her entire being, most would have had difficulty on first glance recognizing the sad creature before them as Hope, but Mike, unfortunately, had seen this side of Hope once before.

CHAPTER 26—WE TRAVELED HERE BEFORE

May 1984

Hope quickly threw her books in her locker, slamming it shut as she turned to rush home in time to get ready for a date. As she turned from the locker she came face to face with Rob Stinner. Surprise flashed across her face, and she shoved down her dislike for him into her stomach as her natural capacity for compassion bubbled forth. "Oh, Rob...you surprised me." She regretted the words as they worked to remind her of her brothers confronting him a month earlier about that very thing. He seemed to have a habit of following her, even to her own home, where they had ordered him to leave her alone.

She put a hand on his shoulder, but quickly pulled it away as bile seemed to form in her throat at the touch. "I heard about what happened to your parents last week. I, uh, I'm very sorry, Rob. I can't believe you came back to school so soon."

The cold smile that spread across his face chilled her. "Well, life must go on." He leaned in too close to her as his eyes traveled the length of her body. "The pain at times is horrible. It might help me to recover if I had someone to lean on...someone to hold me."

Hope felt shock at his obvious attempt to use his parents' deaths to convince her to become involved with him. She suddenly felt as if between the two of them, she was the only one who felt any sadness for the loss of his parents. "I'm sorry, Rob, about your parents, but I must be going home." She started to walk past him when he abruptly grabbed her arm.

Rob's voice was hard as his hand bit into her. "Running away, again? You going to go tell your big shot brothers that I was picking on you?"

"Rob, my brothers don't have anything to do with this. *I* don't have anything to do with this. You and I are not in a relationship and never will have a relationship. I'm sorry you're having a hard time right now, but you have to leave me alone."

"I'll do whatever I want." He sneered as he pulled her close, trying to kiss her and grinding her lips into her teeth. Hope pushed with all her might against his shoulders.

"What's going on here?" Mr. Mathews came down the hall.

Rob let go of Hope and turned to the teacher angrily. "It's none of your business." He turned and walked down the hall, his every step an outward display of his anger.

"Are you okay?" Mr. Mathew's look of concern was comforting.

"I'm fine…thanks, Mr. Mathews."

"There's something wrong with that boy." Hope was surprised to see such a look of hatred on a teacher's face.

"He's upset. His parents were murdered last week, you know."

"Something's been wrong with him long before last week." As if suddenly realizing he was speaking to a student, he gathered himself together and paused to straighten his tie. "Well, you should be getting on home now."

Hope drove home slowly, unable to shake her feelings of sadness and confusion. The more she thought of Rob and the feelings of dislike she felt whenever he was around, the more her head ached. The pain began to grow and she pulled over to the side of the road as it intensified.

Images began to flash before her eyes and the view of the green fields and old maple trees on the side of the road were overlaid with a haze of dripping red and a feeling of rage. Hope breathed deeply trying to push the images out of her head. They had occurred in the past as fuzzy shadows that were fleeting and lasted for mere seconds, but lately the flashes were more frequent and intense, especially when she was around Rob Stinner. Suddenly in her vision a knife flashed and the image became focused so that she could now discern that the red was blood dripping from the blade as it stabbed deeply into Rob Stinner's mother's chest. A man walked into her vision from the right, rushing forward shouting angrily, grabbing, but the knife was faster as it plunged into his stomach and then quickly across his throat.

Suddenly, Hope found she was laughing, but it wasn't really her laughing, it was the person she was inside of in the image in her mind, it was Rob Stinner laughing as he hacked and carved his parents with the butcher knife his mother had been using to prepare dinner. Tears filled her eyes. Hope grabbed frantically at the handle of the door before running to the edge of the road and leaning into the tall grass of the ditch as she came face to face with her school lunch for the second time that day.

Hope wiped her mouth and sat limply on the road, weakened from being sick moments earlier, but also from the piercing images that had enveloped her as she had struggled forcibly to block them from her mind. She heard the sound of a car and glanced to the side of the road as Mike got out of his deputy's car and rushed over to her.

"Hey kid, you okay?" Mike wiped her hair out of her face and helped her to stand. Hope had grown up with his protective nature and was used to Mike's concern as he leaned her against her car. "What's wrong?"

Hope looked up into the face of the big brother she had trusted to protect her since she could walk and it all came out. The dark halos she sometimes glimpsed around people, a sense of all of a person's darker deeds, the images of Rob Stinner murdering his parents.

Other individuals might have felt some form of doubt and a definite disbelief if their sixteen-year-old kid sister suddenly claimed she could see images of things that had happened to someone else, but to Mike it made perfect sense. In a way, he had been waiting for this kind of revelation for a long time. The Rhineholdt children had grown up knowing that they were different, along with their cousins, aunts, and especially Mama. It wasn't something they ever discussed, but it was something of which they were all aware.

The fact that Mama almost always knew when someone was lying to her was only one of her somewhat psychic skills. The way Luke, Ty, and Mike all seemed to react a little faster to situations than most seemed to indicate that they could determine a need before it existed. This had been beneficial in the fire department, army, and police department for each of them on numerous occasions. Kate's skill as a surgeon, her ability to determine what should be done in a quick and decisive manner, had saved many lives. A cursory glance sometimes was all she needed on which to form her opinion, while others would have spent a much longer time on a diagnosis.

So the fact that Hope had not seemed to have any such innate skill had actually seemed odd, when any of them had thought of it. Mike was actually relieved that one had finally showed up in his youngest sister. It was this relief and a desire of his own that pushed the look of Hope's despair from his mind. It allowed him to look past her need and focus on one of his own.

It was the last item of Hope's itemization of her situation that Mike latched onto. The Stinner murders were a big deal. Especially if they went unsolved in such a small town. He was also sure in his mind that the officer who solved the case would probably find himself with a raise and promotion. He would be the town hero, and probably in line for sheriff, especially since Sheriff Roberts had just mentioned the day before how he was thinking it was about time to retire. "Hope, you said you could see the Stinners' murders?"

Hope nodded. Her eyes dark as she looked past Mike's shoulder, focusing on a hawk circling the air over a nearby field.

Mike drew her attention back to him. "See, the thing is, Hope, how much do you see? Do you see what happens to the knife? Where he put it? No knife, we got no case, and so far we have no knife. Hope, do you know where the knife is?"

Hope's eyes were filled with tears and she shook her head, "No, I was able...I was able to block it before he finished."

"Hope, I need you to bring it back. I need for you to find the knife. Otherwise...it's likely this guy is going to walk."

Mike didn't see the anguish as it poured through her body, but he could hear it in her voice. "You don't understand...what it's like. I'm—I'm him when it's happening. I feel what he feels. So while part of me wants to wretch at the evil of it, there's also him laughing and loving every moment of it. It tries to push through...and I try to block it. I'm just barely able to get it to go away—and you want me to *bring it back*? I can't. I can't do that, Mike."

"Hope, this thing you can do…it's a gift. If you can help me solve this case, you have to do it. You see that, don't you?" Mike stared into Hope's eyes.

"But…it's awful, and I'm not sure I can stop the visions again." Hope looked up at her older brother, seeing the need in his face and sighed. She thought of Rob Stinner and the evil she had seen inside of him. Guilt began to close off her throat as she thought of him getting away with murder. She sighed, looking up at Mike's hopeful face and nodded her agreement to try.

Hope closed her eyes, not sure exactly how to bring the images back. She had never wanted to see the horrible things that people could do, but she thought back, remembering the way Rob had stabbed his parents and the feelings that had flowed through her. At first the images were blurry memories of what she had seen before, but then they began to clear up, and she could tell by the sensation of no longer being in control that she was going back into Rob Stinner's murders.

Again, she felt his exultation at the demise of the two people he most hated in the world. He glanced around the scene, wiping away incriminating evidence, careful not to touch the bodies themselves. He grabbed a rag from a drawer in the kitchen and used it to cover the knife. After a stop at the garage for a small spade, he walked into the woods. He stopped at a log, lifting it and carefully moving one end to reveal the bug infested muddy area beneath. Rob quickly dug a shallow hole and placed the knife in it before replacing the dirt and the log. A person could walk past that log a hundred times without any idea of the bloody knife hidden beneath it.

Hope slumped against the car, dizzy and disoriented. She pushed at the darkness that was surrounding her. She felt as if the evil she had seen somehow covered her body in a tangible film. It gagged her with its poison. She returned her focus to the hawk, still circling overhead, only now she noticed its intense concentration on its purpose. It was hunting, looking for prey that was weaker which it could snatch up in its mighty grasp, crushing it, squeezing out its life. She smiled at its power. Her face pinched around the smile that seemed sinister beneath feverish eyes. Mike grew concerned and placed a hand on her shoulder.

She stared past the concern in Mike's face, looking deeper inside at his need to be the hero. She knew that he wanted the praise of the capture, and that his ego needed it. He would feel joy and excitement as the town patted him on the shoulder, saying that now they could feel safe, while the murdered couple, who really had never done anything for anyone other than themselves, would quickly fade from memory.

Hope pushed his hand away. "About a hundred feet behind his house, in the woods, there's a fallen log. Under the far side you'll find the knife. His fingerprints are on it because he was sure that no one would find it. Who would suspect him, right? Go along now, Mike, and play hero."

Mike was shocked at her bitterness. "Hope, are you okay?"

"Okay? You concerned now? Do my feelings somehow matter more now that you have the information you need? You were only thinking about yourself. Even in worrying about me now, you just don't want me to do or say something that will mess up your case."

"Hope, that's not..."

She interrupted him, laughing. "True? That's what you were going to say wasn't it?" She didn't wait for an answer. "Don't try to tell me what's the truth. I can see it *inside* of you Mike. You're actually glad that it's Rob. That way, not only do you get the glory, but you get to be rid of someone you have always hated."

"I hate him, yeah—because he's evil, he killed his parents, and he would like to hurt you."

Hope looked at him, not seeing the hurt or concern on his face, only seeing the greed and pride that shadowed his features. She felt the dizziness worsen and swayed on her feet. Mike caught her before she could fall and lifted her into his arms. "I'm going to take you to my place. You don't look so good." Worry gnawed at his stomach. All Hope saw was his fear of the disappointment his parents would have for him when they found out that he was somehow to blame for Hope's condition. She allowed him to lead her to his car, not wanting her parents to see her in this state, but only after having Mike promise to come back with a friend and get her car.

Mike dropped Hope off at his house, tucking her into bed, where exhaustion overcame her body. He thought about how to handle the case, and left the house to make his way across town. He used a pay phone to make a call to his cell phone, not saying anything but giving himself some time, so that phone logs would later corroborate his statements of an anonymous source. He couldn't have his "psychic" sister ever be on the witness stand. He wouldn't do that to her. He found the knife, exactly where Hope had said it would be. Fingerprints matched Rob's, and Mike picked him up. As he put him into the car, he couldn't keep from voicing the emotion deep inside of him. "Now you won't be able to bother my sister ever again." He knew it was a mistake, as soon as he saw the burning hatred in Rob's eyes intensify, but he couldn't recall the words.

Hope seemed to be okay the next day, but Mike couldn't help thinking that the brightness usually found in her eyes and smile had somehow faded. He felt as if he had stolen part of her innocence. The bridge between them remained, and after she moved away to attend college, he felt as if the move was in part so that she could put distance between herself and the memories of a murder that she had never really witnessed, but one that would forever be vivid in her mind.

CHAPTER 27—TO PROTECT AND TO SERVE

Mike took Hope's limp hand, gently lifting it from the white, coarse, hospital sheets. "Hey, kiddo." He tried to keep a teasing note in his voice, even though the sadness he felt at seeing her like this choked the words off in his throat. He tried again, "So, you finally found a way to stop Mama in her tracks, huh? Man, I have to say I wish I had thought of doctor's orders to ban Mama from pestering me." He gave her hand a squeeze, hoping for a smile as she turned her head towards him.

"I was afraid." The frailty in her voice tore fresh anguish into Mike's lungs. "I don't want to know."

Mike listened to the quiet, not wanting to ask, but the quiet demanded it from somewhere deep inside. "Know what, Hope?"

"I don't want to look at all the people I love and know the evil that lurks inside."

Mike wasn't sure how to answer, so he said nothing.

Her tired eyes peered into his, and he felt a chill as if an ice cube had dripped down his back. He felt an urge to run from this creature in front of him. The idea that this really was his little sister battling with the darkness she seemed to emit caused an ache of protectiveness inside him. He stayed sitting, but gently removed his hand from her touch.

"You remember how I can see evil don't you, Mike?" Her voice was flat and emotionless as she continued to stare at him with her dead eyes. "After all, you're the one who made me do it the first time."

Sadness enfolded Mike. Even at her angriest, bitterness had always been an alien quality to Hope. Now she seemed to be thriving on its acrid taste. He almost expected her to lick her lips to taste the salt from the wounds her words were inflicting. "Hope, what happened?"

A smile spread across her face, so devoid of any humor that it pulled her face into a sad caricature of the person she usually was. "Why, don't you know? I killed someone."

"Hope, you didn't kill anyone." Mike took her hand again, willing her to feel his strength and the sureness of his voice, praying for her to take it inside of herself.

"You weren't there." She looked away, a tear pooling, hanging damply from an eyelash.

"God, Hope, I wish I was there. I wish anyone were there besides you. You've been put through too much for any one person to deal with these past few days."

"You were right."

Mike felt as if he had missed part of the conversation. "Right about what?"

"The day I was attacked. You wanted me to reach out then, see if I could tell who had attacked me. Even if I didn't recognize him then, I would have been able to feel him before he came up behind me in that parking lot."

"You don't know that Hope. You don't know how things would have turned out. You might have been the one who died in that parking lot." Mike's voice broke at the thought of how close he had come to losing her.

"It should have been me...he wanted to hurt *me*." Tears began to silently fall down her pale cheeks. "And he probably has no understanding of how much he did."

"Hope..."

"It was Rob Stinner, Mike. He was after me...and I was so scared of him. He's changed his face, but I know it was him. He could never change the look in his eyes. I was just so scared. So scared of the memories and feelings that I didn't even try to fight back." She began to openly sob. "I didn't even *try*."

Mike pulled her close in a hug. He softly rubbed her back in a small circular rhythm, trying to comfort, trying to support her, trying to swallow down the guilt of a hastily spoken taunt years ago. He could hear his own voice in his head, taunting Rob with the knowledge that he would never be able to bother Hope again. His own eyes grew damp as he felt the weight of Hope's despair. She clung to him, the pain too great for words. They sat that way for minutes, and when the minutes turned into an hour, Hope finally quieted and fell asleep. Mike laid her back gently on the bed, wiping her face with a tissue. He sat watching, knowing that others were waiting, but unable to face them. How could he explain what wasn't his to share? The guilt that was his was too bitter for the words to leave his mouth. So, he sat and watched his youngest sister sleep, and he hated Rob Stinner more in that moment than he thought a human being should be capable of hating.

CHAPTER 28—SAM'S DOVE

Mike had told the others that Hope had been sleeping and that he didn't want to disturb her rest. Mama had looked at him as if she wanted to say something, but let the matter drop. He had tried to comfort them, lying about how she looked, claiming she seemed to be resting peacefully. That was all that he could manage before returning to his bedside vigil. Now he didn't know if he wanted Hope to wake up and tear fresh wounds open inside of him, or if he wanted her to remain in the troubled sleep she was in, where at times she would call out and kick at some secret demon. He waited.

When she opened her eyes to peer at him from the desolate place she found herself, he felt surprise and an ache. What was he expecting? A ready joke and a great big smile beaming up at him from the hospital bed? Maybe not that, but maybe a spark of something, a hint of some of her spirit, a bit of spunk—ready to fight her way through this, a little hope. It was the bleakness that quietly peered back at him that was the hardest thing for him to take. He wished she would yell and scream because at least that would be a glimpse of life.

"It's not a gift." Her voice was a mere rustle.

"What?" Mike wasn't sure he had heard her correctly.

"It's not a gift." A whispered echo.

"What's not a gift?" He was puzzled and craving a drink. Hope being this dark, sad creature was like a black hole. Where once she gave off energy to all around, she was now draining him of it.

"You once told me that my visions were a gift, remember that?" There was no blame in her voice, just an ancient sadness.

"Yeah, I remember."

"It's not a gift. When I looked into Rob's eyes, all these memories took over, and then all the blocks I put up just washed away and I was feeling it again. I saw the evil in him, surrounding him. It washed over me, and it touched me. Then when I was there with Jimmy, dying in my arms. I couldn't turn it off. I was looking at this kid, this kid I adore. He got his life together, you know. He was gentle with his brother. I've seen it. He was good and kind, but when I looked at him all I saw was this haze surrounding him. I saw the drugs, and the theft, and him hitting people. That was all years ago, Mike. He had changed. I know he had. But all I could see was the darkness. This kid died trying to protect me, and instead of seeing his beautiful young face, I saw the mistakes of his past. What kind of gift is that?" Hope turned sad eyes to him, eyes that were begging for an answer.

Mike would have given anything to have an answer for his young sister, but looking into her dark eyes he couldn't think of a single thing that would lessen the pain, so he found himself uttering one of the cruelest sentences in the world. "I don't know."

Hope nodded. She had not expected an answer, and that fact only made Mike sorrier that he couldn't provide one. He tried to change the subject. "So, are you ready to see the others, Hope?"

The stare she turned on him was the teacher look she had given students when they had given ridiculous answers to questions they should have known. "I can't turn it off, Mike, and I don't want to look at the faces of all those I love and just see the lowest moments in their lives."

"How long are you going to hide in here?" The thought of Hope running away from her problems brought back enough anger to allow it to slip beneath the folds of his protectiveness.

"However long it takes."

They stared at each other as they realized they had reached a standoff. They were so focused on each other that they didn't hear the whisper of the door sliding open. Mike jumped as the touch of his father's strong hand gently squeezed his shoulder. He gazed into the eyes of the man he admired more than any other, feeling lighter at the reassuring smile he saw there. "Son, why don't you take a break and go get yourself a cup of coffee?"

"I didn't think they would let you in." Mike glanced down at his now wrinkled uniform and wondered why the doctor would have broken Hope's request for Sam.

"They don't know I'm here." He smiled down at Hope. "But she's my little girl…so here I am."

Mike breathed in a calming breath, relieved to no longer have to bear the burden of Hope's well-being alone. A cup of coffee sounded really good. He craved its warmth as much as he ever had on a cold winter's night on patrol. And again he was saddened as he realized that he also craved an escape from the despair that was currently Hope.

Sam waited for the door to close before sitting in the chair vacated by his son. He looked at Hope and smiled. She refused to meet his eyes, or look his way. Sam propped a foot up on the rail of the bed and leaned back, his manner easy and sure. He slowly unwrapped a piece of watermelon bubble gum, chewing with relish before softly blowing a bubble.

Hope could smell the watermelon scent waft in the air as her father's bubble popped. A hint of something stirred inside of her as she remembered long ago summer days, walking with her father, his huge hand holding her smaller one. They would go out early in the morning, keeping a watchful eye for any animals, hoping for a glimpse of a fawn or squirrel. They would often sit by a stream and chew gum, having contests over the largest bubble. Sam had taught her how to blow bubbles, but he had also taught her how to sit still, to become part of the quiet, and to really see what was around her. Her cabin in the woods was her reminder of those walks and of the love given to her so readily by her father, a strong, quiet man.

They sat like that for a long time, quiet. Sam was watchful as ever. A sense of peace surrounded his frame. Hope thought she caught the scent of cedar and flowers from his clothing. She thought of the stream and the woods and began to relax, a reflex born of a long time habit.

Sam's voice was soft when he finally decided to speak. "Do you remember that bird?"

Hope tensed slightly, still not looking at him, not wanting to see if there was something hidden inside of her father now visible to her cursed eyes. She tried to recall the bird he was talking about. There had been many. They had owned a parakeet at one time. They would go bird watching, looking for nests, but never touching the delicate eggs inside. She had seen robins, blue jays and cardinals and at the zoo, penguins, flamingos and ostriches. Still, she knew exactly what bird he was talking about. "The dove."

"The dove." Sam smiled as if she had won the final question on Jeopardy, even though she was still avoiding looking at him. "Just a baby, really, when we found it, the poor thing with its wing broken." Sam returned to his silent gum chewing.

Hope thought back to the dove. It was a beautiful pearly white. She had watched Sam as he had carefully lifted it and carried it home. He had set the wing, and every day for weeks, he and Hope had fed it and talked to it, wishing for it to heal. Then one day, the wing had mended, and Hope felt tears on her cheeks as she watched Sam open the cage, holding the bird up to the sky and letting it fly away free. He had put a hand on her shoulder, the gentle smile on his face beautiful as he watched the bird glide overhead and circle away. He had patted her head before squatting to her side, eye-level. "That's the beautiful thing." Hope remembered her young voice as she looked into his smiling eyes. "What is, Daddy?" The look on his face was reverent, and Hope felt something calm touch her inside as he answered. "The way God helps all creatures to heal."

Hope thought of the dove and glanced over at Sam. There was no hazy aura seeping over his body. No visions of past mistakes flashed before her eyes. She hadn't had the strength to push the evil back. It hadn't been the battle she had imagined, but a breath of release as her father reminded her that all creatures have strength inside. Sometimes they just need the time to find it and the gentle waiting love of a father.

"I didn't try to help him, Daddy. I should have, but I didn't." Hope felt tears welling in her eyes.

"Bad things happen that we can't control, but that doesn't make us responsible. Maybe if you had tried to do something you would have saved the boy, but maybe you would both be dead now. You can't live in the maybes, Hope. You have to live in the what you can do now."

Sam's voice was gentle as he lifted a strand of hair from her forehead gently tucking it behind an ear.

"What can I do now?" Hope's eyes were not their usual brightness, but they held within them a positive sign. They held trust for her father's wisdom.

"Heal." He leaned forward brushing his lips across her cheek, and before he had fully pulled away he gave a soft chuckle, "Oh, and you could let your Mama and the rest of the family see you before any doctors get hurt."

A corner of Hope's mouth twitched upward. It was the beginning of a smile.

CHAPTER 29—UNEXPECTED PUNCHES

Mama and Aunt Agatha fussed over Hope as she returned home. They cleaned, cooked and fluffed pillows. The boys all worked on her arbor and swing, while Kate checked on her constantly, taking her vitals as if she was recuperating from pneumonia instead of stress.

Hope had plenty of cheerful company, and together they had watched a lot of comedies. She had taken several relaxing bubble baths, and the cut on her head had turned from an ugly black and blue to a shade of aqua green that reminded her of sea foam. The house smelled of pineapples and brown sugar. Hope had put on her Snoopy house shoes, and feeling hungry for the first time in days, she had begun to follow the enticing aromas wafting through the house from the kitchen. She half smiled as she heard the voices of her aunt and Mama arguing about cake batter. She took a deep breath and sighed, recognizing the sadness still in her heart, but also comforted by the familiar.

She was passing the phone when it rang and automatically picked it up. Mama and Agatha had both rushed towards it, thinking she was still asleep and wanting not to wake her. Hope put the phone to her ear and listened to the voice of her principal, after assuring him that she was okay. Kate must have somehow determined from her mumbled okays that something was not right because she put her arm soothingly around her younger sister before she hung up.

Hope's glazed hazel eyes looked at her sister, aunt, and mother in a fashion similar to the shock they had seen on her face in the hospital. "Well…" Hope took a breath before continuing. "It seems in light of some questions raised by the newspapers, the school board would feel better if I was to take a leave of absence until things were figured out."

"What do you mean a leave? You're on summer vacation." Mama scrunched a dishtowel into a tight ball in her hand before tossing it on the counter.

"I've been suspended—while they investigate my connection with Jimmy." Hope stared into space.

Agatha was flustered. "They can't believe that…that crap… that stupid reporter at the hospital was spouting!" She gave Hope a commiserating look before turning angrily back to Eavenly. "You shouldn't have smacked him. You should have kneed him in the balls!"

Hope started laughing…and didn't seem able to stop.

Kate patted her shoulder and took her by the arm. "Let's go lie back down, and maybe you should take one of those pills the doctor gave you."

Agatha stood next to Eavenly as Hope was led down the hall. "Eavenly, your daughter is cracking up."

Eavenly huffed. "Agatha, *Rhineholdts* do not crack up." But she couldn't hide the concern in her voice.

"Eavenly?"

Eavenly turned with exasperation, "Yes, Agatha?"

"Doesn't Sherlock own a newspaper here in town?" Their eyes met, and they held a gleam.

"Yes, Agatha. She does."

CHAPTER 30—MONEY AIN'T EVERYTHING

"I need a cigarette." Sherlock rapped her fingers angrily on the table while glancing around the kitchen.

"You don't smoke." Eavenly calmly reminded her from the other side of Hope's kitchen table.

"Then someone better bloody-well get me a Dr. Pepper." Sherlock was fuming. She was so angry that she didn't even notice the cold soda that Agatha had brought her earlier. Instead of arguing, Agatha went to the refrigerator and removed another can quietly and set it beside the first.

"So what's this reporter's name?" Sherlock angrily pulled back the tab on the can as she waited for more information from her sisters.

Agatha spoke first, "Well, we've mostly been calling him 'Asshole'."

Eavenly interrupted, "His name is James Brown."

Agatha added, "Like the singer."

"Only white." Eavenly contributed.

"And we really don't know if he can sing or not." Agatha finished.

"And he claimed to work for my newspaper? The name doesn't sound familiar, but I have to admit that I leave all the running of it up to the editor."

"Well, he doesn't really work at your newspaper." Eavenly said.

"Actually, he had a camera, so he probably worked at a television station, right?" Agatha looked at Eavenly for support.

Sherlock sighed. "And you thought I could help, how?"

"Well…" Agatha paused. "It would be really great if you could run a front page explanation of, you know, how he's an asshole."

Sherlock and Eavenly exchanged looks. Eavenly's tense voice bespoke her concern over the treatment of Hope by the press. "When he was talking I had this feeling, you know, like he really didn't care if he had the facts of what he was reporting or not. If he was like that with us, then he's probably been the same way with others. I thought maybe one of your guys could do an article evaluating the ethics of the television station and its news crew."

"Especially the asshole." Agatha added.

"She knows that, Agatha."

Sherlock slowly nodded her head thinking it over. "I think that's a good idea. Give them a little taste of their own medicine, only in our case it's even better, because the truth is on our side. I'll call my editor. So, is it true that you slapped the guy?" Her eyes sparkled, as she looked at Eavenly, the petite picture of composure as she sat sedately in the kitchen chair.

Eavenly nodded. Her face reddened at the memory. Now that Hope was home, she was appalled at her own lack of manners in public, even though the smack was well deserved.

Sherlock, sensing this, patted her hand. "He deserved it. Look at all the trouble he's causing our Little Hope. I just wish you would have kicked him where it hurts."

"That would have been *so* much better. That's where the characters in my books always get kicked." Agatha agreed. "You know men, the easiest way to control them is through their…" Her voice broke off as she looked up to find Joe standing uncomfortably in the doorway.

"I knocked, but nobody answered." Joe offered by way of explanation.

"It's okay…" Eavenly searched her memory for his name. "…Joe. We were just talking about the reporter who gave Hope's attack such a negative slant on the news."

Joe's face grew taut, his hands tightly clenched fists, held at his sides. "I would like to get hold of both that reporter and the man who attacked her. How's she holding up?"

"Actually, I think she was doing a little better until this morning." Eavenly wasn't sure what she thought of the man, but felt she should give him the benefit of the doubt. After all, he had carried her daughter home after she had been attacked in the woods, and now he looked as if he would murder the next person who even thought of hurting her. "Would you like to sit down? Can I get you a soda, tea, or some coffee?"

"No, thanks. I really just wanted to check on the kid. I've been worried about her. She's a special person, and it's just wrong that these things have happened to her lately."

All three looked at Sherlock as a loud laugh erupted from her, "She is definitely a wonderful person. But if you're surprised that these things have happened to my niece, then you must not know her that well. Hope attracts trouble. Or at least," Sherlock paused giving Eavenly a pointed look, "She always seems to be around those who go looking for it." She looked up to find Joe staring at her. He quickly closed his open mouth when he noticed her returning his look.

"I must say, your resemblance to Hope is amazing." Joe, like Eric, had seen the briefest spark of Hope in Sherlock's smile and sparkling eyes.

Eavenly and Agatha looked at each other in shock before Agatha blurted out cackling, "You must need glasses, Joe. There aren't two people on this planet more *unlike* than Sherlock and our sweet Little Hope."

"Blind." Joe thought as he looked again at the aunt from whom Hope obviously got part of her looks. "These women must be completely blind."

"She's sleeping now. I gave her another of the sedatives left by…" Kate stopped as she turned the corner to the kitchen and saw Joe standing inside. "…the doctor. You're Joe, right? I guess you saw the attack on the news."

"I called Eric, right after it happened. I would have been by sooner, but he said she had been mostly sleeping, and then this morning he called and said she might do with a little company." Joe shifted on his feet. The kitchen was quickly becoming more crowded than he had been used to the past few years.

"She was doing better." Eavenly tried to reassure Joe, wanting him to know that his visit was welcome.

"Until she got fired this morning." Agatha added.

Joe was shaken. "Hope was fired? Why?"

"Actually, she was suspended. And the reason is because most people believe anything they hear whether they know better or not. You would think an educated man, such as a principal, would know that the press isn't always accurate." Sherlock's voice dripped with censure.

Eric followed by Sam and Uncle Bob had walked into the kitchen, after finally completing the arbor just in time to hear Sherlock's remarks.

"Hope got suspended?" Eric leaned against a wall in shock. Hope loved teaching. This was going to kill her.

"Don't worry, Honey." Agatha tried to reassure him. "It's not like you're going to go broke. Hope has plenty of money."

"I know Hope has some money. It's not…"

"Hope doesn't have *some* money, sweetie. Hope is swimming in money." Agatha felt Eric would feel relief at the information.

"Well, we have lots of money. I've always known that." Eric was puzzled at Agatha's emphasis on Hope's money.

"Agatha, Eric isn't worried about money. He doesn't care that Hope is richer than any of us. He's worried about her feelings about losing her job." Eavenly calmly explained to Agatha.

Eric nodded, not surprised that Eavenly understood what he was feeling. Then he latched onto the words she had used. "What do you mean Hope's richer than any of you?"

"She's never told you the joke?" Agatha asked.

"What joke?"

"Well, it started with our Grandmamma. She loved Hope. When Hope was two years old, Grandmamma said you could see it in her eyes, that she was a good person. We said of course she is Grandmamma, but she said not good like a good baby, but good as in a kind human being. So, Grandmamma decided that since we all pretty much had all the money we needed, it just seems to grow with each

generation, she would leave half to her children, and half to Hope."
Agatha looked at Eric, expecting this cleared everything up.

Sherlock could see his confusion. "Well, it became like the
family joke. Everyone's will leaves half to Hope. Because you know,
being the person she is, she would do more good with it than anyone
else, and we all have enough money anyway. So over the years, we've
had a few deaths. Aunts, uncles, Granddad, and Cousin Jake, who ran
his motorcycle into a tree, so Hope had her share, plus she got all these
halves."

"And she does well on her own investments." Kate added.
"Most of us get stock tips from her."

Eric sat down in a chair. "So how much…how much does she
have?"

Agatha laughed, "Enough so that you two never need worry
about a piddly teacher's income. I doubt Hope even knows. She
spreads it out, a lot of charities."

Eric looked hurt. "She never mentioned how much. I mean, we
have joint checking accounts and I see those balances, and she says her
trust just keeps growing, but she never said she was so rich."

"She wasn't trying to keep anything from you, son." Sam
clapped him on the shoulder. "See, that's the real joke. Grandmamma
was absolutely right. Hope doesn't ever consider the money that's
added up from everyone's wills as her money. She thinks it's her
responsibility to use it to help save the world and make it a better place.
She probably thought she was saving you from a burden. You know
Hope wouldn't want to lie to you. You okay?"

"There was a fire. Hope almost drowned. Hope was attacked.
One of her kids died. She was suspended, but it's okay because we're
rich? I would rather be dead broke and not have my wife depressed in
the other room and my nights filled with nightmares that someone is
trying to hurt her." The weight on Eric's shoulders was almost visible as
he slumped at the table.

"And that's why she loves you."

CHAPTER 31-KEEPING WATCH

Mike stared at the house belonging to the two Mr. Smiths. He took a sip of coffee that had turned cold hours before. His back and neck ached from the hours he had spent sitting in the same position. Patience did not come naturally to Mike. His frustration made the inside of the car feel more enclosed, and the stale smell of the Big Mac he hadn't finished from dinner was unpleasant in the hot air. He couldn't get rid of the gut feeling that, although Hope was attacked by Rob Stinner, somehow her problems had really started when Mama got suspicious of the Smiths. He started the car with an angry twist of the keys. He had been watching the house for hours without a sign of anything criminal going on inside. Without just cause, he had no reason to ask for a search warrant. So instead of tearing the place apart in order to find out what the Smiths had to do with Hope's attack, he was unofficially watching the house on his own time.

He pulled away from the Smiths; dissatisfied and with a deep sense of anger that he was no closer to Rob Stinner or to ending the potential danger to Hope. He drove through the small town, as was his habit even when off the clock, driving past areas with the most frequent trouble. He was slowly cruising past the "Squealing Pig", a local dive of a bar with dim lighting, sticky floors, and old sixties music on the jukebox, when he recognized the unsteady gate of the man stumbling out the door and down the street. The man stumbled a few times and seemed to be having real trouble remaining on his feet.

Mike followed quietly for a few blocks, when suddenly the man stopped stumbling and began to walk without even a hint of a lean. He pulled up alongside, rolling his window down as he looked into the man's surprised face. "Hey, Ty. Why don't you hop in the car and tell me what you're doing walking around town pretending to be drunk?" Ty looked up and down the street nervously before rounding the front fender of Mike's personal car, a mint-condition '66 cherry-red Mustang convertible. Mike reeled back in disgust and rolled down all the windows at the overpowering smell of sweat and stale beer coming from his brother as he climbed in the passenger side.

"Hurry, up. Let's go." Ty slouched in the seat as Mike pulled away from the curb.

"Okay." Mike said, "You want to tell me what you're doing walking out of The Pig as if you're plowed?"

"I had a few drinks." Ty's voice was tense.

"Uh-huh, you sober up fast little brother. I watched you go from falling over drunk to stinky sober in five minutes."

"Look, Mike. Drop it. Give me a ride over to Glendale Street. That's where I parked my car."

Mike was quiet for a moment, his thoughts churning. "Hey, you weren't really drunk that morning Hope punched you, either, were you?"

"What do you know about it?"

"I know enough to know that if you had drunk enough to smell the way Hope described you, there's no way you could have survived shopping with Mama most of the day. Why are you trying to act the tough guy—because you got tossed from the army?" Mike glanced over at Ty's face, his gut instincts kicking into overdrive as he watched the muscles in Ty's neck bulge as he tensed up. "Hey, Ty."

"What?" Ty's voice had an edge to it.

"Why are you lying about being thrown out of the army, and why are you going around town tonight acting like the bad ass town drunk home for a visit?"

Mike's car pulled up beside Ty's convertible. He turned in his seat so that he could see Ty's face better in the soft glow of the street lamp. The face that looked back at him belonged to a stranger.

"Thanks for the ride." Ty got out of the Mustang and got into his own car without a look back in Mike's direction. Mike watched as Ty pulled away from the curb and drove away. He sighed and headed home. He now had two siblings who weren't acting like themselves, and he only knew of one who had a reason for it. How many other secrets was he going to have to uncover? As he neared the street where he lived, Mike sighed and pulled over to the side of the road. The dead look in Hope's eyes and the ugly bruise on her head as her haunted voice told him Rob was after her floated before his eyes like a video. There was no way he could have the police search for the new face of Rob Stinner based on the instinctual recognition by Hope, and since Hope wasn't good at drawing he was still uncertain what Rob now looked like based on her sketchy description. He rubbed his fingers against his tired eyes. Rob Stinner would be in town, loving the fact that he was hiding under Mike's very nose. At this thought, Mike got his second wind, and turned the car around to continue his search for the man he hated more with each passing moment. Several times he had to stop and remind himself that he wasn't just Hope's oldest brother, but also an officer of the law. For the first time since becoming sheriff, Mike felt at odds with his occupation.

Ty walked around his parents' house, taking in the work still to be done. The garage would have to be rebuilt and one wall of the house already showed the signs of beginning repairs. The smell of smoke, amazingly, was now gone, and all of the singed and smoke-damaged furnishings had been removed. Ty made his way upstairs to one of the guest bedrooms. A smile flickered for a breath of a moment across his face as he spied the set of binoculars sitting on a table near the window. The smile vanished as he remembered how serious the situation truly was. Strolling to the window, Ty hesitated a moment and looked over his shoulder before picking up the binoculars and glancing briefly through them at the Smith's house. Ty sighed and set them back on the table, knowing that he wouldn't see anything suspicious from the Smiths at this time of night.

As Ty walked down the stairs, he glanced at the pictures on the wall that his parents had named the wall of fame. Pictures of little league teams, plays, graduations, and birthday parties competed for the eye of anyone walking up or down the stairs. Ty's eyes focused on a picture of his farewell party the day he left for boot camp. God, he looked so young sitting there with one arm around Hope and another around Pops as the family smiled for the camera. He ran a finger down the side of the frame and frowned. That picture contained everyone who mattered the most in life to him, and here he was putting them in danger with every moment he remained. "I should have stayed in the army." His sad voice echoed through rooms emptied by the cleaning crew.

The look of disgust that had passed across Mike's face when he had picked him up outside of the bar stuck in his gut. He would be lucky if his family didn't decide to disown him when this was all over. Ty locked the door and slowly drove away, heading back in the direction of the city and Hope.

Mike had returned once again to keep watch on the two Mr. Smiths. He was surprised to see Ty pulling away from his parents' house. He decided that he and his youngest brother were going to have to sit down and have a real talk sometime in the near future, but he rubbed his eyes and decided that he had spent enough time trying to figure out what was going on for one evening.

Mike walked into his house, careful to tread softly enough not to wake Kathy and the twins. He pulled off his clothes and got into bed next to his wife. He spent the next hour listening to Kathy's steady breathing while he tried to force himself to get the sleep that his body was demanding. His tired mind kept telling him that there was something he wasn't seeing, something he should know. As he finally fell into an exhausted sleep, he felt that he was no closer to figuring out what it was that he was missing.

CHAPTER 32—FOR BETTER OF WORSE

It was morning. Fresh dew kissed the grass and moistened the soles of Hope's feet as she stood in her backyard. She had risen earlier than normal and quietly slipped out of bed so as to not wake up Eric. No sound had come from the guest bedrooms as she slipped down the hallway and out into the morning air. Hope felt as if she had been sleeping for years. The spreading glow of the sun as it danced amid the clouds lacked its usual sparkle, in Hope's eyes. She noticed the mama bunny as it hopped from the hole Pops had shown her days before. Days now stretched behind her in an endless haze of time. Hope breathed in deeply and quickly scanned the nearby tree line for anything amiss. The site of a sleepy Scout and Jaspers lying on the porch watching her was reassuring.

Hope evened her stance and began to concentrate on her breathing as she performed the first movement in her T'ai Chi routine. A brief image of Jimmy flashed into her mind and caused her movement into the second position to be clumsy and jumpy. Hope concentrated on her center just beneath her navel and moved into the third position more smoothly. A soft morning drizzle began to fall. Hope ignored the rain, continuing with her exercise. A tear fell down her cheek, unnoticed. She felt none of the normal peace or centeredness that usually accompanied her T'ai Chi ritual, but the normality of the routine helped to fight the surreal feeling she had upon awakening. By the time she finished, her clothes were wet and clinging to her body. She squinted against the drizzle to glance up at the last location of the sun now hiding behind a cloud. She closed her eyes as the rain began to fall harder, allowing it to wash over her face.

Eric stood framed in the doorway, watching Hope go through her movements. His heart ached and he started to go to her but had stopped as she raised her face to the rain. Eric rested his head on the glass of the storm door. For the first time since they had met, Eric felt a distance between them that he wasn't sure how to cross. The person standing in the rain was a stranger to him, and that knowledge caused him more sadness then he ever remembered feeling. He turned from the door and walked back into the bedroom, hoping that giving her some time alone was the right thing to do.

Hope lowered her head and glanced toward the house. She stared at the door where she knew Eric had stood moments earlier. She took her ability to sense his presence as a sign that she still could not control this thing hiding inside of her. Hope felt anger, at the lack of control, begin to form in the pit of her stomach.

"Hope?" Eavenly stood on the porch watching her youngest child.

"Yes, Mama?"

"Honey, come back inside. It's raining." Eavenly wasn't sure what else to say except to state the obvious.

"Okay, Mama." Hope walked onto the porch and stopped to stand in front of Eavenly.

Eavenly knew that Hope was in pain and pulled her close, unmindful of the dampness soaking through her own clothes. "It's okay, Baby. You're going to be okay."

Hope looked at Mama through tear-filled eyes. "I can't even go to the funeral. Reporters would just turn it into a circus if I showed up today."

"I'm sorry, Baby." Eavenly had to pull Hope's head down to cradle it on her shoulder, since Hope was several inches taller. "Come on. Let's go inside so you can change out of these wet clothes." She glanced out at the gray morning, cold and damp for a summer day. "It looks like today is going to be nasty."

Hope looked down at her clothes and then at the sky as if she hadn't realized until that moment that it was really raining. "You know, Mama. I'm glad it's raining. It would be wrong somehow if it was sunny on the day they put Jimmy into the ground. It's right that the world weeps and people feel the blues of a rainy day."

Eavenly was quiet for a moment before taking Hope gently by the arm. "Come on, Sweetie. Let's go inside."

Eric sat on the bed, listening to the sound of the shower as he waited for Hope. It was long moments before she stepped into the bedroom, fully clothed in a dry pair of shorts and a T-shirt as she dried her hair. Seeing Eric, Hope paused from rubbing the towel against her head and sat down beside him.

"You okay?" Eric asked the question, almost out of habit, fearing that he wouldn't know how to answer if she said she wasn't.

"I will be." Hope leaned over and gave him a gentle kiss that was barely a feather-light caress against his lips. "I'm, sorry. Things have really been messed up lately, huh?"

Eric put his arm around her in a gentle hug, offering his comfort, knowing that Hope felt she was to blame for everything that had occurred.

"I just keep seeing Jimmy lying there on the pavement. I wish I could go today." Fresh tears began to fall down her face as she looked into Eric's eyes. "He's in a better place, though, right? I mean at least he doesn't have to suffer anymore. He's in heaven."

Eric felt a tightening in his chest as he looked into Hope's sad eyes, knowing that she needed his reassurance, saddened that she was asking for the one thing he couldn't give her. He had always stepped around the topic of religion with Hope. She tried often, thinking that he was just lax about practicing his religion, believing that her faith would bring him around. Now, looking into her face, he couldn't lie to her. Even though he knew his answer would cause her more pain, he couldn't pretend to be someone he wasn't when she was at her weakest. "I'm sorry, Honey. I don't believe in heaven."

Hope stared at him, an uncomprehending expression on her face.

"To believe in heaven, I would have to believe in God. I don't. How could I? Just look at all of the horrible things that have happened to you the past few days. You're a good person. The kindest I have ever known, and all of these evil things have happened to you. How could there be a God who would allow all these bad things to happen?"

Hope sat staring at him. Her eyes now dry. She waited as if expecting that time would change the words she had heard. There must be some kind of mistake. She stood, distancing herself from her husband, feeling more alone than she had ever felt in her life. "How can you not believe in God? How have we been together this long without you ever telling me this little detail? How could you have kept something like this from me?"

Eric didn't have an answer, except the fear he had developed that this would be the one thing over which he could lose her. He didn't want to mention the fear, believing to let it breathe the air as it passed his lips would give it life and power to materialize, so he remained sitting on the bed as she turned and walked out of the bedroom. Each step she took away from him only emphasized the distance he had glimpsed in her eyes.

CHAPTER 33—LOST

Eavenly sat at the kitchen table, her hands circling the mug of black coffee. She looked down into the black liquid with her heart aching. The image of Hope standing in the morning rain, looking lost and broken, was a sight no mother wanted to experience with any of her children. Hope had struggled so much in her life and had overcome so much turmoil to become the bright shining light of a person that she was. To see that light dimmed by the evil in the world from which Eavenly could not protect her made it more heart-wrenchingly sad.

She thought a moment of crawling back in bed next to Sam, knowing that he would pull her close and she would feel warm and safe in his embrace. She took a sip of coffee. The hot liquid scalded her tongue and scorched the soft tenderness of her throat. She welcomed the burning punishment of the liquid as it ate away the tears she had been choking down deep inside. She couldn't go back to bed. She knew that Hope was hurting. Instinct told her that Hope was going to need her, so she sat at the kitchen table, the mother's altar of late night worries, whispered prayers, and early morning answers. The early dawn light falling through the windows gave Eavenly pause that this might be the beginning of a vigil longer than any she had experienced in the past.

Hope rounded the corner into the kitchen. A sharp pain shot through her chest and it suddenly became difficult to breathe. Her head ached and the room began to spin before her eyes. Interspersed with the image of Eavenly jumping up from the table were images of Jimmy lying on the street dying, Rob Stinner smirking, and the sad guilt in

Eric's eyes. She felt Mama's hand wrap around her arm and was surprised by the strength in the hand as Mama held her tightly, keeping her from falling to the floor as she led her to a chair at the table. Hope heard the fear in Mama's voice as the words came to her as if from a long distance away, "Hope. Hope, you're having an anxiety attack. Come on, Love, calm down for me. Focus on your breathing. You can get past this."

Hope panicked again as she was trying to breathe, causing the band across her chest to tighten in response. She felt light headed, and her pulse was beating so rapidly and with such force that she could feel it in her neck, wrists, and temple. She felt Mama's hand as it tightly gripped her by the chin, forcing her to stare mere inches into her Mother's eyes. "Hope, damn it, I did not raise any fragile children. You're going to give me a heart attack if you don't calm down right now."

Guilt surfaced as Hope saw the real concern in Mama's eyes. The flood of guilt washed through her veins slowing the blood, opening her lungs, and doing what she hadn't been able to do with will power alone. She took a deep shaky breath and straightened. "Sorry, Mama." Hope, ever the worrier, was able to halt a panic attack at the thought of causing her Mama any added stress.

"Hope, you okay?" Mama's eyes watered as she watched the struggle on Hope's face.

Hope began to look at Mama when she began to get the sensation back. Gray edged her vision in the corner of her eyes. Hope felt weakened. She couldn't push the sensation away. Knowing the possibility of darkness lurking inside of Mama was too much to take. She felt a tear fall down her face as she turned without answering and walked out the back door. Eavenly started to follow her daughter, but stopped after a few steps. She wasn't what Hope needed right now, but she would need all of them later. She peered through the mist as the retreating figure of her daughter entered the woods. She stood at the door long enough to see the tense figure of Hope's quiet neighbor move through the trees following her daughter. She felt a small amount of relief that, at the very least, Hope wasn't alone. She turned back to the kitchen, her shoulders sagging under the burden of her concern. She went to wake the others. Eavenly decided that Hope would return to a house full of life and activity.

Joe, having kept a careful vigil after Hope's attack, stood at the edge the woods, concerned as a tearful Hope walked off of her back porch. As she reached the woods, Hope began to run. Tears falling blurred her vision, mixing with the softly falling rain, turning the trees and branches of the woods into a soft palette of colors, softer than they felt as she tripped over a root sticking out inches above the grass. She picked herself up, ignoring the burning in her knee and the palms of her hands where abrasions bled.

She ran in a direction parallel to the cabin, wanting to avoid any contact. She paid no heed to the lone male figure who detached himself from the trees to follow her. Once Hope had reached a dark section of the woods far from home, she sank to her knees on the muddy ground. She kneeled forward grasping at the grass and clawing handfuls of dirt, which she raised above her head in an angry display. Her torment was expressed in a short guttural howl that left her weak. She began to sob into the dirt. Never had she been more confused or angry, and she had never felt so hopelessly lost.

She knew Joe was standing behind her, watching her cry. She had felt his presence as he ran after her deeper into the woods. "Joe, leave. I can't see you right now."

Joe didn't answer as he sat on a small log, unmindful of the rain. "Joe, damn you, leave!"

"I can't, not with you like this." Joe's voice was gruff, unsure of how to handle this emotional display.

Hope turned angrily to him and started to hit his arms and his chest with her small, tightly clenched fists. "Leave, leave...you have to leave."

Joe pulled her close, pinning her arms to her sides, accepting her weight as she sobbed into his shoulders. "Honey, that's the one thing you could ask of me that I won't do." He rocked her in a manner of a man who had just found a newborn baby in his arms. He eased the grip he had on her arms and began gently stroking her hair. A small bit of wonder passed through Joe as he held Hope, waiting for her to cry herself out. He was staying around when it got tough. He was sticking. There was hope for him after all.

They sat like that for a long time until Hope's sobs subsided. Hope had difficulty meeting Joe's eyes. Joe noticed this and reached forward to brush a strand of wet hair from her face, "Kid, you could never do anything that would make me think less of you." He felt her hesitation. "After all, you're talking to a man who's had to eat bugs, even slimy slugs to survive. I've had to use tree leaves more often in my life than Charmin. I once had to remove a piece of shrapnel from another soldier's private areas. I understand embarrassment, and Kid, you have no reason to be." Hope peeked at him briefly through her lashes. He stood up, pulling her up with him. "Now, how about you let me walk you home before I have to resort to sharing really disgusting information with you?"

Hope nodded. Her hand tightly held his until they reached where the woods met her back yard. Joe hesitated as she removed her hand from his grasp. He let her walk on alone, but his eyes never left her as she made her way back home.

CHAPTER 34-COPE

Hope left a confused Joe standing at the edge of the woods and began a solitary walk home. She felt angry with herself for so many things it was becoming a small loathing. She blamed herself for Jimmy, and the look of concern on Mama's face tore fresh flaps of guilt into her burdened soul. Her attack on Joe had convinced her that she was losing her mind. Even if Joe never mentioned the scene, she believed she would forever feel the base humiliation of another human being seeing her diminished to mere animalistic instinct.

Hope pulled a patch of grass and mud from her cheek, trying to think of a way to resolve the events of the past few days. Grief and anger began to once again envelope her, causing her attempt at logic to drown beneath another wave of immobilizing emotions. Hope swam through the feelings of fear, confusion, and pain she had been living in and grasped onto the one feeling in the deep darkness that offered any buoyancy. Hope latched onto her anger, pulling it close, fanning its flame, praying it was strong enough to push back the tidal wave just beneath the surface.

Hope straightened her shoulders and took a deep breath as she mentally prepared herself, picturing herself as a female Rambo, or at the very least a Charlie's Angel. She felt her equilibrium begin to return as her anger swelled to an equally dizzying height as the emotions that were ready to suffocate her beneath their surge of sadness.

She felt surer of herself as she forced her soggy shoes to step onto the porch. She stepped into the kitchen to a scene out of a

Norman Rockwell painting. Mama and Aunt Agatha had every burner on the stove covered with the sinful greasiness of fried green tomatoes, fried chicken livers, fried taters, and some fried June apples. The oven was also on, but Hope couldn't determine what was inside over the heady sound of pans screaming and popping in their joy and the smell of apples caramelizing in sugar. Hope felt every cell in her body rise in cholesterol levels upon her arrival into the kitchen. As her eyes scanned the room, they stopped at the site of Pops and Uncle Bob carefully setting up a checkers board and her Connect Four game. Sitting near them, Eric seemed to be concentrating very hard on what appeared to be a stack of every Dolly Parton, Kathleen Turner, and Meg Ryan video she owned, a sleepy-eyed Ty looking over his shoulder. This was so like her family, offering support by their mere presence.

They all seemed to notice her at the exact same instant. Worried, eager, reassuring eyes peered intently at her. The room was suddenly strangely quiet. Ty went to the freezer pulling out a small pint of Breyer's Reese Cup ice cream. He offered it to Hope, breaking the awkward silence, "Ice cream?"

Hope glanced at the clock on the microwave, confirming her belief that it was only eight forty-five in the morning. She glanced at the ice cream and spoon offered by her brother, along with everything offered by everyone else in the room, and her anger suddenly left her. In one swift, caring stroke, her family had stripped away the only defense she had been able to find within herself.

Hope sighed, pushing a lock of wet hair out of her eyes, suddenly very aware of a coldness that went deeper than the layer of wet clothes clinging to her body. She moved a suddenly heavy leg forward and took the ice cream from Ty. The energy it took to force a reassuring smile onto her face left her exhausted as her lips curled up, the tightness causing her jaws to ache in the spots usually reserved for a spattering of dimples. "Sure, thanks." She took a bite as all eyes watched the spoon slowly travel from the container to her lips. Hope forced the sticky glob into her mouth, swallowing quickly to allow the cold treat to slide down her throat and settle uncomfortably into the icy pit that was her stomach.

She heard the soft splat as a clump of mud dislodged itself from her clothes to land on the spotless hard wood floor at her feet. Not a single eye left Hope's face, giving her the distinct feeling of a zoo animal during feeding time. Hope pictured herself as an ostrich, mentally sticking her head beneath the sand, as she strode out of the kitchen mumbling about needing a bath.

As soon as she walked into the hallway, all eyes quickly turned to Eavenly.

"Well, she seems okay now, doesn't she?" Agatha blurted.

Eavenly turned to her sister, knowing that she was only trying to be reassuring. "Agatha, don't be a dote."

With that, everyone quietly turned back to the task of creating an environment that would help Hope cope with her grief.

Hope sat in a corner of the shower stall, her head bent over her knees as the pounding spray beat down from above. She watched the murky swirl of water as a small, watery tornado circled the drain. She was thinking of all the people who had hurt her, or bullied her, or even cut her off on the interstate. Every grievance she could remember since first grade was tallied in her mind as she tried to locate the rage from earlier, wanting it to return and melt the icy block in her stomach. She noticed her skin turning pink from the intensity of the almost scalding water beating down on her. It was as if her body and soul were living in two different climates. Briefly she wondered how she would manage to get back to the person she was before everything that had happened.

"You won't."

Hope jumped at the bitter voice that had answered the question she hadn't asked aloud. It was then that she recognized the voice was her own.

CHAPTER 35—OUTSTRETCHED HANDS

Hope concentrated on the intricate design of lines and curves she was penning in her sketchpad. The clarinet playing a Mozart minuet was turned up loud enough on her Walkman to drown out any other noise. The piece was one she had been practicing lately on both the piano and on the clarinet. The bouncy beat with its half steps and offbeat tempo was light and airy. She listened with a close ear to every breath and note. The page before her was almost completely darkened with the strong black strokes of her pen. Hope's hand hesitated for a moment, as she suddenly noticed that beneath the layers of symmetrical patterns of lines and loops were dozens of small eyes peering out toward her. "Hmm…wonder what Rorschach would make of that?" Hope turned to a clean page and began quickly sketching with clean strokes the outline of trees, but as a forest, dark and somewhat murky, began to form before her eyes, she quickly shut the sketchpad and tossed it onto the floor beside the bed.

Hope looked around the bedroom for something else to occupy her. She didn't feel up to facing the others. She felt on the verge of becoming diabetic as a result of the continual syrupy sweetness of her family as they tried to cheer her up. Mama and Aunt Agatha tried to feed her every moment she was in their presence, while Uncle Bob and Pops tried to keep her mind occupied with games and trivia. For the first time in her life, she was sick of being asked obscure questions that caused her to rack her brain for answers. Eric and Ty, however, were the worst. They hovered, ready to attend to her every need, while an air of guilt hung heavily across their faces. She steered her brain away from Eric's guilt over his lack of faith and the difficulties this added to their relationship, a problem that was too painful for Hope to even consider. Ty, however, was also acting guilty, and Hope was puzzled as to what could be causing him to keep darting glances at her, his face set in a smile that did a poor job of hiding the concern and confusion Hope saw in his eyes.

Hope picked up the remote and began to flip through the channels. Her finger paused in mid-push as a picture of herself flashed upon the screen. She turned up the volume in time to catch the announcer's voice-over. "An article in today's issue of *The Seconds* has taken issue with the slanderous attack on Hope Jamison's character by Channel 94 which gave false implications about her relationship with a former student who was recently murdered. Our own investigation of this matter has not only contradicted this version of events, but we have also determined that Hope Jamison's connection to the young man who was murdered was purely that of a mentor and benefactor, including a scholarship that had been awarded to the young man. She has on numerous occasions been the source of anonymous donations to the school. We go live to the school where Mrs. Jamison was a teacher to talk with some of the staff and students."

Hope watched in shock as teachers and students alike declared Hope to be a wonderful teacher, but how they had no idea she was so wealthy. Even though it was summer vacation, a large group of students had formed at the school, all trying to have their schedules changed to include one of her classes.

Many of the students, along with two of the teachers, mentioned plans for asking Hope for financial assistance in the future. Hope watched in horror as a couple of students began to first argue over who was the more worthy of the next scholarship offered by Hope, then quickly escalate into a fist fight. Hope sighed as she turned off the television.

Her name had been cleared, and for that she was truly grateful. But if she ever went back to teaching at her old school now, she would spend most of her time dealing with everyone wanting her financial help.

She could already picture the problems as parents tried to make sure students were placed in her classes solely for the hope of attaining money. Hope ran a hand through her hair, frustrated at the press. Now, even though she could go back to teaching for one reason, she couldn't go back to teaching at any school in this area for another.

Mama poked her head in the door. "Honey, you okay?"

Hope grunted and lay back on the bed pulling a pillow over her head.

Eavenly took a deep breath and opened her mouth to say something. She looked at the form of her daughter, Hope's legs pulled up in a fetal position, the pillow covering her head. Eavenly closed her mouth, deciding now wasn't the time to mention today's paper. She closed the door, leaving Hope alone. Hope didn't notice. She closed her eyes and listened to the silence, trying to lower the volume of the guilty thoughts circling her brain as she thought of Jimmy's death, Rob Stinner, and the students she would leave behind if she didn't return to teaching.

CHAPTER 36—PASSER-BY

Hope stared at the spinning ceiling fan, quickly coming to the conclusion that it had at least an eighth inch of dust on the upper side of the blades. She hadn't thought about cleaning the fans lately, and it was obvious that the maid service that cleaned every two weeks hadn't remembered either. Hope glanced over as the bedroom door was suddenly opened. She quickly sat up, surprised to see Aunt Sherlock enter, closing the door behind her before she crossed the room to sit beside Hope on the bed. Her aunt eyed her up and down, a frown forming. "Pouting, huh?"

Hope stiffened at the comment. "I'm not pouting." She consciously attempted to pull her lower lip tightly against her teeth.

"Humph."

The two women stared at each other for a long moment before Sherlock broke the silence. "So, if you're not pouting, what are you doing?"

"I'm…" Hope paused. "I'm thinking."

"Ah-ha. Thinking."

Hope nodded and the silence returned.

Sherlock again studied her favorite niece before speaking. "Me, I don't think I would be thinking. Grieving, fuming, doubting, praying…maybe, but not just thinking. What are you thinking about?"

"What a stupid question." Hope's voice flattened with the heaviness of her sarcasm.

"Anger, that's better, but am I really the one you are angry with?" Sherlock looked at her; a small smile, the first sign of compassion she allowed herself to show, flitted across her face before she changed topics, not allowing Hope time to answer her question. "Your young fellow seems to be pretty worried about you. He's beside himself with your pain. You know, I envy you. Anybody can take one look at the two of you and suddenly believe in all those old fairy tale romances by the brothers Grimm."

Hope remained quiet. Eric's lack of faith and his purposeful withholding of it from her created an ache in her heart that brought back images of her earlier panic attack.

"My Harold and I, we didn't have that kind of love—the passion you two have. Not many people do. I think…no, I know, that kind of trust and selflessness would be rather frightening for me. But you and Eric, it's truly as if you are two halves of one whole. I would almost believe it possible for you to be cut and for him to bleed. My Harold and I were very good friends. We were comfortable together, and when I lost him…" Her voice broke, "when I lost him, it was one of the darkest periods of my life. It was at that point in my life that I ran into Chris. I don't believe I've ever mentioned her to you have I?"

Sherlock glanced at Hope as she slowly shook her head. Sherlock stood up and moved to the dresser, fingering the jewelry lying around, smiling at the Snoopy watch lying next to a pair of diamond earrings that had to be worth a couple of thousand dollars. "You would like Chris. She likes to think about things, too. We have wonderful conversations. When Harold died, I felt alone. I was angry. Then, I bumped into Chris at a bookstore. I thought she was quite the free spirit. You can always recognize one; it's in the eyes. She had these tranquil blue ones that look right into you."

"Before I realized it, I was telling this stranger about Harold and my fears, my doubts, and my anger. She just listened, every now and then asking a question that focused my feelings and thoughts. I felt calmness then, a real sense of tranquility. I still do whenever I talk to her. She has a very peaceful effect on people. She has this faith that God is really in control and things work out the way they're meant to.

She has so much faith that it seems to rub off on any who are near, even those among us who are a little more...cynical. She has convinced me that even the sad and frightening moments in our lives result in beauty and goodness in some way."

Hope stared at her, her voice quiet without any of its former bitterness, "Why are you telling me this?"

"It seems to me that in life we are always given what we need, when we need it most. I needed a calm listening ear, and Chris, a passer-by in a bookstore, was there. At one point in my life, I felt suffocated by this ability I have which for whatever purpose allows me to see the blackness of men's souls. I didn't think I could connect with people any longer, and then this amazing child was born who had the same gift in her eyes...and I was no longer alone. I watched her grow with this gentleness and cheerfulness inside of her. I saw her jump over every hurdle life threw at her with a joy and faith in the beauty around her that nothing seemed able to diminish. I don't believe anything ever truly could."

Hope stared into Sherlock's eyes, understanding for the first time the strange connection she felt to this quiet, reserved, and very private aunt. "You're like me? You see the mistakes people have made?"

"I see, but I'm not like you. I hide from the world, not letting many close. Chris and the family are the few people who know me, and even from them I need breaks, time alone. You, you are the embodiment of the cliché of wearing your heart on your sleeve. You give yourself freely to others, even when you know you'll be hurt. You allow others to see your soul and you carry their failures as if they were your own."

"You're wrong. I've been running from this *gift* my entire life. I kept it locked away, but now it's in control. It's grown stronger."

"No...think about it, Hope. There's a positive side to this gift. You've never fallen for a con artist or a scam in your life. You find people others see no value in and you prove their goodness to the world. You've been using your gift your entire life. You just haven't been aware of it."

"I don't want to know others' secrets."

"No, neither did I, but you can't hide from it now, Hope."

"Why not?"

Sherlock smiled as she turned from her study of the items strewn across the dresser. She returned to the bed and pushed a lock of hair from Hope's face. "Because you, my dear, are a lot like my friend Chris. You have too much faith that things are meant to be to hide from them. You, Hope, are a seeker and a believer, most definitely not a hider."

Hope's words stopped Sherlock as she reached the door. "So, do you believe your friend Chris? Does everything happen for a purpose? Will something good come from this?" Hope's eyes peered into those of her aunt.

"You can make yourself believe in anything, if you try. I made myself believe that God sent Chris to me to help me deal with Harold's loss and to get on with living. This gift…I've never thought of it as anything but a burden. I would much rather have your Mama's foresight, or even your Aunt Agatha's instinct for making people laugh. Now, looking at you with this same burden as myself, yeah, I guess I do believe good must come from it, because that, my darling, is what you do. You bring us all hope. Your Mama gave you the perfect name."

"What if I don't want to be the provider of everyone's hope?"

Sherlock smiled. "You don't have a choice. It's who you are." Her smile broadened, "Look on the bright side. You could have been named Chastity."

Hope felt a small smile. "Or Glory?"

"Possibly, Trinity?" Sherlock added.

"Or Joy?" Hope laughed.

"Or even…" Sherlock shuddered. "Claire."

Hope was puzzled. "What's wrong with Claire."

"I knew one in high school. Spiteful girl, I've hated that name ever since." Sherlock grew serious. "So, you know what I think you should do now?"

"What?"

"I believe you should think about what I've said." Sherlock smiled as she headed toward the door.

"You told me not to just think."

"Yes, but that was before you had the benefit of a wise aunt's advice to consider. And Hope when you figure out the good that comes from this gift, and you will figure it out, let me know."

Hope smiled as Sherlock left the bedroom. She thought about her words for a long time. Her decision became clear. Hope picked up the phone and dialed before she could change her mind.

"Yeah-lo?" the familiar voice answered on the other line.

"Mike, come pick me up. You and I are going to try something."

CHAPTER 37—BALANCE

Mike looked over at Hope's focused features as he slowly drove past first Mama's house and then the Smiths'. "So, young Jedi, how does this work? You just reach out with the force searching for the dark side?"

Hope quirked an eyebrow, "This isn't *Star Wars*, and I haven't tried this before, but yeah—that's basically the idea."

Mike was quiet for several moments longer as he turned the car in the direction of town. "So you're using this mind meld thing now? You trying to pick up Rob?"

"That's *Star Trek*, and yeah, I'm trying now."

The silence was longer this time. Hope turned to Mike and gave him a gentle smile. "So, ask."

"Ask what?"

"Ask me what it is you really have on your mind."

"Okay."

The silence returned and Hope waited patiently. Mike cleared his throat. "So, since you're sitting there with yourself open up to all the bad things in the world, are you picking up anything about me?"

"As a matter of fact I am." Hope nodded her head sadly. "You're destined to fall in love with one of those sand people things, and become back-up singer in an alien band."

"I'm serious."

Hope's smile left her face. She considered for a moment before answering. "It's different with you Mike. I know you. So yeah, I know that you drive past the speed limit with your lights flashing just because you don't like to sit in traffic, and I know you sometimes lie to Mama about what your day at work was like, and that sometimes you would like to put the cuffs on a little more aggressively than called for, but you don't. Everyone knows those things, though."

"There's more, though, isn't there?"

Hope stared at Mike for a long time and sighed. "Once you hate someone, you will always hate him. You feel responsible for more than you should. You feel that the law should be bent at times, and then the guilt of thinking that eats at you. You lied once about evidence to protect your kid sister from going to court, and you want Rob Stinner to hurt in ways that aren't considered acceptable force." Hope reached over and gently squeezed Mike on the shoulder, her voice a soft caress. "You try to protect everyone you meet. You're a faithful husband, a good father, and a great big brother."

"You see all that?"

Hope nodded. "I always have." The smile returned, "Except for the great big brother part. That's just something I promised Mama to say."

Mike laughed and reached across the seat to pinch her leg. Hope screamed playfully, swatting at his hand as they stopped at a red light. She tried to push Mike's hand away, turning her head away as he reached for her nose to give it a squeeze. Her eyes locked with the driver in the old gray plumber's van that was stopped next to her. The revulsion was immediate and Hope clawed the door handle, thrusting the door open enough to hold her head down close to the pavement as bile left her stomach to splatter on the hot asphalt.

"Hope...Hope you okay?" Mike touched Hope's shoulder as she began to tremble. The light turned green and after Hope leaned back into the car, closing the door behind her, he moved slowly forward.

"Mike, that man has a little boy locked in the back of that van. He's a kidnapper and a pedophile." Hope ran a trembling hand against her lips.

Mike didn't hesitate before flipping on his lights and siren. He sped up behind the van, and pulled it over to the side of the road.

He started to get out of the car, when Hope's voice stopped him. "What are you going to say caused you to pull him over?"

Mike hesitated for a moment before frowning down at her. "Don't worry, I'll think of something. Use the radio and call Justine for backup."

Mike cautiously approached the driver's side door. His own revulsion at Hope's words caused his stomach to churn painfully. He stepped up to the door, his hand near his gun. "Sir, could I ask you to step out of the vehicle, please?"

"Sure, officer." The brown-haired, thirty-something man could have passed Mike in the store without giving him any reason to suspect him of Hope's claim. He seemed so clean cut and polite as he stepped out of the van that for a moment Mike felt doubtful.

Mike took a deep breath, looking back at Hope's tortured eyes, which were still focused on the rear door of the van. "Sir, your tail light was flickering as you pulled away from the light. I think you may have a short in it."

The man visibly relaxed. "Oh, thanks, Officer. I'll be sure to have that checked." He started to walk back in the direction of the driver's door.

"Sir, it's probably just a loose wire. If you could just open your rear door, I might be able to help you repair it."

"No...No that's really okay, Officer." Sweat began to bead on the man's forehead.

"Sir, is there a reason you don't want me to look inside your van?" Mike's hand moved closer to his gun.

The man broke into a run just as Mike's deputy came down the street in the opposite direction. Hope watched from inside Mike's police car as he and his deputy tackled and then handcuffed the man. Mike walked back to the van as Dave put the man into the back of his police car. Mike opened the rear van door, revealing a bruised and beaten young waif of a boy lying against an old dryer, toolbox, and piles of boxes. Hope's heart ached as his frightened eyes briefly met with hers before staring at the policeman who had just rescued him from the most awful thing he had experienced in his eight young years of life.

Hope never moved. She sat quietly as the EMS team showed up and checked the boy over. She watched as Mike talked to his deputy and the EMS team. She watched Mike walk slowly toward the car as the others pulled away, one going to the hospital, one to jail. Mike got in the car and sat silently for a few moments before turning pained eyes to his sister. "That poor kid, he was the about the same age as the twins. He could have been one of the twins." His eyes watered momentarily as Hope sat still unmoving. "Hope, you saved that kid's life. I could see it in that man's eyes. He has a warrant in three states, and is suspected of murdering three other children. You saved his life. And Hope, you're not going to believe this." Hope turned dark eyes to her brother. "That kid? His name was Jimmy. How's that for a coincidence?"

Hope sat stunned for a moment, taking it in. "Chris was right." She whispered.

"Who's Chris?"

"Aunt Sherlock's friend."

Mike smiled. "Aunt Sherlock has friends?"

Hope felt a smile of her own form. "Yeah, good ones."

"You want to drive around some more looking for Rob?"

"You know, I think we've done enough for one day." They shared a smile as Mike started up the car.

Mike turned to stare at Hope before he pulled back onto the road. "Just in case I haven't told you lately, I'm really proud to have you as a sister."

"Thanks." Hope choked out the words past the happy tears in her throat. "You're not too bad yourself."

CHAPTER 38—ROBBED OF CHOICES

The two Mr. Smiths sat at the kitchen table across from an angry Rob Stinner and a nervous Kyle Murdock. The scarless Mr. Smith tossed a copy of *The Seconds* across the table at Rob. "The boss isn't going to be happy about all this publicity."

Rob sneered. "Look, you told me to take care of the situation, and I'm taking care of it."

"We told you to locate the missing stuff."

"Yeah, right." Rob took a drink of his beer. "That stuff is tiny. You wanted me to tie up loose ends and that's what I've been doing."

"You were supposed to keep the Rhineholdts away, not murder anyone." Kyle gave Rob a startled look as he realized that Mr. Smith's words proved Rob to be a liar about their orders.

"Yeah, well, I know the Rhineholdts, *personally*. They ain't that easy to scare."

Scarred Mr. Smith leaned forward, his eyes holding a hint of menace. "You're not getting paid to get revenge on some broad who dissed you."

"Look, you hired me because I know this town and the people in it. I know how best to handle the Rhineholdts." Rob crushed the beer can in his hand and tossed it onto the table.

"Instead of getting us our stuff back, you've caused unwanted attention. The sheriff's car drives by here almost every night."

"I wouldn't be too concerned about that. He's probably just keeping an eye on his parents' house, since they moved out after the fire."

"The sheriff is the Rhineholdts' son?"

Kyle could sense that the conversation was taking a turn for the worse.

"Look, I've told you I have the Rhineholdts under control."

"The boss comes into town this week, and you better have all of this taken care of before he gets here." The scarless Mr. Smith tapped the newspaper. "And no more publicity."

Rob stood and walked toward the door. He paused, waiting for Kyle to follow him. The two got into the black pick-up, Rob slamming his door closed with angry fierceness. Kyle started the engine and waited until he had pulled onto the road before shooting a nervous glance in Rob's direction. "So, what are we going to do now?"

Rob lit a cigarette, inhaling deeply before answering. "We're going to take care of it just like I said. Dead people can't talk to the press, now, can they?"

Kyle felt a knot of uneasiness form in his stomach. He wanted out, but it was obvious that Rob enjoyed killing, and one more murder wasn't going to make a difference to him, even if it was Kyle's.

CHAPTER 39—FORGIVENESS

Hope sat in the porch swing with her eyes staring out at the flower garden and small pond, but her vision was turned inwards to the events of the past few days, especially the young boy that she and Mike had saved. She was so deep in thought that she hadn't heard Eric open the back door, and neither had she noticed as he walked towards her carrying two glasses until he was standing in front of her offering them to her.

"You have two choices. You can have ginger-ale/orange sherbet surprise, or a pink lemonade fizzy."

Hope contemplated the two cold glasses before her before taking the pink lemonade fizzy from Eric's hand. She took a sip and smiled at the refreshing citrus burst. "What's in this?"

Eric sat down beside her taking a sip of his own drink. "Chef's secret." He smiled at her before continuing, "But I guess I can tell you. Ginger ale, pink lemonade, and just a splash of key lime juice."

Hope took another drink. "It's good."

"Thanks."

They sat silently next to each other, their feet gently rocking the swing in a languid rhythm. Hope looked up at the puffy clouds, squinting against the brightness of the sun, before turning her attention back to Eric. "So, you getting tired of a houseful of Rhineholdts yet?"

Eric's smile broadened. "You know, you probably won't believe this, but at times it's really been nice. Your Mom and Aunt Agatha keep feeding me, your Dad's been taking care of the yard, and Ty showed me this morning how we had the surround sound set up wrong, so now we don't have to watch TV through the VCR anymore."

"Honey, you're a computer programmer. You couldn't figure it out without Ty?"

"Everything with a plug is not the same, you know."

Teasing Eric about his everyday lack of mechanical expertise, such as programming the remote controls or setting his watch, was a constant source of amusement for Hope, given that he could write computer software that was far more innovative than the competition.

"I'm just glad my family isn't getting on your nerves, yet."

"I would trade childhoods with you in a second. At least you know that your family really cares about you."

Hope would have liked to argue with Eric, but his parents were two of the most self-centered, cold people she had ever met. It always amazed her that Eric grew up in such an environment and still turned out as wonderful as he had. "You know that they've already adopted you. You couldn't get rid of them now if you tried." She thought of how much her family really loved Eric.

Eric took another sip of his drink, his voice hesitant. "It's good to see you smiling again."

Hope's smile widened and she leaned back looking up again at the clouds. "I was just thinking, if this was a musical instead of real life, I think this would be the part where Annie would break into "Tomorrow", or maybe that song in *The Sound of Music* where they are all laughing after it begins to storm outside." She leaned over against him, resting against his shoulder.

"Is there a song for when the wife forgives her stupid husband for not being there for her?" Eric's voice was wistful.

"You've always been there for me." Hope's eyes looked deep into his. "We just have to find a way to work through this issue of faith, together."

Eric grew serious again. "Any suggestions? I can't just make myself believe in something. If it was possible, for you—I would."

Hope closed her eyes for a moment, longing for wisdom she didn't think she had. "Okay, how about this. You promise me to keep your mind and heart open to the possibility."

"Just keep an open mind—that's it?"

"And keep your heart open for a sign." Hope wasn't sure where the words had come from, but she knew they were right.

"A sign?"

"A sign that there is a God. I'm sure He won't let you down."

Eric paused, considering. His need to be honest forced him to measure his ability to do what Hope was asking of him. "Okay. You've got it."

The smile that spread across her face was the closest to her ordinary brightness that Eric had seen in days. It warmed his heart that he was able to remove some of the pain he had caused her and replace it with that smile. They sat on the swing, his arms cradling her for long minutes, her shampoo and sweet scent comforting to him as he rested his chin on top of her head. "If this was my musical, this would be the part where they play that 'boom, pa-chic, boom, boom, pa-chic song."

Hope's brows furrowed as she tried to place the melody. "What musical is that from?"

"It's that song they always play in dirty movies when the sweaty young pool boy finds the scantily clad woman at home alone." Hope quickly turned her head to look up at him just in time to catch him moving his eyebrows up and down in his best imitation of a dirty old man.

"Sex addicts. I knew it!" They both jumped, neither having noticed Agatha quietly listening in the doorway until she spoke. "Humph." She turned to go back into the kitchen. "I told Eavenly about the two of you. You can just see it on your faces, sex maniacs."

Hope began to giggle and she could feel Eric's body shake behind her as he joined in laughing. "Well, Eric, still welcoming the family's extended visit?"

Eric laughed, "Okay, I'll admit it. There are times when I could do with a *little* privacy."

CHAPTER 40—LAUGHTER AND HOPE

The sound of Hope's laughter wafted across the porch, through the kitchen door, and circled to rest at the kitchen table where Sam and Eavenly sat drinking tall glasses of iced tea. Sam's smile was reflected in his eyes as he looked at Eavenly, checking to see that she too had heard their daughter laughing again.

Agatha walked from the back door and plopped into a chair next to Eavenly. "Sex addicts, I tell you."

Eavenly smirked, "They're having sex on the back porch?"

"No, but they're talking about it."

Hope's giggles as Eric began to tickle her grew to a louder level causing the three of them to begin to laugh themselves. Eavenly breathed out a great sigh of relief. She smiled at Sam before turning to Agatha. "She always has been rather resilient, you know."

"You don't have to tell me, Eavenly. I told you that she was going to be okay."

"*You* said she was cracking up."

Agatha gasped. "Eavenly, what nonsense! You should be ashamed for uttering such a lie."

"Agatha, you're such a nitwit that you can't even remember what you've said from one day to the next."

"Nitwit?" Agatha placed her hand against her chest in an exaggerated display of shock. "Moi? A woman who has a solid white Christmas tree with only crystal ornaments should never dare call anyone else a nitwit."

"What in the blue blazes does a Christmas tree have to do with your inability to remember what you say?" Eavenly sputtered.

"Exactly my point!" Agatha taunted triumphantly.

"Point, what point?" Eavenly leaned towards Agatha touching her shoulder with an accusing finger. "You don't even know how to argue properly."

"Ladies." Sam's gentle voice interrupted the escalating flow of the argument. "If you please, I'm listening to the sound of my daughter laughing, and your arguing is making it difficult."

Anger left as quickly as it had flared up, and in its place was the simple pleasure that often accompanied those in the presence of Hope.

CHAPTER 41—BROTHERHOOD

Luke shifted against the uncomfortable feel of his seatbelt, raising his hand to stifle a yawn. "What are we doing, exactly?"

Mike turned his attention from the "Squealing Pig" to look at his younger brother. "We're watching to see if Ty is in that bar."

"And we don't just call him on his cell phone and ask him where he is because…"

"Because, he's up to something. I get the feeling that Ty has been lying to us lately, and that makes me very nervous. Maybe he's not thinking too straight since he got kicked out of the army."

"Ty lying?" Luke sat up straighter. "I don't know. You know, he took that whole Eagle Scout thing pretty seriously. Did he ever tell you exactly what happened to get him kicked out?"

"See, that's the other thing." Mike frowned. "He hasn't told anyone. Just spent the past few months wandering aimlessly from place to place, hardly ever called or visited, and then he just suddenly shows up at Hope's drunk, or pretending to be drunk, after Mama and Pop's house is set on fire."

Luke snickered. "You thinking he had something to do with the fire?"

"No, of course not, Stupid." Mike paused. "It's just none of this feels like Ty, you know? He was always the easygoing, responsible one. Something's wrong." Mike rubbed a hand across the beginning of a five o'clock shadow. "I'm worried about him."

Luke nodded seriously. "You're the one with the cop instinct. If you're worried, well then, I'm right there with you, Man."

Mike smiled. "Thanks, it helps to have someone else to talk to about it."

Luke grinned. "You could always have told Mama."

"She would be mad enough just to know he was hanging out at this dive to give him down the road. I think his dishonorable discharge was the closest anything has ever come to breaking her heart."

Luke shook his head. "No, I think all of this stuff with Hope lately tops the list."

"I worry about her, too. None of this adds up, you know? Mom and Pop's house, Hope being attacked twice, Rob Stinner showing back up. I feel like I'm missing something."

"Mama said Hope was in better spirits since you guys saved that kid. How's he doing?"

Mike's face saddened. "He went home to his parents, and the slime ball is looking at a long time behind bars. We extradited him today. I would like to see that police car crash in some remote place and that man suffer a few scenes from *Deliverance*."

"All those guys that could even think of hurting women or kids like that should be castrated." Luke's voice held an unusual amount of vehemence.

Mike nodded in agreement.

"So what is it you think you're missing?" Luke unhooked the seat belt, and stretched his tired legs out as far as he could beneath the dash.

"Why don't you just ask me what it is that I don't know? If I knew what it was I was missing, then I wouldn't be missing it."

Luke grinned at Mike's irritation, "Yeah, but I know you. You've got some connection going, or you wouldn't admit to missing something."

Mike sighed. "I think maybe it all has something to do with Ty."

Luke straightened in his seat as a man stumbled out of the bar, falling into the brick wall before regaining some balance to sway down the street away from Mike's car. "Speak of the devil."

The two brothers exchanged a worried look before Mike started the car.

"So we going to stop him and talk to him?" Luke glanced over at Mike's sharp features.

"No."

"We going to just follow him all night?"

"No."

Luke sighed, "So, Man, what are we doing here?"

Mike looked back at the Squealing Pig, "We're going to wait and see if we can figure out who he's been meeting here."

They only had to wait fifteen minutes before the two Mr. Smiths walked out of the bar.

"Damn." Mike pulled away from the curb, shaking his head in confusion.

"Know them?"

"Yeah, they're Mama and Pop's neighbors. The ones Mama thinks are dealing drugs, Pops thinks are smuggling jewels, and right after Hope was found on their property all of the bad stuff started happening."

"So, maybe Ty was just in the bar at the same time. You know, a coincidence." Luke was trying to be reassuring.

Mike grunted. "Except for that this is the third time I've seen him leave this dump, closely followed by Mr. and Mr. Suspicious."

"Okay, so what would Ty be doing hanging out with suspect one and suspect two?"

"Don't know."

"You guys aren't going to get in a fist fight are you?" Luke tried to lighten the mood.

"I hope it turns out to be something that can be handled that easily."

CHAPTER 42—MESSAGES

Hope sat up in the hammock, lifting her sunglasses and peeking over the top of the book she was reading to smile at Scout and Jaspers who were wrestling in the grass. She took her hand and plumped the pillow before lying back and turning a page. She hadn't been in the mood for a suspense novel, or even an adventure, so she had picked out books by Erma Bombeck, Bill Cosby, and the one in her hand by Garrison Keillor. She felt her mood lighten as the sun warmed her skin, the breeze blew the gentle scent of lilac blossoms over her, and the lighthearted words whispered through her thoughts.

Joe stood at the edge of the woods, eyeing the book in Hope's hand, along with the two additional ones lying next to her. Even with Hope's speed in reading, Joe felt that she would be lying in the hammock for a while. He began to briskly walk back to his home, deciding to take a break from his vigil to shower and take a small nap. Hope's family was on guard and she was safe at the moment.

Joe went straight to the upstairs bathroom as soon as he entered the house. He turned the shower on letting the water grow hot before stepping beneath the spray. His tired muscles began to unknot beneath the massage of the hot water. As Joe lathered himself with soap, he realized that he was growing too old to stand guard so long without sleep or rest, and it had forced his body to rebel in a display of aches and pains.

Joe stepped from the shower, grabbed a towel, and rushed from the bathroom as he heard the shrill ring of his telephone.

"Yeah, Joe here." Joe didn't get many phone calls, so he was surprised when the voice belonged not to a telemarketer but to his friend Mac.

"Joe, hell, where have you been? I've been trying to reach you for the past two days."

Joe felt frustrated as he realized that in his concern over keeping an eye on Hope, he had left his cell phone on the dresser beside his bed for the past couple of days. "You didn't leave a message on my machine."

Joe felt Mac's sigh even over the distance connected by the phone lines. "The information I have for you isn't exactly the kind I could leave on a machine."

Joe swallowed a sudden sense of unease. "What have you got?"

"I checked on Ty Rhineholdt like you asked. So his sister, Hope, is she the one who is your friend?"

"Yes, she is." Joe's words were short and clipped

"Well then, it looks like she's involved in something dangerous."

Joe's hand turned white as he clenched the phone tightly, listening to Mac's words with a feeling of growing anger and dread.

CHAPTER 43—BEHIND TY

Mike and Luke had slept in the car, taking turns watching their old home, as they waited for Ty to come out. Luke picked a potato chip bag up out of the floor, only to toss it back after discovering it was empty. "Got anything to eat?"

"No." Mike's answer was short.

"Why don't we go inside and just have some breakfast with our kid brother?"

Mike frowned, "Because he's up to something, and I have to know what it is."

Luke looked at him, "I'm still for just asking him."

"Normally, I would agree, but this time it just doesn't feel like that's an option."

They both jumped before hunching down in the car as Ty came out of the house and headed to his car, even though both knew that it would be nearly impossible for Ty to see them, parked as they were behind a weeping willow down the road. They looked at each other as Ty started the car. Mike gave himself time to be a far enough distance back as to go unnoticed before he started his own car to follow.

Mike was confused as Ty slowed the car shortly after he had started and turned into the driveway of the two Mr. Smiths.

Luke coughed. "Okay, I see your point. This is a little unlike our guy, Ty."

Mike stopped the car and pulled it to the side of the road as he and Luke watched Ty get out of the car and walk to the house. The scarless Mr. Smith opened the door before Ty had even stepped onto the porch. Ty glanced over his shoulder briefly as if sensing he was being watched before following the scarless Mr. Smith inside.

Luke turned to Mike. "So what do we do now—get a search warrant and call in back-up?"

Mike shook his head. "They haven't done anything illegal yet—at least, nothing I can prove. And besides…" His voice trailed off.

"Besides?" Luke looked at him as Mike opened his door.

"He's our brother. It's our job to protect him." Mike closed his door and waited for Luke to follow. "Come on, I'll take the left, you circle around back, and we'll see what we can find out."

Luke nodded and headed toward the rear of the house.

CHAPTER 44—NOT WHAT THE DOC ORDERED

Kate raised a tired hand to push a lock of silky blonde hair behind one ear as she peered intently at the chart in front of her. She took a look at the information before making a note and turning to the nurse standing beside her. "She's fighting off an infection. Double the Augmentin dosage and keep me informed on her progress."

The nurse took the chart and nodded. "Yes, Dr. Kate. Scott, in the lab, called up and asked me to let you know that he needed to see you whenever you get the chance."

Kate nodded distractedly, her attention still focused on her caseload and rounds. She walked into the children's wing, wanting to check on her latest tonsil patient. She grabbed a cup of strawberry ice cream from the cart and popped into Wendy's room. "Hey, kiddo. How's the throat feel?"

The young brown-haired girl smiled up at her while reaching for the ice cream she was holding. "Hey, Dr. Kate!" Though her voice was still scratchy, her smile was bright.

Kate smiled and sat on the hospital bed next to Wendy. "So, you doing okay?"

Wendy smiled and nodded. "It hurts a little, but the nurses are nice, and I get all the ice cream I want, just like you said."

"That's good. The video cart will be around soon, and I'll be around a little later to check on you again." Kate continued on her rounds. She had already changed back into her street clothes before she remembered the nurse's message that Scott wanted to see her. She changed directions and headed back down the hall, only to find a nurse walking in her direction with Leslie. "Hey, Doc Kate. You didn't forget that Tom was dropping off Leslie, did you? He said something about the two of you going to visit your sister. I hope she's alright. I saw on the news all about that student of hers getting murdered. That's just awful."

Kate smiled as she took Leslie's small hand. "Thanks, Nurse White. I appreciate your bringing her to me." She glanced down and smiled at her young daughter. "Honey, we have to run a quick errand and then we can go check on your Aunt Hope."

They walked into the near empty lab and up to the lone figure whose attention was fully focused on the microscope in front of him.

"Hey, Kate." He glanced down at Leslie before returning his attention to Kate. "You're not going to believe what we've got here."

"What we have where?"

"The shiny green gems you gave me, remember, Dr. Kate?"

Kate felt momentarily flustered as she realized she had completely forgotten about dropping off the stones Pops had given her as she had focused on the events surrounding Hope and the attacks. She stepped closer to the microscope and gave Scott her full attention. "So I guess I was right that they aren't emeralds. What are they?"

"Well, the chemical name—even I can't pronounce it, but here's the gist. These little babies are bad news. He picked up one of the green gems and held it up for Kate to view. "Like this, they're pretty much harmless, but mix them with chlorine and fluoride and they're toxic."

Kate frowned gently guiding Leslie away from the table. "How toxic?"

Scott set the gem back on the table. "Toxic as in *one* of these could kill hundreds, maybe a thousand. I've never seen anything like it. These compounds shouldn't be combined. Who ever made these knew what he was doing."

"So, okay, they're bad, but only if someone pours chlorine and fluoride on them. How likely is that to happen?"

Scott grimaced as he picked up a glass filled with clear liquid. "They just have to drop it in this."

"And that is?" Kate was growing more nervous.

"Ordinary, very common, tap water."

"Oh." Kate stood. "Excuse me, Scott, but I've got to go find my brother."

Scott watched them leave before turning back to his microscope. "Hope she meant the cop one. This stuff is bad news."

CHAPTER 45—HEADING HOME

Mama and Pops came out on the deck followed by Eric. Mama's smile was bright. "Well, we got a call. The house is ready. It's amazing what hiring a few extra crews with a bonus for finishing early can achieve. We're all going to drive down and see how it looks and quite possibly move back in tonight. Your Aunt Agatha and Uncle Bob went shopping. They're going to pick up some barbecue stuff, and we're going to have a cookout. I just hope Agatha doesn't forget the mustard for my potato salad. I wouldn't be surprised if she forgets it on purpose so that we would have to eat that bland version of hers. Come on, grab your stuff and let's go."

Hope glanced to the last place Joe had been standing, knowing that he would have been disappointed if he knew she had been aware of his constant protective gaze. If she left now, he would be overwhelmed with worry not knowing where she was or if anything had happened to her. She decided to wait and let Joe know where she was going. "Tell you what. Why don't the three of you go ahead and drive down, and Scout and I will follow you in about an hour. I want to finish this chapter and then I would like to take a quick shower."

Eric's face crumpled in concern. "I'll wait and drive you down."

"Nah, go ahead and go. I'll be okay. I promise." She smiled reassuringly up at the three.

Eric struggled with his emotions, worried about leaving her alone, but also not wanting to suffocate her. "You sure?"

"Positive."

Mama leaned down to give her a quick kiss on the forehead. "You be careful on your drive down. You hear me?"

"Yes, Mama. I promise I'll be careful."

CHAPTER 46—CHOOSING SIDES

Mike circled around to the front of the house and was about to peek in the window when he heard a cough from behind him. He turned to find Luke grimly facing him, the scarred Mr. Smith standing behind him, a Berretta 9 mm visibly jabbed into Luke's side. "Very slowly, hand me your gun."

Mike felt his stomach lurch as he pulled his revolver from his holster and handed it to the scarred Mr. Smith who took it from his grasp, quickly turning it so that it was pointed back in Mike's direction. "Now, the three of us are going to very quietly go inside together." Mike and Luke stared at each other hesitantly, but the gun in Luke's side was all the motivation Mike needed to urge him through the door. The scarred Mr. Smith led both of them down the steps to the basement, where they came face to face with the scarless Mr. Smith—and Ty.

"We have company." The scarred Mr. Smith shoved Luke from behind before glaring at Ty. "You were followed."

Ty swallowed nervously, trying to regain his composure, his voice condescending. "They didn't follow me. If anyone was followed, it was you." The look he gave Luke and Mike was that of a stranger. "So, what are we going to do with them?"

Mike lunged at Ty, "Why you son of a…" His words were cut off by a punch in the face from Ty.

Luke jumped forward, when a slight shake of Ty's head stopped him. Their eyes met for a brief moment. It was in that instant that Luke noticed the fear and the hurt in Ty's eyes. He and Mike weren't the only ones in a bind. Ty was stuck in this situation, too. The look of pain in Ty's eyes increased as the scarless Mr. Smith answered his question. "We have no choice now but to kill them."

"Wait! You can't kill them!" Ty shouted.

"Why?" The scarred Mr. Smith shifted the gun towards Ty.

"Why?" Ty swallowed. "Okay, I'll tell you why." He hesitated before he looked at Mike who returned his look with a glare that was venomous. Ty's thoughts scrambled until he latched onto Mike's gun holster. "You guys said you wanted to hire me because I know this town, and I'm more stable than your last guy. I know them. This one is the town sheriff. We don't know how many people know where he is, or even if there are more of them out there somewhere. If things go down bad, we may need hostages."

The scarless Mr. Smith stared at him a long moment, considering. He then walked to a corner where small boxes wrapped in plain brown paper stood stacked in a corner. Ty could see that one of the boxes hadn't been wrapped yet, and inside was a small purse, with a bead design made up entirely of small green gems. His throat tightened as he mentally began estimating the number of those gems that must be in the stack of boxes before him. There was much more than he had thought there would be. His attention was brought back to the scarless Mr. Smith as he picked up a roll of twine, which he tossed at Ty. "You may be right. Tie them up with this while we have a look around outside."

Ty started circling Mike's wrists with the twine, making sure it was tight—knowing that one of the Smiths would check—as the two Mr. Smiths left the basement and went back upstairs. As soon as they were out of sight, Mike gruffly whispered as he jerked his hands away from Ty. "Ty, what the hell is going on!"

"Ssh. You're going to get us all killed."

Luke whose hands weren't yet tied poked Ty in the shoulder with a finger. "Seems like you're doing a good job of trying to clinch that for Mike and me."

Ty's haunted eyes stared into those of his brothers. "It's not what you think."

"What exactly is it then?" Mike growled.

Ty opened his mouth to answer but the sound of the two Smiths as they started back downstairs stayed the words before they could be uttered. He only had a brief moment in which to implore his brothers both with his eyes and with his whispered, "You have to trust me."

Mike and Luke glanced at each other for an intense moment before both turned back to Ty and gave a brief nod of agreement.

CHAPTER 47—HOME ALONE

Hope closed her book and sighed as she glanced towards the trees, still seeing no sign of Joe. She was worried that if she waited much longer, she would be late for the cook out. She nudged Scout, who was asleep beside her, out of the hammock and started gathering up her things. As she went into the kitchen, she grabbed a notepad and a pen to leave Joe a note. She jotted down directions to her parents' with an explanation of the cook out and an invitation, believing that with his concern over her since the attacks, Joe might actually suffer through a group event in order to keep a close eye on her.

She smiled as she thought of Joe's protectiveness of her, and though she was still slightly embarrassed over his seeing her at her lowest moment in the woods, she was extremely proud of Joe for standing his ground and being there for another person in an emotional situation she knew was hard for him to deal with. She taped the note to the outside of the kitchen screen door before taking a quick look around through the house, making sure that the coffee pot was unplugged and that all of the doors and windows were closed and locked.

Outside, Kyle and Rob sat inside the black truck watching the house. Rob reached for his door handle, "Come on, they've all left except for her."

Kyle hesitated, "I don't know, Man. You heard the Smiths. They don't want no more trouble or publicity."

Rob grabbed the front of Kyle's shirt and pulled Kyle close, "You know what I tell you to know…and know that with or without you I'm going to take care of this bitch, once and for all."

Kyle swallowed. An ache in his stomach turned into an angry, turbulent burn. He opened his mouth, unsure of what to say, when he saw movement out of the corner of his eye. Both Rob and Kyle turned in surprise as Hope hurried out of the house, followed by her dog, jumped into her Jeep, backed out of the driveway, and drove off. Both men paused a moment before Rob loosened his grip on Kyle's shirt, shoving him back towards the steering wheel. Rob glanced at Kyle, a look of anticipation in his eyes. "Well? What are you waiting for? Follow her."

CHAPTER 48—LEAVING AND ARRIVING

Joe ran through the woods, a shiny sheen of sweat appearing on his body, as his panic and concern caused his heart to beat faster than normal. He ignored his surroundings, his only thought to get back to Hope and make sure she was okay. He knew that she had no idea what her brother was involved in, or she would have mentioned it to him. She had no idea how much danger she was in. Rob was only the tip of the iceberg, and Joe had to make sure that, unlike the Titanic, Hope wouldn't hit it head on. He broke through to the clearing line of trees that surrounded Hope's back yard. He paused for a moment, training kicking in, as he took notice of his surroundings, looking for any sign of potential danger. Hope's empty hammock caused his breath to leave him for a moment, before he forced himself to run to her house. The sight of the note on the back door gave him momentary relief until he read the line explaining where he could find her. "Damn, she's heading right into danger."

Joe swung around, running with newfound speed back through the woods. When he reached his own house, he ran inside, stopping only long enough to run up to the bathroom and pick up the gun he had left there when he had taken his shower earlier, angry that he hadn't taken it with him in the first place to Hope's. He grabbed his cell phone from the nightstand in the bedroom and ran outside, hopping into his car and speeding off in the direction Hope had taken only moments earlier.

Eavenly, Eric, and Sam had already covered the distance Hope and Joe were attempting to travel. As they neared their home, Sam noticed Mike's car pulled over on the side of the road. The three stopped, worriedly looking around the car for any sign of what had happened to Mike. As Eric turned, his eyes searching for a sign of Mike, he noticed a shiny black Porsche parked farther up the drive, near the front door of the Smiths. "Guys, isn't that Ty's car?"

Eavenly frowned as she squinted in the direction Eric pointed. "This can't be good."

Sam went back to the car fumbling around in the trunk. Eavenly came up behind him as he removed the tire iron. "What are you doing?"

"Jewelry smugglers or not, those are my boys, and something about this doesn't feel right. I'm going to go see what's going on."

"Drug smugglers." Eavenly corrected. "And not without me."

Sam started to argue, but upon seeing Eavenly's determined face he merely nodded and looked over at Eric. "Why don't you take the car up to the house and give Mike's deputy a call."

Eric hesitated. If he left Hope's parents and brothers here and something happened to them, he didn't think she would ever forgive him. The look of disappointment on her face as he had told her about his lack of faith had nearly torn him in two. He didn't think he could live with the look she would give him if he stood by and allowed her parents to come to any harm. Eric looked past Sam and grabbed a small spade from the trunk, "You lead the way, sir."

The three of them very carefully and quietly worked their way up the path to the house. Just as Eavenly stopped to eye the very window Hope had held her up to a few days earlier, they all heard the sound of a gun being cocked behind them. The three slowly turned to look into the face of the scarless Mr. Smith. Eavenly took a controlled step forward, her eyes darting back and forth from scarless Mr. Smith's face to the Beretta 9mm he held in his hand. "Mr. Smith, I would think you would realize just how inappropriate it is to hold a gun on neighbors stopping by for a friendly visit."

Scarless Mr. Smith pointedly eyed the spade and tire iron held by Eric and Sam. However, he did uncock the gun. His voice was sardonic, "Why don't you guys drop those, and then you can follow me to your own private family reunion." Sam and Eric looked nervously at each other before they loosened their hands to hear their only defenses drop with dual thuds to the ground.

No one said a word as the three were led down to the basement, their wrists bound before being told to sit next to Mike and Luke. Eavenly even somehow managed to keep her comments to herself when Ty walked past her as if she was a stranger. Instinct seemed to clue in all three of them that identifying Ty as a family member would at this time do more harm than good.

Kate tossed her cell phone back into the top of her purse, before giving Leslie a nervous glance. "Well, it seems that neither Kathy nor the sheriff's office are sure where Mike is, but Kathy says he's been spending a lot of time the past few days patrolling downtown and near your Grandmamma's house. So we're just going to swing by there real quick and see if we see him, okay?" Kate wasn't expecting an answer so she was more than a little surprised when Leslie suddenly began pointing out the window. Kate slowed down as she noticed Mama and Pop's car, Mike's car, and closer to the neighbor's house, Ty's. Kate was for the first time in her life panicked. Without thinking, she slowly drove her car close to Ty's and turned to Leslie, her only thought to help her family. "Listen, I want you to get down in the floor and stay there, you understand?" Leslie nodded, her eyes growing wide as Kate felt around in her purse until her fingers clasped around her container of mace.

She gave Leslie what she hoped was a reassuring smile, "Stay put." She hesitated outside the open front door before cautiously walking into the house. She heard her brother's voice coming from downstairs and had made it all the way to the basement door before scarred Mr. Smith came up behind her. Kate whirled spraying him squarely in the eyes before running down the steps into the basement only to come face to face with the scarless Mr. Smith and his gun. He quickly grabbed the mace from her before turning to the rest of her family. "Just how many more of you are there?"

They glanced nervously at each other as they all simultaneously thought, "Just one…Hope."

CHAPTER 49—OLD PLACES

Hope smiled over at Scout as she sang along loudly and a bit off key with the radio. As she began her descent down the long expanse of highway from the peak that she often thought of as the barrier which marked the beginning of her home town, Hope smiled. She loved the way the hills seemed to stretch out, offering their beauty of soft pastures, tall pines, and vast acres of mostly untouched land up to the crisp blue sky above. She was feeling more upbeat at the idea of a cook out and a little relieved that her parents would soon be returning to their own home, even though she guiltily pushed that last thought from her mind.

The solitude of the drive, except for the silent companionship of a sleeping Scout, had recharged her, and as she looked around, lighthearted memories of her youth filled her mind, pushing aside the dark days of the present. At a ragged wooden sign, proclaiming the "best darn fishin hole any man could wish for," Hope quickly glanced at her watch before pulling off onto the dirt road that wound about, curving back on itself before nearing an old wooden dock, reaching daringly out onto the lake.

Hope had spent many days of her youth at this exact spot, swimming, laughing, and dreaming. She opened the door, her breath momentarily knocked out of her as Scout jumped on her belly before quickly making his escape to sniff a nearby tree and relieve himself. "You stay close, you hear?" Hope smiled at a hazy memory of Scout the last time she had taken him near a lake. "And don't knock any turtles into the water expecting me to get them back out for you, either."

She allowed herself a good stretch, reaching her arms skyward, and twisting until she felt a small pop in her back. She took her shoes and socks off and quietly walked to the end of the dock, the water beneath reflecting the calmness she had located within which she was holding tightly onto. Maybe it was her focus on the beauty of her surroundings that blocked out all indicators that Rob and Kyle had followed her. Suddenly, a chill ran up her spine, and she felt as if a cloud had passed before the sun as from behind her she heard the oily voice that could never entirely conceal the beast lying just beneath. "Hope…alone at last."

CHAPTER 50—NO PUNCHES PULLED

Hope closed her eyes in a moment of disbelief as she registered the voice coming from behind her. She slowly turned to find Rob Stinner smiling at her, an evil gleam in his eyes. She glanced for an instant at the man standing a small distance behind him, Kyle Murdock, recognizing him as being an older student at her old high school, before quickly turning her attention back to Rob. She couldn't quite make herself believe that Rob had managed to get this close to her without some inner warning kicking in to alert her. She felt anger over Jimmy burn in the pit of her stomach and knew deep in her heart that this time Rob wasn't going to be allowed to hurt her without a fight.

She took a defensive stance, silently glaring at the man who had weaved in and out of her life bringing destruction and despair. Scout came running from the trees where he had been playing, the fur on his back standing on end. He was growling as he leapt at Rob, his teeth bared. Scout, though not a guard dog, had sensed the danger to his master, and instinct led him to protect her. Scout sank his teeth into Rob's arm, refusing to let go. Rob slung his arm out, giving the dog a vicious kick in the ribs, the crack as they broke an explosion of pain in Hope's heart. Scout whimpered once before lying unconscious on the dock. Hope screamed and raised her fists in anger.

Rob eyed the way she was standing, a smirk spreading across his face as he tossed back over his shoulder. "Look at that, Kyle. Princess here thinks she's going to give us a fight."

Hope noticed Kyle swallow nervously, unable to meet her eyes as he glanced away, mumbling a barely audible "Remember what the Smiths said."

Rob's jaw clenched at Kyle's comment, and as he turned to face his partner, his face was a flush of angry red. "*We* will do what *I* say." He pointed an angry finger toward Kyle's face. "You got that?" Rob noticed the surprised widening of Kyle's eyes as if he noticed something over Rob's shoulder, an instant before he felt the impact of Hope's kick as she squarely planted her foot into his back, bruising a kidney. Rob growled with pain and anger as he swung back to face Hope, but before he was able to turn all the way around she had already begun to drop into a rotating crouch that allowed her to sweep his unbalanced legs from beneath him.

He reached out as he began to fall and grabbed Hope's leg, pulling her off balance and causing her to hit the dock, hard. He kept his grasp on her leg as he pulled her toward him, using the leverage to throw himself over her. He grabbed a handful of her hair and used it to pound her head three times into the coarse unyielding wood of the dock. Hope's vision began to swim before her as the old injury on her head split open, releasing fresh blood to accompany that of her now bleeding nose and split lip. She groaned as she struggled for every small memory of Joe's training, using her hips to leverage Rob away from her. She placed her hands on the deck, but a kick in the ribs from Rob with her hands gripping into the wood beneath her caused fingernails to be torn as her grasp slipped with the momentum of her body rolling away from the impact.

She cradled her ribs, gasping for breath. She felt a shadow pass over her and looked up to see Rob once again standing upright before her. She spit blood, wiping a hand across her mouth, thankful for a moment as she realized that Kyle had yet to join in the fight. A glimmer of hope sprouted inside. She feinted with her body, and then swung forward, shifting all of her weight into the punch she landed in Rob's groin. As he leaned over, retching with the pain, Hope took the reprieve from his onslaught to stumble to her feet. She wobbled for a moment, before steadying herself to move in on Rob. Just as she got within reach of him to plant a punch to his face, he pulled a butterfly knife from his back pocket and quickly twirled it open. Hope was too late to stop her momentum, only able to throw her hand up to ward off the knife as Rob stabbed toward her side. Hope cried out as the knife sliced the tender flesh of her left palm, blood dripping from the wound to stain the wood beneath them.

Rob launched himself at Hope, throwing her off-balance so that she landed with him lying on top of her, the knife against her throat. Rob stared into her eyes, the menace in his body emitting a scent that arose from his skin. Hope, gagging slightly on the blood as it began to run down the back of her throat, spit a mouthful of it into Rob's face. Rob wiped away the blood with his free hand, a malicious smile spreading across his face. He called over his shoulder to a stunned Kyle who had not moved an inch during the fight. "Get me that piece of rope from the truck. We're going to have some fun with Princess here." Kyle hesitated.

Rob jabbed the knife in Kyle's direction. "Go, or you'll be the next one I stab to death." Kyle gave Hope a brief look before trotting back to the truck for the rope.

Rob traced the blade of the knife softly down one cheek, careful not to press hard enough to break the skin. Hope's stomach churned in fear, knowing the things Rob was capable of, which made the gleam in his eyes a hundred times more frightening.

Hope tried to keep calm, knowing that a clear head was important in a situation like this, as Rob dragged her to her feet and began tying her hands together in front of her with the dirty piece of rope that Kyle had brought. Hope eyed her surroundings, the solitude she once thought beautiful now a taunt, as she knew she was too far away for anyone to hear if she screamed for help. Rob pulled on the rope, laughing as Hope winced with the pain of the ropes biting into her tender wrists. Hope looked down at her hands, a feeling of despair washing over her, when the image of her bound wrists caused other memories to flash into her mind.

Once Rob let go of her hands, he folded the knife, placing it once again into his pocket. Hope grew sick at the look on his face as he started to unbutton his jeans. "Now for something I've wanted to do for a long time. You're going to enjoy this, Princess." Kyle seemed to be quietly approaching Rob from behind. Hope felt nausea rolling through her body, her mind running from the situation in front of her. She turned her eyes from Rob, back to the water of the lake around her.

Finally, the vague memory blossomed into an idea. Hope breathed in deeply, expanding her lungs, quickly pushing the air out forcefully, and then repeating the process. Without hesitating, she filled her lungs one last time before running to the edge of the dock and diving into the water, leaving a surprised Rob and relieved Kyle behind her.

Hope forced herself to remain calm, allowing her body to descend as quickly as it could to the bottom of the lake, thankful that this section was deep enough to make it impossible for her to be seen from above. Hope turned her attention to the ropes, using her teeth to tug on the knots, thankful for the first time in her life that her brother's had gotten such a kick out of tying her up as a kid, and also that wrestling with them under water combined with playing a woodwind instrument had developed her lung capacity so that she could hold her breath underwater a lot longer than most. Hope felt a small doubt creep into her mind as the knots on the ropes withstood her first efforts. Soon though, like always before, she was able to loosen them and free her hands. Hope remained on the bottom of the lake, using the long legs of the dock as a focal point, pushing off to the right, away from her attackers.

Above the water, Rob screamed in angry frustration. He scanned the water for any indication of Hope. Kyle stood at his side staring unbelievingly at the water. "She must have drowned."

Rob, his eyes flashing with an insane rage, turned and swung a hard punch into Kyle's jaw. "You idiot. She hasn't drowned. I know Hope. This is some kind of trick."

Kyle rubbed his jaw, his hatred and distrust of Rob flaring. He turned back to stare at the water where still there was no movement or sign of Hope. "Some trick." He whispered.

Rob lay on his stomach leaning over the edge of the dock so he could look beneath it. "No way." He muttered as he stood. "No way she's getting away from me." It was as he turned angrily around that he noticed something from the corner of his eye. A hundred yards down the bank Hope was pulling herself out of the water. Her lungs aching from the kick in the ribs and the disoriented feeling brought on by her head wound made it impossible for her to swim any farther. Rob slapped Kyle on the shoulder to get his attention and pointed. "Get her." Both men broke into a run toward Hope, one hesitating a bit more than the other.

Hope heard Rob's voice as she pulled herself out of the water. She focused all of her remaining strength into forcing her aching body to break into a run in a direction away from Rob Stinner. Tears of frustration and despair began to fall from her eyes as her legs began to grow wobbly, while at the same time the sound of Rob's angry footfalls grew closer. In that moment, Hope realized that there was no chance of her being able to outrun him.

CHAPTER 51—LATE TO THE RESCUE

Joe's foot pressed down on the gas pedal, while his hands tightly gripped the steering wheel. Mac's news and Hope's departure were wreaking havoc on his nerves. He had taken a wrong turn before noticing his mistake and was now driving with all the speed he could muster in order to catch up with Hope. He was making good time when he first noticed the black truck slowing down to make a turn in front of him. He veered around it, quickly passing it, but something about the truck and its two passengers triggered a thought in the back of his mind as he glanced in the rear view mirror to see it pull off to the "best darn fishin hole any man could wish for."

Joe had gone five miles farther down the road when the niggle in the back of his head broke its way through. When Hope was attacked, the attacker had jumped into a black truck, driven by a second man. Joe was not a firm believer in coincidence. He swung his car around, spitting gravel and dirt as he floored the gas, speeding back in the direction he had just come from. He picked up his Colt .45 lying in the seat beside him and laid it in his lap.

Hope spun around, her eyes searching for a rock or branch to use to defend herself, refusing to give in to the tiredness and pain encircling her spirit. Her hope deflated slightly as a scan of her surroundings provided nothing that could help her. As she turned her eyes to Rob, who continued to run towards her, she used the only weapon left to her. "You think you can kill me and this will be all over? You think that hurting me gives you control of me?" She saw Rob slow as her words met him. "No matter what happens here today, you will never own anything of me. My heart, my soul, my love, *everything* that *is* me will *never* be something that can be *taken* by you!"

She forced the laugh through her tear-strained throat, refusing to allow him to see her fear. "You kill, and hurt, and hate because you think it makes you somebody powerful? ...Someone important?...You are now and always will be a loser, not even human enough to warrant a tear to fall on your grave on the joyous day someone removes you from this world."

Rob was now only ten feet from her. Never had Hope seen such hatred and malice displayed in another's face. His words seemed wrenched from inside of him. "Maybe—but that day isn't today." He flipped open his knife. His intent was obvious. Hope knew that he wouldn't let anything keep him from killing her this time.

"No!"

Rob turned in the direction of the shout that had sounded from behind him. Hope flinched, her wobbly legs no longer able to support her as her mind tried to take in the sound of a shot. Rob turned back to her, from impact more than will. She could see the bullet wound in the middle of his forehead. The eyes, just an instant before filled with such hatred, were now lifeless. Rob Stinner fell to the ground in front of Hope, dead.

CHAPTER 52—REDEMPTION

Hope lifted her eyes to the hand outstretched before her. She gripped it, pulling herself slowly to her feet. Hope's confused eyes met the anxious ones of Kyle. The small Walther PPK .22 pistol he had hidden in his boot, in fear of the day Rob Stinner would turn on him or go too far, was now held tightly in his free hand. One bullet had been fired.

Kyle searched for words to explain, his heart tearing as he stared at the beaten, but not broken, woman in front of him. "I'm sorry I didn't stop him sooner." Hope remained silent, just staring and listening. Kyle gave a humorless snort of a laugh. "I know you won't believe this, but I'm not like him." Kyle looked at the body lying near his feet. "I don't think too many *could* be like him."

Hope's voice was a hoarse whisper. "I'm glad."

Kyle wondered for a moment if she was glad there weren't more like Rob, or if she was glad that he was dead. He decided that it was probably a little of both. He noticed that she hadn't yet pulled her hand away and he gently squeezed it, wanting her to understand. "I'm sorry about your parents' house. I was told that no one was home. I was told a lot of things that weren't true."

Hope's eyes peered into his, and for a moment Kyle felt as if his thoughts were on display. "You wanted to take care of your boys." She glanced down at the body, lifting her sliced hand to gently probe the wound on her head. "But this...this is not the way."

Kyle began to cry. He let go of her hand and dropped to his knees crying. Guilt and shame overwhelmed him at the gentleness in her voice. They were both startled as Joe screamed from the road, his feet pounding the ground as he ran towards them. Death was in his eyes as he looked at Kyle, the gun still in his hands. Joe's gun now pointed at him, but his feet faltered as Hope gently raised her uninjured hand in a gesture for him to stop, her voice barely loud enough for him to hear. "No, Joe. Don't shoot him." He cautiously approached the pair, checking the body at their feet to make sure it was no longer a threat. He took the Walther PPK .22 pistol from Kyle's hand, before turning questioning eyes to Hope.

Hope leaned into Joe's shoulder for support. "His only crimes have been against me and my family, but if he hadn't been here to save me, I would be dead. Saving me deserves my gratitude."

Kyle's surprised eyes met Hope's as she gently raised his face with her hand. "What you did was wrong, no matter what the reason. And you're going to have to do a lot of good to even the score. I expect in the future, you're going to find that my idea of repayment is fair, but not easy."

"What about Rob?" Joe's distrust of Kyle had not wavered.

Hope took the Walther PPK .22 pistol from Joe's hand. "He's been obsessed with me since high school. He killed Jimmy. He followed and attacked me here. When I shot him, it was self-defense."

Joe took in a deep breath. "You sure this is how you want to handle this?"

Hope nodded, "Yes."

"Okay." Joe gave in, but his voice was harsh as he turned to Kyle. "But if you do anything, and I mean *anything* in the future to make Hope regret her decision, you will settle up with me. You understand?" Kyle nodded, tears still falling down his cheeks in shame—and gratitude for a second chance.

Hope leaned heavily on Joe. "Joe, help me to the dock. Scout…" Her voice broke. "Scout is hurt." Tears fell freely from her eyes as Joe helped her back to where the limp Beagle lay unmoving.

Joe put his hand on the dog, glad when he detected that it was still breathing. He lifted it gently, handing it to Kyle. "You take this dog to the nearest vet. Get there as quick as you can and tell them to do whatever they have to so that this dog makes it. I don't care what it costs." He turned to Hope as she started to follow Kyle and Scout. "Hope, Honey, there's something I need to tell you. It's about Ty and the Smiths."

Hope stopped and turned to face Joe as Kyle pulled away, gravel spraying behind him in his hurry to get Scout to the vet. Joe hesitated for a brief moment. "The Smiths aren't dealing with drugs. It's worse, they're working for terrorists and Ty, he's..."

Hope interrupted him. "But Eric and my parents are going back home. They're going to be right there with the Smiths. We have to warn them." Hope's steps began to quicken as she headed to Joe's truck. She hesitated for a moment looking at Rob's body and her car, her concern for her family winning out. "We'll have to explain all of this to Mike when we get to Mama and Pops. If we call the police now, it may be hours before I get a chance to talk to my parents. Mama might even go next door to spy again. We've got to hurry."

Joe got into the truck beside Hope and started the engine. He had never imagined that after leaving the military he would find himself dealing with dead bodies, terrorists, and damsels in distress. He turned to look at Hope as the last thought flashed through his mind. He corrected himself as he took in the determined tilt to Hope's chin. At that moment, she looked ready to take on a whole slew of dragons.

CHAPTER 53—WHAT HOPE KNOWS

Although she was in shock and was worried about her family, Hope leaned back in the seat and closed her eyes, allowing her battered body a brief reprieve, taking in Joe's words as he continued the news she had interrupted earlier. They had left her car at the lake and now Joe was headed in the direction of Hope's childhood home. "So, Ty wasn't thrown out of the army?"

"No, the CIA recruited him. He's been undercover, and the dishonorable discharge is part of that cover." Joe took a clean white handkerchief from his pocket and gave it to Hope to help stop the flow of blood from her palm.

"So all these past months, when he was supposedly roaming around jobless and without any real goal?" Hope's tired voice lacked any criticism, surprising Joe.

"He's been following up leads, trying to make contact with the terrorist group that the two Mr. Smiths are working for. Hope, it's really serious. The stones your father found are a poison. It's powerful enough to kill thousands. Ty only did what he did to try to save all of those lives."

"Oh."

Joe waited for something else, but Hope sat silently beside him taking in all the new information. Joe couldn't tell if it was exhaustion or acceptance, but it wasn't normal for Hope. "So that guy back there, you really going to take the rap for the shooting and let him get away with what he did to you?"

"He saved my life."

"He helped set your parents' house on fire and was working with Rob to torment you."

"He thought he didn't have any other way, and he never actually hurt anybody." Her voice held a strong sense of resolve.

"He helped Rob get away after he stabbed Jimmy."

"He didn't know that was going to happen, and he's been trying to get out for a long time now."

Joe glanced at her, trying hard to hide his doubt. "You can't know that."

Hope sighed, "Actually Joe, I can—and I do. By the way, that deep dark guilt you feel, sitting home late at night wishing you had been there more for your family—drop it, Joe. You were a good soldier, and when you were home, you were a good father. You spent time with your kids. Just because you weren't the one to kiss their boo-boos or wipe their tears, that doesn't mean you didn't have a hand in raising them. You mistook their grief over their mother's death as disapproval for you. You found some boxes of half-tried hobbies, a few pictures you didn't remember, and you convinced yourself to forget all of the times you were there. Your wife was tired and sick and couldn't fight the illness and help reassure you at the same time. Call your kids, Joe. Imaginary fences—well, they aren't really there, are they?"

Joe sat silently for a long time. "How do you know all that?"

"The same way I know about Kyle. I just do. That's who I am." Hope paused as they turned onto the road leading to her parents'. "Joe, pull over here."

"What is it?" Joe pulled the truck to the side and turned to look at Hope.

"I'm just trying to figure out what Ty's, Kate's, Mike's, and Pops' cars are all doing at the Smiths'. Damn." Hope tossed the bloodstained handkerchief into the floorboard and straightened in her seat, staring at the house.

"I would have picked a stronger word."

Hope almost smiled, but both the situation and condition of her lips stopped her. "That's the worst we were ever allowed in my family.

Believe me, it's meant with enough feeling to curl your hair at the profanity of it." She looked at the man who had come to mean so much to her. "I can't ask you to go in there with me."

"I don't suppose there's some way to convince you to stay out here?" He took a moment to examine her face. "No, I didn't think so. Well, if we're going in there, you're going to need something a little more dangerous than your right hook." Joe handed Hope the Walther PPK .22 pistol and reached for his door handle.

"Joe?"

Joe paused before opening the door.

"Thanks." Hope said.

"No, kid. Thank you."

Both Joe and Hope got out of the car as quietly as they could manage. Hope took the .22 pistol and shoved it into the waistband of her pants, where it settled snuggly into the small of her back. Joe, however, was more comfortable with his .38 held firmly in his hand. With Joe leading, they made their way to the side of the house without incident. Hope felt a moment of irony as she realized that they were currently standing beneath the window Mama had been peering into less than a fortnight ago. She knelt to quickly peek into the smaller window level with the ground. As she peeked into the basement window, Hope felt her pulse race as she quickly jumped back to lean once again against the house. She had only needed that brief glimpse to take in the frightening image of her family members tied and held at gunpoint by the scarless Mr. Smith and Ty. She was grateful for the knowledge Joe had given her about Ty. It gave her a brief moment of hope that he was on the inside and on their side, but the situation was worse than she had imagined.

It was as she stood trying to think of what she and Joe should do next that her eyes traveled across the yard before her, scanning past Kate's car where she glimpsed a small movement through the window. Hope stared at the car for a long moment before the frightened features of Leslie's face became focused, and Hope realized that her niece truly was sitting alone and scared in the car. As Hope's eyes locked on Leslie's, an irrational hope filled her heart. She cupped her uninjured right hand to her ear in imitation of a phone and then pointed at Leslie, hoping she would understand. Leslie stared at her for a moment before understanding crossed her face and her head disappeared from view. She popped back up holding Kate's phone in the air.

A sound of someone stepping heavily on the porch hidden from her view forced a surge of adrenalin through her body as she quickly held up first nine fingers and then flashed her index finger twice at Leslie, praying she would understand. She then signaled for Leslie to hide back down inside of the car. As Leslie disappeared from sight, Hope was grateful that at least the second part of her silent message had gotten through.

Joe tapped her on the shoulder, making several hand signals that looked to Hope as if he was saying he was going to drive doughnuts and then hop like a rabbit. He disappeared around the house in the opposite direction before Hope could ask him what he was talking about. Before she could follow him the scarred Mr. Smith rounded the corner, acting unsurprised to find her standing there. Hope attempted a smile, knowing that the usual force behind it had to be lessened with the bloody lip drawing focus away from her dimples. Although the scarred Mr. Smith hadn't been surprised by Hope's appearance, he most definitely was surprised as Joe tackled him from behind. Joe looked up at Hope from the ground where he was wrestling with the scarred Mr. Smith. He managed to grunt out a few words. "Go help your family."

Hope didn't need any encouragement as she carefully made her way around the house. She peered around the open back door, scanning the kitchen for danger before tiptoeing inside. Hope moved with caution and speed through the kitchen, only slowing as she started down the basement steps in order to make sure to not make any sound that could give her away. Hope made a quick glance in the basement to discover it empty except for her family. She ran straight to Mike going quickly to work untying his hands.

"Hope, run." Mama whispered the words to Hope, her eyes staring over Hope's shoulder. It was then that Hope heard the unmistakable sound of the door swinging closed. She turned to find that instead of having left, the scarless Mr. Smith and Ty had used the door to shield themselves from view. Ty gave Hope a sad, guilty look as the scarless Mr. Smith pointed a twin 9mm, identical to his partner's, at her.

Hope was wondering how they had known she was coming, when a nod of Ty's head lead her gaze to the basement window where a very visible fight was taking place between Joe and the scarred Mr. Smith, and Joe didn't look to be winning. Hope's thoughts churned as she tried to figure out why Ty was still pretending to be undercover when he was left with only one bad guy. It dawned on her then that Ty had no way of knowing that Kyle and Rob were no longer in the picture.

"You might as well turn yourselves in." Mama's voice came from her left where she and the rest of Hope's family were leaned up against the wall, their hands in identical bindings. "I'm sure that Hope alerted the police. They're probably on their way here at this instant."

Hope shared a glance with her husband and her siblings, and in that moment she knew that all of them had made the same mistake of running headlong into danger. None of them had stopped to call the police. Her thoughts turned to her silent niece, and she prayed that somehow Leslie would come through for them.

The scarless Mr. Smith gave a short laugh. "If that's the case, I guess I should just take care of all of you now." He shifted his gun slightly towards Hope, unmindful of Ty's standing behind him, his own gun now aimed at Mr. Smith.

"No!" Eric's frightened cry echoed over the rest of the Rhineholdts as they all began to struggle to their feet.

Hope took a cautious step placing herself squarely in front of Mike, who after working on the ropes Hope had loosened, was now untied. "If you think I'm frightened of you, think again." She glanced at Ty, willing both him and Mike to understand her message. If you think your cronies, Kyle and Rob are going to come help you, forget it. The cops picked them up an hour ago." Hope thought potential stool pigeons might sway the scarless Mr. Smith to give up, but he seemed unmoved by her comment, remaining silent as his eyes went back and forth between Hope and the basement window. Hope only had to wait a minute longer to understand his interest as the scarred Mr. Smith and not Joe, came down the steps to join them, Joe's .38 joining his 9mm as they were aimed at the Rhineholdts.

"Listen, leave my family alone! We don't care about your drugs. Just take them and leave." Mama and Pops had managed to lean against each other coming to a standing position. Luke, more agile, had quickly risen from his sitting position and had been quietly easing along the wall, closer to the two Mr. Smiths. Eric and Kate were struggling with their ropes, still on their knees, when Eavenly's words drew their attention back to the Smiths.

"We'll do anything you want. We can give you money. Just let my children go," added Sam.

The Smiths looked at each other as if considering. The scarless Mr. Smith turned back to the group. "Hey, stop that." He snarled as he saw Eric began to frantically pull at his ropes with his teeth. He swung his gun in an arc as Eavenly and Sam made a move as if they were going to rush the two Mr. Smiths. "Hold it right there. We'll wait and see what the boss has to say."

Hope's hands grew clammy. The two Mr. Smiths didn't look as if they would even consider leaving without causing harm to her family. Looking into the eyes of the two men, she knew that they had reached a decision, one that would not be in the best interest of the Rhineholdts.

Hope met Ty's eyes across the room. Their childhood connection had never been stronger. The look conveyed more than words could, what the boss's decision would be. Ty shifted and began to edge his way closer to the two Mr. Smiths. Hope wrestled with scenarios, all of them risky, before taking a new tact. Her voice was brittle as she turned to her worried parents and a frantic Eric. "Just do what they say. It's going to be okay."

After watching to make sure her parents, Eric, and Kate were still standing to the side against the wall, she turned back to the Smiths. She took a small step backwards, appearing frightened and unsure, bringing herself closer to Mike. "I grew up with bullies tougher than you. You're all the same. You don't care who you hurt. Well, we've dealt with worse than you." She called over her shoulder, "You remember them don't you Mike? Carl Smith and his friend Little Wesson—the two of them were always on my back." She tossed her next words in the direction of the wall where the rest of her family stood. "I would always have to hide under anything I could find when they were around."

Hope's eyes were on Ty, a slight incline of his head the only indication that he understood. As Mike's voice quietly came from behind her, she felt his hand brush her back, unseen by the Smiths.

"Yeah, Hope. I do remember them. You would take the low road, but I would always take the high road....now!" Hope dove to the floor, unsurprised to find that everyone else followed her lead as Ty swung his gun hitting the scarless Mr. Smith hard in the back of the head. Mike pointed Hope's .22 at the scarred Mr. Smith at the same instant that a still tied, but fast Luke ran forward, slamming his shoulder into scarred Mr. Smith's knees, causing both guns to skate across the floor, where Eric threw his body on top of the 9mm as Eavenly kicked the .38 into a corner.

The shot was deafening, causing everyone to jump. All eyes turned to find that Ty's hit had not been enough to knock the scarless Mr. Smith out. He had been able to get one shot off, hitting Ty in the shoulder, before Mike returned fire. Mike's shot hit the scarless Mr. Smith in the side, as Luke rushed over to kick the 9mm from his hand before he had a chance to fire again. Hope untied Luke's hands. Luke retrieved the scarless Mr. Smith's gun, which he kept trained on the two Mr. Smiths, while Hope set to work untying everyone else. The instant he was untied, Eric captured Hope in a tight embrace, his gentle hand shaking as it touched her wounded face. His fear for her safety and relief to hold her in his arms was almost tangible as he exhaled the breath he had been holding for so long. Mike leaned down to get a closer look at Ty's wound. "Well, Bro. It may hurt, but you'll live." Sam hugged Eavenly close, relief evident on both of their faces that their children were okay.

The scarred Mr. Smith growled, "Bro? Brothers!" He turned to glare at the bleeding scarless Mr. Smith. "You hired a psycho you couldn't control, and then you hired a relative of the people who were giving us trouble as his replacement? Why didn't you just put an ad in the paper or invite the FBI?"

Ty stood slowly, a hand pressed against the wound in his shoulder. He took his wallet from his pocket, flipping it open to display his badge. "CIA, actually, and you're both *so* under arrest."

Eavenly clapped her hands in delight. "So putting your family in danger and hanging out with these lowlifes was all part of your job? That means you weren't kicked out of the army? You're not a worthless disgrace!" She lunged forward hugging Ty tightly. Ty smiled through the pain she was inflicting to his wounded shoulder.

Mike stood next to Luke, his own gun aimed at the two Mr. Smiths as he leaned closer to whisper in his brother's ear. "Talk about having your priorities out of whack."

"You shot my baby!" Eavenly walked over to the bleeding Mr. Smith and started to smack him on the head, until Sam took her by the arm and pulled her away.

Kate sighed as she had a close look of her own at Ty's wound. "I'm just glad that the whole thing is finally over with." She looked up to gesture at the boxes of purses lying in the corner. "I mean can you imagine how horrific it would be if any of those things had fallen into the wrong hands?"

"As a matter of fact I can." All eyes turned in surprise to stare at the man standing in the doorway, a Kalashnikov AK-47 in his hand. "Now if you would, please drop your weapons, I believe my men would like them back." As Mike and Luke dropped their weapons, The man bent to pick up the small .22 tossing it in the air lightly before it landed back into his sure grip.

Hope's startled hazel eyes flew to meet those of the stranger. The dark evil they held within was suffocating. She suddenly felt sheer panic and the feeling of drowning in their cruel blackness. Never had she felt such total darkness. This man had murdered many and enjoyed it. He was without a conscience and compassion was alien to him. She found that she could not force herself to break eye contact, even as images of tortured faces passed before her eyes and the man's euphoria at the death and destruction he had caused flowed around her in a painful embrace.

A smile formed on the man's face, doing nothing to warm the icy hatred he was emitting in waves. "Ah…allow me to guess. You must be Hope. I hate that name." The man looked down at the .22 in his hand. "Doesn't look big enough to even sting does it? Let's find out." A shot rang out as the .22 went through the center of Hope's right hand, which she had thrown up as if to stop the bullet. "You have caused me a bit of trouble." He turned his attention to the wounded scarless Mr. Smith. "A good man wounded—a shame, really." He raised the gun and shot again. This time the bullet left the wounded scarless Mr. Smith dead.

The man turned his malevolent attention back to Hope as she pressed the hem of her shirt against her newly wounded hand. "I wouldn't want to see him have to suffer any further."

Ty in an effort to shift the man's attention from Hope, spoke through clenched teeth. "You're the Camel, the Palestinian terrorist who hired the Smiths."

"I am." He glanced at Ty before he returned his gaze to Hope, who for the first time in her life felt the sudden creeping of a fear that bordered on hysteria. This man planned on killing them all, and there was nothing she could do to stop it.

CHAPTER 54—LIGHT EXTINGUISHED

Hope looked around the basement. Everyone was tense, and looked on the verge of attacking the man only known as the Camel. Her eyes scanned the protective glimmer of her three brothers, the concern of her sister, the prayerful eyes of her parents, and the frightened look of unconditional love in her husband's worried stare. She felt the heat of their bodies pressing in on her as if they were willing her their protection. All of this took but an instant, an instant in which Hope realized that they would all die without hesitation if they thought they could save her or each other. The knowledge of such love brought a smile that reopened the cut on her lip, allowing droplets of blood to once again form.

A realization formed in her heart, pushing away the fear and hysteria, the realization that they had more at that moment with each other's love than many would find in a lifetime. She felt no fear as she made her decision. If anyone was to be sacrificed to save the others, it would have to be her, for she was the only one now who was left with any kind of weapon.

Hope looked back at the Camel, her gaze unblinking as she allowed the evil to wash over her, seeping inside of her. The evil crept inside crashing against her spirit, pushing despair inside her heart. Her mind balked at the blackness. The nausea that threatened her was pushed down with sheer will and determination. Hope looked inside the darkness of the man in front of her, searching for a weakness, praying that there was one, believing that she would be able to find something.

"The Camel?" That's a pretty stupid name. "What…you able to drink a lot of water or just have a really big hump on your back?" Hope attempted to keep the fear she felt out of her voice as she tossed the flip words at the terrorist.

His smile was icy. "Actually, my moniker is an invention by your CIA." He glanced at Ty. "I believe the allusion is to a brand of your cigarettes. You see—I have been linked to more American deaths than even your tobacco can claim."

"Yeah, with all that gas you're blowing I'm surprised they didn't name you Pinto Bean." This added by a restless Mike.

The scarred Mr. Smith stooped to retrieve his own 9 mm before turning to the Camel. "Okay, let's hurry up and take care of these guys. I want to get my payment and get out of here."

It was as Hope, open and naked to the evil around her, momentarily focused her attention on the scarred Mr. Smith, that a realization pushed its way through her mind and out of her mouth. "He doesn't know!" She turned an astonished brow to the Camel. "You told them it was a new kind of drug." Her eyes traveled back to the scarred Mr. Smith. "Of course! Even a scum bag like him wouldn't help you if he knew how many Americans you were planning on murdering."

Surprise crossed the scarred Mr. Smith's face. He turned toward the Camel. "What's she talking about?"

Ty followed Hope's opening, realizing that the scarred Mr. Smith wasn't aware of who he was working for. "This guy's number one on our most wanted list. He's the head of a large terrorist group bent on destroying America."

"Shut up." The Camel spat.

"The green gems on the purses are a poison, a very strong, very deadly poison." Kate hurriedly added.

"I said shut up!" The Camel spun his gun to aim it at Kate.

"Don't talk to my daughter like that!" Eavenly started to move toward the Camel, but Sam stepped in front of her, his own hands clenched into fists.

The scarred Mr. Smith frowned. "You said this stuff was some new kind of drug. You never said nothing about poison."

"He's going to put it in the water system. He could take out whole cities. The symptoms take days to develop, a couple of weeks before you die. Thousands of people would be infected before anyone knew there was a problem." Hope's words rushed past her lips. She had to get the scarred Mr. Smith to realize the full intent of the man he had been working for.

Mr. Smith's gun rose steadily to point at the head of the Camel. "I ain't into killing Americans. This ain't what I signed up for. Did you think we would just go along with this?"

The Camel stared hard at the scarred Mr. Smith and opened his mouth as if to answer, but the bullets firing rapidly from his gun were the only answer the scarred Mr. Smith ever heard. Bullets continued to pummel and pierce the body of the scarred Mr. Smith until the AK-47 jammed. The Camel turned quickly aiming the .22 at Hope, halting everyone before they could react. Again his focus turned to Hope. "You American bitch! You think you're smarter than me?! You Americans sit in your big houses, with your cars, eating till you're fat, watching your televisions. The rest of the world suffers while America prospers. You are a stain on this planet, a disease that can't be allowed to continue to spread."

Hope stared back catching a flicker of movement at the top of the stairs. "Do you hate all Americans, or just the rich? I bet you can't stand me—the rich, powerful, *woman* who got in your way? Because from where I'm standing all I see is a weak, worthless man who hates what he doesn't have, and you're the only one in this room who deserves to be hated, to be murdered for your sins. You're an aberration of humankind, unworthy of my spit."

Hope saw the glassy glare of madness in his fiery eyes as he raised the .22, angered out of control. She took a breath to steady herself for what she knew was next.

Eavenly rushed forward, her instincts a moment too slow as she tried to throw her body in front of her youngest child. Hope heard the two distinct explosions at the same instant fire seared through her chest. Her eyes latched onto Joe as he leaped. Hope's tirade had held the Camel's complete attention long enough for Joe, after regaining consciousness, to move in close behind him. She saw the flicker of Joe's double-edged EK knife as it sliced across and into the Camel's throat, blood flowing in waves from the severed artery. The brief flicker of surprise in the Camel's eyes was muffled as the blanket of death covered him.

Hope saw all of this as her body, overcome with the force of the gunshot wounds, began to fall back through the air. She stretched her hands out to her side as if to catch herself, barely feeling the impact as her body hit the floor. The thought that she had been shot flickered through her mind, and she waited expecting the pain to return.

Eric's heart stopped. Time stood still as he watched Hope with her bloodied head and her wounded hands, one with the red slash of Rob's knife, one with the small hole of the .22, sail softly through the air, a brief replica of the cross she wore around her neck. "No! God, no...not this." Eric thought he was screaming, but the words were just a mere whisper. Disbelief anchored his feet to the floor, the effort it took to move incredible as he started toward her.

Hope felt as if she was trying to breath with a heavy weight pressing down upon her chest. Although she could see movement from the corners of her eyes and bright faces moving in and out of her line of vision, and she could feel hands touching her, pressing against her, she could hear no sound over a steady thumping that was roaring in her ears. She felt no fear, peaceful with the knowledge that her loved ones were safe and that they were near. She stared at the moving images of her family above her, the dark gray shadows diminished by the bright glow that seemed to be emitted from their very core. She would have to remember to tell Sherlock how beautiful it was to look past the dark edges into the beauty that lie in the center. "Inside", she thought, "people truly are good." She pushed the contradiction of the Camel's dark soul from her mind, focusing on the light in front of her instead.

Her thoughts shifted back to her body and the wounds that she could no longer feel. "It's odd." Hope thought. "How can I be so cold with so much warmth surrounding me?" She felt her body start to shiver in response. She focused on the thumping. It was growing softer—the beats farther apart. A hazy veil fell over her vision, replaced by an image of her wedding. Eric laughing beside her flashed in front of her eyes. That had been one of her happiest days, shared with those she loved.   The images faded and were replaced with Jimmy's face, no longer the dark blank stare of death, but in its place a smiling, healed, peaceful, young man. Then she was ten again, running through the woods, running with all her speed, knowing that she had to keep going forward but unsure of why. She dove into the lake, diving down deep into the cool water. The thumping was still there, muffled by the water. She felt her lungs aching for air. She kicked hard with her feet swimming towards the surface, the bright light from above guiding and warming her as she swam. The thumping grew quieter, farther apart. She burst through the water into the bright glare of the light, the brilliance of it blinding her. Sound became her only sense, and she suddenly realized that the thumping sound was her heartbeat—then it stopped.

"No!" Eavenly screamed. The moment that life left Hope's eyes, her face took on the appearance of a stranger, her spirit having been so much of her character that it had defined her features. "No!" Sam caught Eavenly as she slid, sobbing, to the floor. They held each other, weeping at the pain every parent dreads, the reason parents often pray to not outlive their children. The pain seeped into every molecule of their bodies, forcing their hearts to skip a beat in denial.

Eric fell to his knees at Hope's side, feeling disbelief followed quickly by anger ending in grief. The pain was more than he believed possible to bear, and he howled in anguish, his voice joining the astonished gasps and cries of the others. The Rhineholdt siblings stood paralyzed with uncertainty and disbelief. Joe sat in numb silence on the stairs, stunned. None had believed it possible—that they could ever lose Hope.

CHAPTER 55—THE TRUE FIGHT

It had taken but a few moments for the bullets to enter Hope's body and take her life. It took only a brief moment longer for her family's disbelief to turn to defiance and led by Kate, to begin doing all that they could to force life back into her still frame. Luke and Mike helped administer CPR while Kate focused on the challenge of ceasing the flow of blood from Hope's wounds, her medical training telling her that time was not on her side. The sound of sirens peeling through the silence as they approached the house was almost, but not quite, as welcome as the sound of a gasp as Hope—on her own—drew a ragged, rasping breath. The EMS crew was beside Kate before she realized it, applying an oxygen mask and placing Hope's body onto a stretcher. Hope had a pulse, but it was weak. The EMS crew, followed by the family, hurried outside.

The sight that awaited them as they walked through the door of the Smiths' house was shocking. The yard was quickly filling with people. State police cars, fire trucks, and ambulances together created a frightening tumult of desperate sound with their sirens. Men in civilian clothes pushed their way forward, guns drawn, badges waving from flapping wallets held in tense hands. One agent, with the haughty air of a man used to being in charge, made his way to stand in front of the stunned Rhineholdts. His eyes flickered across their stricken faces, dismissing each in hand until he came to Ty. "Agent Rhineholdt, have the hostiles been taken into custody?"

Ty, still holding his bleeding shoulder started to push past the man, his eyes not leaving the stretcher that carried Hope to a waiting ambulance. "The hostiles are dead."

The agents formed a human barrier in front of the desperate family. "We are going to need to debrief each of you, before we can allow you to leave."

Joe took the situation in, his anxiety over Hope making him desperate. He stepped back into the shadow of the doorway, and pounded the keys on his cell phone before quietly whispering into the mouthpiece.

Mike raged forward, "Debrief this." He shoved the nearest agent only to have three more wrestle him into submission.

Kate's voice was sharp with desperation. "We have to go with Hope. You have to let me help her."

Kate was startled as Leslie's small hand tugged on her arm. "I called 911 like Aunt Hope wanted me to. She'll be okay now, won't she, Mommy?" Kate's eyes watered at the sound of her daughter's voice, which had not been heard for over a year.

"Mommy will take care of her, Sweetie." Kate choked as she looked up at the men standing between her and the ambulance. As if of one mind, Hope's loved ones began to push their way forward.

The agent in charge was unmoved and gave his men a brief glance that was all they needed to move forward, each attempting to detain a different Rhineholdt. A crazed Eric thrashed out angrily while trying to rush past them to Hope. The agent's cell phone was barely discernable over the angry yells. His eyes widened as he listened to the caller, before yelling to his men, "Let go of them immediately. Let them go to the hospital." His eyes scanned the faces of the angry breathless men in front of him. "It seems that one of you, a Colonel Joe Salinger, has been put in charge of this operation." The agent listened intently to the person on the other line of the phone as a calm Joe stepped forward. "Yes, Mr. Vice-President. Here he is, Sir."

Joe calmly took the phone from the agent's outstretched hand and placed it to his ear. "Yeah...thanks, Mac. I'll make sure everything is taken care of on this end...and I definitely owe you that beer." Joe looked at the group of surprised faces, both those of the agents and the Rhineholdts, turned his way. "An old friend." He nodded to Kate,

"Take care of her." He put a hand on Eric's shoulder as he turned to the rest of Hope's family. "All of you…go with her. I'll be there as soon as I clear all of this up. Go with Hope."

CHAPTER 56—WAITING ROOMS

Sam breathed in the unusual scent of hospital antiseptic mixed with the freesia of his wife's shampoo as he looked over Eavenly's head, scanning the quiet faces of his family. An angry Mike leaned back against the wall, his hand tightly gripping that of his wife Kathy. The twins looked like small statues of themselves, their eyes wide with worry and their bodies unusually still. Leslie sat between them, her fingers tugging at the seam of her shirt. Ty sat alone in a corner, his shoulder now bandaged. Sam grimaced as he remembered the fight Ty had put up before Mike had finally pulled him away to have his arm taken care of by the ER team. Luke stared out the window, his eyes unblinking as Kate's husband Tom offered him a cup of coffee. The only Rhineholdt sibling missing was Kate.

Never had anyone seen Kate as angry as she had been when they had first arrived at the hospital. Administrators had, following policy, tried to prevent her from going in to perform the operation on Hope. It was only after Eavenly had entered the battle demanding that the hospital provide as good a surgeon as Kate, in her place, that they had acquiesced and allowed Kate to break the rule of operating on a relation.

The only one who stood a chance of saving Hope was her sister. Kate's eyes as she had turned to Sam before rushing away, had torn at his heart. In them had been enough worry, fear, responsibility, and doubt to cripple a normal person, but Kate wouldn't allow herself to fall apart when Hope's life hung in the balance. Sam didn't know how Kate would be able to live with herself if she wasn't able to save her sister, but then he didn't know how any of them would go on living without Hope.

He squeezed Eavenly tighter against him, again breathing in deeply the scent of her shampoo. It had been four hours since Kate had left to operate on Hope. They had held their breaths the whole time in dread after being informed by a nurse that Kate would not only have to remove the two bullets but that she would also have to repair the punctured lung and the wound in Hope's heart where one bullet had cut a gash. Sam thought of how big-hearted Hope was. He knew that soon, more family members would be here with them, waiting with them for news. The family would support each other. They had always been there for each other, but Sam didn't think any amount of support would be enough to withstand the pain if Hope were to…he pushed the thought from his mind. An image of the two dark red circles in Hope's shirt flitted once again through his mind. Sam looked over the head of his wife, scanning the quiet faces of his family. A tired Mike stared back at him, their eyes connecting for a brief moment before Sam began for the hundredth time his scan of the waiting room.

Eric sat alone in the small hospital chapel, his gaze steady on the solemn figure of Christ staring back from his cross in the front of the room. The image of Hope, her arms outstretched as she fell, continued to play and replay before his eyes, accompanied by Hope's whispered plea, "And keep your heart open for a sign." Eric kept turning this over and over in his brain, along with his own instinctual cry for God to not let Hope die as she fell before him. Logic warred with his first thought that, somehow even when facing death, Hope had tried to convince him to have faith.

But Eric had to admit Hope hadn't had time to even think of him in that moment, which brought him circling back to the idea that kept whispering inside of him. Again Hope's words echoed in his mind. It was in that quiet moment that Eric came to believe—to believe with his heart and his mind that Hope was right, there must be a God. Eric had no choice but to come to this decision because his soul wouldn't allow him to believe in what it would mean if there weren't a God-that if

Hope was gone, she was just gone. A being like Hope couldn't just exist and become nothing—there had to be more.

Images of Hope, full of life and laughing, flooded his brain. He slowly pulled out one by one his most precious memories: the first time he had held her hand, their first kiss, the first time she had laughed at one of his silly jokes, the first time she told him she loved him, the weight of promise in her voice as she had repeated after the minister, "till death do us part." A tear fell down Eric's cheek, unnoticed as he let out a choked laugh, the sound tinny and unnatural in the quiet of the chapel. "Hope, if this were a musical, it would be the part where someone sings about how the woman was perfect and completed the man's life in a way that could never happen with anyone else, while the man's heart is shredded inside of him." Eric's voice was scratchy as he softly sang the words. "Hope, you are the one, the only, till death do us part and wherever we go from there."

Joe ran a frustrated hand through his hair as the agent in charge put a fresh cassette in the tape recorder, turning flat eyes on Joe. "Okay, Colonel Salinger, for our report…from the beginning."

Joe slammed his hand on the table. "Look, the bad guys are dead, you have the dangerous stuff all rounded up and taken care of. I have to get to the hospital."

"Colonel, as you must realize, this is a matter of national security, and since you got our superiors to okay the dismissal of all the other witnesses, I'm sure you can understand why we need to make sure we cover all the facts with you…now again for our records." The agent took a calm drink of his soda.

Joe sighed, his attention straying from the man in front of him as his eyes flickered for the hundredth time to his watch. "Have you heard anything, yet? How is she? How's Hope?"

"Sir, I told you, we'll let you know as soon as we get any new information from the hospital." He pointedly tapped on the tape player.

Joe sighed. Not knowing, he suddenly realized, was even more of a torture than sitting beside a loved one who was dying, especially when Joe's imagination kept dreaming up worst-case possibilities. He attempted to push the frightening thoughts from his mind, and he began to once again repeat his story. "Rob Stinner was a wanted felon who had recently began stalking Hope Rhineholdt and her family."

"And that was the reason he jumped her at the lake…forcing her to defend herself by shooting him?"

"Yes."

"Where did she get the gun?"

"Rob had it on him, but dropped it in their struggle."

"How exactly did she wind up at the Smith's?"

"She was on her way to the sheriff, when she noted her family's cars were in the driveway."

"Sir, I'm sorry, but you're story just doesn't add up."

Joe stood glaring at the younger man. "Then I believe at this point, it's your job to write it down so that it does. I'm finished here." Joe never looked back as he walked out of the room. After years in the military, he had an intuition about whether or not his orders would be followed, and he knew that in this case, they really didn't have a choice—Mac would see to that.

Mike felt as if there wasn't enough air in the crowded waiting room, but he couldn't risk stepping out for fear that he would miss news about Hope's condition. His eyes scanned the room, stopping briefly on his parents. Mama looked so frail and helpless as she leaned up against Pops. Looking tired and old, it was as if she had aged in the past hours. Mama had been an instant too late in catching the bullets meant for her daughter, and that was weighing heavily on her. Aunt Agatha and Uncle Bob had arrived with grave expressions. It was the first time Mike could recall his Mama and Aunt being in the same room without arguing. Agatha just patted Mama's hand from time to time, not saying much. Sherlock sat in sober silence, unmoving.

Mike leaned forward handing the twins and Leslie some money, telling them to go grab something from the vending machines. His eyes followed them as the three shuffled off. It was as if without Hope, no one had any energy left to do more than pray. He carefully eyed Ty making sure he looked like he was holding up. Concern over Ty's wound helped to focus some of his protectiveness and shift it to someone he still could help in some way. His eyes moved around the room, sharing a look of concern with Luke, before locking with Aunt Sherlock's steady stare. Mike was astonished at the helplessness he saw on his toughest aunt's features. They stared at each other a long moment, which is perhaps why Mike didn't notice as Ty quietly walked out of the room. If he had noticed, his protective big brother mode would probably have pushed him to follow his wobbly brother who had recently lost so much blood.

Eric continued to hum to himself. He stared down vacantly at the candle he held in his hand. The tears that had yet to fall turned the small flame into a round halo of color. He looked deep into the circle of fire, allowing his thoughts to dwell on happier times, rather than focusing on the feelings of despair that threatened to overwhelm him. He jumped when a hand closed over his shoulder and was surprised as Ty sat down on the pew beside him. They sat silently together, both staring forward as Jesus stared silently down from above.

Ty cleared his throat as he turned to Eric. "Hope ever tell you about the priest, the rabbi, and the Baptist minister?"

Eric growled. "Ty, this isn't the time for a joke."

"It's not a joke." Ty softly stated. He waited until Eric returned his stare before continuing. "When Hope was, I don't know, maybe nine or ten, she came to the realization that not all of her friends attended the same church that we did." A smile crossed his mouth at the memory. "Well, you know Hope, she asked Mama why everyone didn't go to the same church, so Mama tried to explain to her how different people had different beliefs. Hope didn't get it. She wanted to learn more, so Mama arranged for her to attend the different churches in town with some of her classmates. But the thing is, every time she went to a different church, she drove us all crazy afterwards with even more questions."

Ty paused making sure he still had Eric's attention. "Well, then suddenly Hope stopped asking us questions, but she spent a lot of time riding her bike, so I decided to see what she was up to...I followed her around. She knew I was there, but she didn't mind. Hope had started visiting the town's rabbi, priest, and one of the ministers. And let me tell you, Hope was really asking them some pretty heavy stuff—you know, real deep spiritual stuff. Anyhow, this went on for a few weeks, then Hope just stopped her visits, went to our church, and didn't ask any of us any more questions." Ty paused, remembering.

"So one day, I followed her out to this small creek we have that runs behind the house, and I asked her if she had given up on her study of religion. She turned to me—nine years old, remember—and she told me she hadn't given up on it, that she just understood it now. So, I asked her what she understood. She closed her eyes and smiled at me and told me to close my eyes. 'Feel it?' She asked me. 'Feel what?' I asked. 'God...It doesn't matter where you are, or what church you're in...He's always there.'" Ty stared into Eric's eyes. "Hope has had that unquestionable faith since she was a kid. Nothing could shake it. Makes you feel like you have to believe, too, doesn't it?"

Eric nodded, his eyes sad. "Ty?"

"Yeah?"

"How do you pray?"

Ty paused thinking. "You kind of just let your mouth say what's inside of your heart."

Eric nodded before turning back to the sympathetic gaze of Jesus. "God, if it's time for Hope to leave..." His voice broke. "Those of us left behind...we're going to need a lot of help. And if it's possible..." Eric begged for the first time in his adult life. "...Please let this not be her time. Let her come back to me."

A young nurse opened the chapel door. "Are you with the Hope Jamison group?"

Ty squeezed Eric's shoulder tightly as they both nodded.

Dr. Kate has finished with the surgery. She's on her way to the waiting room to give you guys an update. The nurse turned and walked back out.

Ty closed his eyes, his voice shaky. "Lord, let it be good news...and please let Hope forgive me for all of this." He opened his eyes to find Eric staring at him.

"You know Hope," Eric consoled. "You've already been forgiven."

A tired Kate pushed a shaky hand through her hair as she removed her surgical gown and booties. Facing her family in this situation was more difficult for her than any such waiting room visit had ever been before. She pushed through the doors, all eyes immediately upon her. She took a deep breath in a rush to get it all out. "I removed the bullets, and took care of her heart and lung. It was a difficult surgery. She's still critical…and during surgery she slipped into a coma. I've admitted her into the ICU unit where we'll keep a close eye on her. Prog…prognosis is not good." Her voice broke as tears began to fall. Tom rushed to her side pulling her tight, her voice muffled as she wept in his shoulder. "There's only a twenty percent chance she's going to make it."

The room was an orchestra of sobs and gasps.

"She'll make it." All eyes turned to the surprisingly strong voice of Eavenly Rhineholdt. "She'll make it. She's my baby." Her voice grew stronger with each word. "She's Hope."

CHAPTER 57—INTENSIVE CARE

Eavenly sat beside of the hospital bed holding Hope's hand. Although Kate had overridden the policy of a five-minute visit per hour, they were still only allowed one visitor at a time in the ICU room. Equipment beeped and sighed from every direction. Eavenly was the first one to enter the small unit. The pale features of her unmoving daughter had brought fresh tears to Eavenly's eyes. Not wanting to cry in front of Hope, Eavenly had pushed them away, but the unshed tears could still be heard in her voice. Although Hope was unresponsive, Eavenly chattered on as if Hope was listening intently to every word. "That was a brave thing you did, Sweetie, brave, but stupid. What were you thinking, getting shot like that? You've got us all just worried to death, you know. Your poor father is a nervous wreck—everyone is. And can you imagine just how hard it would be on Kate if you don't pull through this? She would blame herself forever for not being able to save you. You couldn't do that to your sister, now could you, Sweetie? You see, Hope, you really don't have any choice. You have to snap out of this coma, Dear. You just have to. Come on, Dear, fight back."

Eavenly paused as she gently trailed a finger down the curve of Hope's cheek, very much like she had when Hope was a baby. Her voice dropped to a whisper, and she leaned closer to Hope's ear. "The truth is, Honey, I can't deal with this…this is too much. I know you can hear me. Be stubborn a little longer and fight this. Come back to us, my baby, my Hope." Eavenly leaned forward and kissed Hope on the forehead, pushing a lock of hair behind her ear, before remembering how much Hope hated when she did that. She waited a moment half expecting Hope to sit up and complain or to run her hand through her hair, disheveling it once more. When Hope remained unmoving, Eavenly sighed and leaned back in the chair. She began to hum soft songs to Hope, her hand never breaking its grasp with Hope's.

Luke and Kate stood in the doorway, then both stepped back into the hall, saddened by the image of Eavenly and the still Hope. Luke's soft smile belied the ache in his chest. "You know, nothing can happen to Hope. Mama won't allow it. She loves Hope more than anyone, enough to battle the Grim Reaper himself."

"Mama loves all of us just as much." Kate leaned back against the wall, her shoulders and back still aching from the tension of surgery and the long, agonizing hours on her feet.

"Come on, Kate. It's not like it hurts my feelings or anything, but Hope's always been the favorite. She's the baby. It's kind of expected."

Kate raised tired eyes to stare at her younger brother. "You really think that's it, don't you? The reason Mama looks the way she does? The reason she grieves over Hope the way she does?"

"Well isn't it?"

"No, I've seen that look on the faces of too many parents to not recognize it for what it is." Kate massaged her temples. "You were so young that I don't even know if you remember it that much, but when Hope was born…we didn't think she was going to live very long. The doctors didn't think she would make it. Then later, when she was older, we almost lost her to pneumonia."

"I remember that." Luke scrunched together his brows as if trying to focus the images of his past.

"Well then, you should understand. Mama loves all of us just as much. Hope's not her favorite. The reason she looks at Hope the way she does is because with Hope…Mama has been forced to really picture what it would be like to lose her. To think of all the things she would never be able to do, and to play in her mind all of the wonderful things she is. When Mama looks at Hope, she doesn't just see who she is like the rest of us, but Mama sees what could be, what almost wasn't, and when she thinks of all the moments she's shared in Hope's life…each one of them are felt to be a special gift. Every parent who has almost lost a child…they all have that exact same look."

Luke sighed. "Wow, that must really be hard on Mama."

Kate smiled, "It's not been that easy on Hope either."

Luke grew serious. "So really, what are Hope's chances?"

"Are you asking me as her sister or as a doctor?"

"Both."

Kate's aching shoulders grew tight with new tension. "As a doctor—the odds are against her."

Luke's voice ached with raw emotion. "As her sister?"

Kate's eyes conveyed the intensity of her belief. "I don't think Hope believes in odds."

Sam now sat alone in the chair next to Hope's bed. He had been sitting there for an hour, staring at his little girl. Eavenly had encouraged him to talk to Hope, believing that somehow she would hear their words from deep inside of herself and that their voices would bring her back to them. But Sam wasn't much of a talker, especially with Hope. He had never needed to be. The peaceful silences they had shared throughout Hope's life had often held a communication on a deeper level. They had always understood each other, and the other's company was often all they required of one another. So Sam took his time, searching for words to utter. "What you've been through, well, it's been really rough on you, I know." He allowed the silence to creep in, pausing for long moments, letting his words sink in. "And if you need this time, alone, inside of yourself to get yourself together? Well, that's okay. Because, Hope, Baby, we'll wait for you, as long as you need—I'll wait." Sam sat back in his chair, making himself more comfortable, his hand gentle as it cradled Hope's. His calloused fingers gently circled her bandaged palm. Hours passed, but Sam sat on. If she could somehow sense…anything, Sam wanted to make sure she never felt as if she had been left alone.

Eric had sat for hours in the chapel praying after Kate's prognosis. But now as he sat beside Hope, some of his newfound strength faltered. Eric, a morning person, always woke up long before Hope. He would often spend long moments in the morning just watching her sleep. He awoke every morning somewhat amazed and overjoyed that Hope truly was his wife, cuddled close in his arms. He would breathe in her scent and wonder at the dreams beneath her long lashes. As he leaned toward the hospital bed, both hands gently embracing hers, a chill of apprehension skated down his spine. The battered, frail creature lying in the hospital looked nothing like the warm sprite he awoke to every morning. He leaned in closer peering intently at her closed eyes. Eric hoped that her dreams were peaceful. The thought of Hope trapped in some form of nightmare cut into him.

"Hope, honey." Eric's voice was strong. "You were right. I believe now, and I thank you for that. But I need you to come back to me. I need to share this with you. I need to share everything with you. I need your strength and your smile. I need you to tell me everything's going to be okay. I need for the sun to come up again tomorrow, but that can't happen as long as you're away from me. I searched my whole life, searching for who I am. I know now, Hope. I'm the man who belongs with you. We're meant to be together. I feel deep inside that that's true, so you can't die. It doesn't work with just one of us, so you have to make it, and the thing is, I'm not really that scared…because you've never let me down in your life, and you won't now. The words were wrong, Hope. For us there is no death do us part. We're meant to be together. I believe that."

Mike and Ty stood outside the door, both hesitating. Mike patted Ty on his un-bandaged shoulder, "Look, you go ahead and take this turn."

Ty stood still. "No, that's okay, you can go ahead."

Mike stared at Ty. "Afraid that she's mad at you?"

"Is it that obvious?"

"Only to someone feeling the same way. I keep thinking she's going to be upset at me for not doing more, for not keeping her safe." Mike ran a hand across his tired eyes.

"I think she'll be more focused on the brother who lied, knew about the terrorists, you know, the one working undercover for the CIA?"

They looked at each other for a long moment before giving each other a sheepish grin. Mike broke the silence first. "You know, she would never be able to hate anyone the way we're imagining, don't you?"

"Not in her nature." Ty agreed

"Probably use it for leverage for a few days, though."

Ty smiled, "Probably more like months."

Mike glanced up and down the hall. "Don't see any nurses. Want to sit with her together?"

"Yeah."

They sat together quietly, both having difficulty looking at Hope. Ty cleared his voice. "She's going to be okay, right?"

Mike finally stared at the bruised face of his youngest sister. "She's tough."

"So, she's going to make it?"

Mike looked at his younger brother, guilt once again rearing its clawing grasp in both of their hearts. "Yeah, sure she is. She'll be okay."

"You think she knows we're here?"

Mike stared at the unmoving features of Hope's face. "Maybe."

Ty nodded and leaned forward. His mouth inches from her ear. "Hey, kid. How about letting us see those peepers of yours, huh? I can't live with this guilt. Wake up and yell at me, hit me even."

Mike sighed and looked at Hope's ragged fingers as he gently kissed the cuts the way he had when Hope had skinned her knees as a kid. His eyes glanced over her still body at Ty. "She put up quite a fight, didn't she?"

Ty forced a smile. "Looks like she went a few rounds with Tyson."

Mike nodded and looked back at the face of his kid sister. "She's not down for the count, yet."

"She's just taking a breather."

Neither brother knew who they were trying to convince more, themselves or each other.

Joe stood at the door of the room, self-conscious. Worry had creased his features. He had never experienced torture as excruciating as having to answer endless questions while waiting to find out how Hope was. He glanced at Sam, unsure. "It says family only."

Sam nodded. "Yep."

"I shouldn't go in there."

"If saving my family's lives doesn't make you family, then I don't know what does." Sam patted the other man on the shoulder. "Go on inside…and talk to her. It helps." Sam paused. "It'll help you both."

Joe stepped into the dim hospital room, memories of his wife's final days opening old wounds. He pulled up a chair next to the side of the bed. His practiced eye scanned her bruised face and bandaged hands, seeing nothing that wouldn't quickly heal. He knew that it was the damage inside, in more ways than one, that was causing her pain and weighing on her spirit.

"Hey, kid. Well, it looks like we got the bad guys." His body was restless as he stood and walked to the window. I told them what you wanted, about shooting Rob. This is really some mess you've gotten into, you know? It's like you're a trouble magnet."

He began to pace back and forth. "If you're feeling guilty about my killing again, don't. That man was evil, Hope. We saved thousands of lives. *You* saved thousands of lives. Man, what you did. Getting him mad like that…keeping his attention…I could see it in your eyes. You knew he was going to shoot you. You knew there was no way I could get to him in time. That has to be the bravest thing I've ever seen. You were staring death in the face, and you didn't even blink." Joe stopped his pacing and sat again in the chair, scooting it closer to the bed. "Is death there now, Hope? Are you still staring him down? Well, you tell him that you've done your part. You're through. You hear me? Your duty is over. It's time for you to come home now, Hope. Hope? Come on now…wake up. I've been thinking…and I want you to meet my kids. I'm going to tear down that fence. It wasn't really there, you know, just in my mind. That fence there between you and the rest of us? It's not really there, either. Kick the hell out of it if you have to, kid, but come on back across."

Eavenly sat beside the bed watching as Kate checked Hope's vitals. "How is she?"

Kate hung her stethoscope back around her neck. "Much the same. You know, it's a miracle she doesn't have a single broken bone from all she went through."

"You've done all you could Kate. It's up to the Lord now." Evenly stood and hugged her daughter, feeling her quiet sobs. "What is it, Kate? What are you keeping from us?"

Kate wiped her nose. "We ran some blood-work, standard admission stuff, some other tests. Mama, she's pregnant. Probably only two months, if that. I don't think she even knew."

Mama nodded. "Yeah, I thought she looked like she might be. She had that glow about her, even through the bruising."

Kate sniffed as she looked at her younger sister. "They've wanted a baby for so long."

Mama stretched to embrace Kate. "They're going to be okay, Kate. Hope and her little girl are both going to be fine."

"Little girl?"

Mama smiled. "I think Faith sounds like a good name, don't you?"

"Sounds beautiful." Kate wiped tears out of her eyes, keeping her thoughts positive as she pictured her future niece.

Hope walked on the grassy bank. Her bare feet soaked in the feel of the cool grass beneath them. She felt as if she had visited this place before, but she couldn't quite place it. She had been walking for a long time, but she wasn't tired. She was content and warmed by the brightness of her surroundings. She followed the curve of the river. She felt as if she was supposed to meet someone here, that this was just a resting place in the middle of her journey. She felt that just up ahead, just beyond the bend in the river, lie the end. "It's not time, now. You must go back." The wind in the trees whispered the words. She paused, tilting her head, listening. She thought she had heard Mama calling to her, from a great distance. She began walking again, when she heard voices, louder this time. One of them most definitely was Mama. She sounded worried. Others were worried, too. She had been gone too long. They were growing concerned. She glanced around, feeling sad that she was going to have to leave this place. She listened carefully again to the voices, following them to the edge of the stream. As she glanced down at the water, without even moving, she found herself once again swimming in its cool depths. The voices were louder, coming from under the water. Then she found herself being sucked under, her chest screaming with pain. She clawed out, gasping for breath as her eyes flashed open to find herself in a hospital room. A tearful Eavenly grasped her and hugged her close. Kate rushed toward her, a syringe in her hand. Kate leaned over her arm for a moment, then blessedly the pain began to subside and Hope once again closed her eyes. This time, however, it was only sleep that welcomed her.

CHAPTER 58—VISITING HOURS

Nurse Riley pointed the young, black woman and her son in the direction of Hope's room. She watched her walk in the right direction before turning to the other nurse on duty at the desk, Tiffany. "Well, there goes another one. Have you ever seen anyone have so many visitors? I mean when they brought her in, they said that three of the waiting rooms filled up and that was just family. You walked into her room, lately? It looks like a flower shop in there."

Tiffany smiled at the young nurse. "Well, it's obvious that you haven't lived here more than what, two months?" She paused at her young friend's nod. "If you had grown up around here, you wouldn't be nearly as surprised. That young woman, Hope Jamison, her maiden name is Rhineholdt." She took in Nurse Riley's blank stare. "As in the Rhineholdt ICU wing, which we're standing in."

"This wing's named after her family?"

"Well, it should be. They paid for its addition. But it's not just that. I mean you couldn't grow up in this town without bumping into one of the Rhineholdts. They're the friendliest family on the planet."

"Luke Rhineholdt, he wouldn't be related would he?" Nurse Riley smiled shyly.

"He's her brother. I'm surprised you haven't seen him around. The entire family has been taking shifts staying with her since she came out of her coma. How do you know him, anyway?"

"He's that guy that was visiting one of my neighbors when I moved in. The fireman who got a couple of his buddies to help me carry up all of my furniture, remember?"

Tiffany smiled. "See, they're all nice that way…but especially Hope. I went to high school with her. Sweetest person you ever met."

Nurse Riley smiled, "Sweet or not, if Nurse White catches all of those people walking in and out of her room, she's going to throw a fit."

A voice intruded from behind, "Now, why would I do that? She's in a private room, and as a matter of fact, Dr. Kate believes that visitors are helping her condition. Speaking of which, did the priest, rabbi, and Baptist minister leave already?"

Both younger nurses waited for the punch line. When one wasn't forthcoming, Tiffany spoke up. "Uh, I'm not sure. We just came on duty."

"Well, okay then. You two go ahead and get back to your duties."

The two nurses looked at each other and smiled before turning back to their rounds.

Hope took in a breath, listening to the unusual quiet of the room. She had sent Eric and Luke on errands to get her lunch and something to read. An open window allowed a gentle breeze to dilute some of the perfume from the hundreds of flowers that sat about the room in dozens of vibrant arrangements. Hope smiled at the bounty of get-well wishes her friends and family had sent her. Her eyes scanned the room, stopping at the door where a young black woman, not much older than herself, stood hesitantly. Hope had never met the woman, but her features were too much a reflection of Jimmy's to be anyone besides his mother. Her lips trembled as she motioned the woman to the chair beside the bed. The woman turned to say something to someone standing beyond Hope's line of vision on the other side of the door before turning back to the room and moving to take a seat in the chair Hope had offered.

Hope felt a sad smile form on her face as she met the other woman's eyes. "You're Jimmy's mother." It was a statement more than a question.

The other woman gently nodded. "I am. And you're Hope."

They sat there staring at each other for a moment longer. Jimmy's mother broke the silence first. "The news has been full of stories about you and…some terrorists of some kind?"

Hope nodded. "I've had a bit of trouble lately." She mentally kicked herself over her poorly phrased response, hoping that Jimmy's mother didn't take offense at her words.

Jimmy's mother nodded. "You look pretty bad. Does it hurt much?"

Hope met her eyes. "It could have been worse. I'm sorry I wasn't able to attend Jimmy's funeral." Hope turned her eyes away, a fresh wave of guilt washing over her.

"Mrs. Jamison, are you under the impression that I blame you for what happened to Jimmy?" When Hope was unable to meet her eyes she continued. "I understand about the funeral. The press showed up anyway, wanting to make my baby's death their news story of the day. My relatives ran them off."

Hope looked up. "Families truly are wonderful to have."

"I would have come to talk with you sooner, but I needed a few days…to absorb it all, you understand?" At Hope's nod she continued. "When Jimmy first mentioned you, I thought you were some white woman handing out charity." She continued when Hope would have interrupted her. "It didn't take me long to change my mind. You see, when you met Jimmy, he was already lost to me. He was hanging with the wrong crowd, wouldn't listen to me when I was around, and unfortunately that wasn't too often. I had to work two jobs, just to keep some food on the table, and during that time Jimmy turned into a hard, troubled boy that I didn't want to recognize as my son. You changed him. It was a little at first, but I saw it. And then a few years ago, my son had returned to me, and I know that you had a great deal to do with that."

Jimmy's mother hesitated for the first time in a speech she had obviously intended for Hope to hear. "I always wanted to thank you for my job, but I wasn't sure of what to say." She saw the look of surprise cross over Hope's face. "It didn't take long to figure out that Mrs. Hope Jamison, my son's teacher, and the cousin Hope my boss referred to were one and the same. I know that you're probably blaming yourself for what happened to Jimmy, but if you hadn't came into our lives, my Jimmy would have died on the streets a long time ago. Instead, my Jimmy died a hero, and he was a good person again. You gave us that, Mrs. Jamison. There's someone I want you to meet." The young woman went to the door of the hospital room, returning with a young boy standing beside of her. "This is Jamal. Say, hello, Jamal."

"Hello, Mrs. Jamison." Hope's heart broke as the boy smiled up at her with Jimmy's smile and bright eyes plastered across his face.

Jimmy's mother smiled down at her, tears in her eyes. "This one has my full attention and I have the time I never had for Jimmy, thanks to a job you gave me. He grew up with a big brother he could be proud of, a man to look up to. My baby is going to be a great man, Mrs. Jamison. You gave me that."

Hope felt the tears falling down her face. "I don't know what to say."

Jamal stepped forward handing her a piece of folded construction paper. Jimmy's mother's words explained as Hope stared at the folded paper. "Jamal saw pictures of you on television."

Hope's fingers trembled as she unfolded the paper. Inside the young boy had drawn a picture of his family. The mother in the picture stood holding the young boy's hand, while an angel, his brother Jimmy outfitted with wings and a shiny halo, smiled down from the sky above. And to the side, a figure with green eyes and beige skin stood smiling, looking up at Jimmy. It was Hope. When Hope raised her eyes from Jamal's picture the room was a blurry haze of flowers, and Jimmy's mother and Jamal were gone, but the peace they had brought with them remained.

"Okay, you ready?" Kate's bright smile peeked around the door to the hospital room where Hope, Eavenly, Sam, and Aunt Agatha sat waiting.

"Hurry up, Child, before I add another candle to my birthday cake," Agatha demanded.

Kate rushed into the room, giggling, followed by Eric, Ty, Mike, and Luke, all of whom were wearing fifties style white t-shirts and jeans, their hair greased back. Hope immediately started laughing, until the pain in her chest forced her to squelch her humor. "What are you guys supposed to be?" She wiped a tear from the corner of her eye, laughter threatening to erupt once again, when Eric stepped forward and the other three immediately broke into back up moves and doo-wop riffs, while Eric began to sing. Sam and Eavenly broke into laughter as their sons imitated moves from the Jackson Five and Eric emphasized the lines from the song that had the word "hoping" in them.

Eric moved to the bed, pulling Hope into a gentle embrace. They both looked up as Agatha's voice broke into the moment. "Well, Eavenly, that boy's just daft enough to be part of your family."

"And I wouldn't have it any other way, Agatha." Eavenly smiled at the image of her daughter who, even under the bandages and bruises, was once again beaming brightly.

Outside the door, Nurse Riley and Nurse Tiffany stepped back from the door. "I'm just glad Nurse White didn't see that. She would have thrown a fit."

"Who do you think did their choreography?" Nurse White said from behind them. She laughed at their stunned faces and walked away. She had always had a soft spot for Hope.

Kate draped a blanket over Eric, and carefully closed his laptop, setting it on the floor beside his chair. She turned to meet Hope's eyes. "We told him he could stay with any of us while you were cooped up in here, but he wouldn't hear of it. Two weeks, and he hasn't left you for longer than it would take for him to run over to Mama and Pops to take a shower or go out to grab you guys carry-out."

Hope sighed and smiled gently. "I think he still just wants to make sure I'm not going anywhere, you know?"

Kate moved around the room straightening items, letting Hopes' words sink in, before she sat on the hospital bed beside her sister, gently checking her wounds and changing the bandages. "Just because you get to go home tomorrow doesn't mean that you can overdo it. I want you to be careful, Hope. Get lots of rest while these mend."

Hope met her sister's concerned blue eyes. "I promise to take it easy. I'm going to have people waiting on me hand and foot."

"Let them."

Hope studied her sister for a moment longer. "What is it?"

Kate took a moment to put a strip of tape along the side of a bandage before sitting back to look at Hope. She had known they would eventually have this conversation, but still it felt soon and unexpected. "You were hurt...really bad."

"I know." Hope waited.

"No, I don't think you do. Hope, when I first cut into you and saw the wounds, and the amount of blood you had lost, and—well, I knew in that moment that there wasn't anything I could do to save you."

"But you did."

Kate shifted her gaze to Eric, who was still silently sleeping. "What would you say if I told you that while I operated on you, my hands were doing things my mind hadn't even thought to try?"

"I would say I'm glad." Hope smiled.

"I'm not joking, Hope." Kate's serious eyes held her younger sister in their gaze. "You're making it medically makes no sense. I wasn't in control of that."

"And you can't accept that?" Hope's voice was gentle.

"I am so happy that you're alive and that I was wrong, but I want to understand Hope. Why do some people make it against all odds, and why don't others—when they should?"

Hope hesitated. "You're asking me for answers I don't have."

"You've beat death back three times, Hope. How? What happened to you when you died? What did you see? How did you come back?"

"You're wanting me to tell you how to stop death? I don't know. Why are you asking me this, Kate?"

"Because, I don't know how I would have gone on if you hadn't survived, if you hadn't somehow found life inside of yourself where it shouldn't have been."

Hope took her sister's hand and gently pulled her toward her until their foreheads were softly touching. "That's easy. Things turn out the way they're meant to, and that's a beautiful thing—even if I had died on that table, because that's life. We have to find the beauty in life, Kate. How can we not?"

"What would the beauty have been in your dying, Hope?"

"That I had lived at all. Kate, you can't save everyone. Accept the miracles and, at the same time, accept that life happens. There aren't any guarantees."

"How can I accept that?"

"You have to have faith, and that's not something that can be given to you by someone else. You have to find it on your own."

"How?"

"If I were you, I would probably start with the fact that your hands were able to do things your head wasn't…that had to come from somewhere—didn't it?" Hope peered intently at her sister.

Kate smiled as if reassured. "You know…you're pretty wise to be the baby."

"Thanks…I think."

Kate gave Hope a hug before finishing with the bandages. She turned to the door, ready to go check on her other patients, when she stopped in surprise as she found Sherlock leaning against the doorjamb. "Aunt Sherlock…you startled me."

"I get that a lot, my dear." Sherlock gave a small laugh.

"Well, I have to go check on some patients, but I'm sure Hope will be glad for the company."

Sherlock took the empty seat next to Hope's bed. She glanced over at Eric, a warm smile spreading across her face. "Your young man seems to have fizzled out."

Hope returned Sherlock's smile. "I expected you to come by earlier."

"I was here during the operation. After that, the place tended to be a little crowded."

"Ah…I know how you hate crowds." Hope settled back more comfortably against the pillows.

"Well, actually, there was a little more to it." She glanced up to find Hope waiting for the rest. "I wasn't sure I was up to seeing you in the condition you were in. I was afraid it would be too painful."

"You were afraid to see me because I was injured? I can't imagine you being afraid of that, Sherlock." Hope's tone implied she wasn't buying Sherlock's reasoning.

"Well…" Sherlock paused. "Truthfully, I was concerned about my advice. You know I told you to use your gift, to fight back against the evil in your life, and then after the operation…Well, I talked with Joe. He's a nice man. He said that you took on the terrorist, taunting him. He said he saw your eyes before you were shot, and that you seemed to be expecting it."

Comprehension filled Hope's eyes. "You thought that opening myself up to evil, by using my gift, had somehow caused my coma?" Hope saw Sherlock's reluctant acknowledgment in the way she tilted her head. "Kate said the coma was my body's way of protecting me from all the trauma I had put it through. It had nothing to do with the gift. In fact, I wanted to tell you—when I let loose and really opened up—it's amazing Sherlock. The darkness is just on the surface. You have to let yourself see farther, and when you do, the beauty inside others is breathtaking."

"And that's the basis for your conversation with Kate just now?" Sherlock's expression was intense.

Hope smiled. "No. I thought maybe you and Chris had covered that in one of your conversations. The way she feels that things work out the way they're meant to be—you can't base that on anything that happens, or that you see."

"No?"

"No, Aunt Sherlock. Faith is the thing you find deep inside when you have absolutely no reason to believe in anything. I was finally able to see past the dark shadow of others mistakes and sins only *after* I believed that goodness was the center of most people and *after* I allowed myself to believe things would work out the way they were meant to. Even in a desperate man who was willing to burn down a house, there was a good part that wouldn't let him see another person murdered. And a man who would distribute drugs wouldn't let innocent people be destroyed by a terrorist. And my getting shot allowed everyone I care most about to live."

"And the terrorist?" Sherlock's voice remained cynical.

"He wasn't your average person. But if you think about it logically, if true evil can exist…wouldn't you also have to believe in true good?"

Sherlock studied her favorite niece. "Your sister was right, Hope. You are wise for your age."

"Let's not forget funny, beautiful, kind, brilliant, and a fast healer," Hope quipped.

"It would be impossible to let it slip my mind."

Hope laughed, and this time it didn't hurt nearly as much.

CHAPTER 59—FULL CIRCLE

Eric moved to push some things out of the way as Mike and Luke carried Hope into the living room to gently lay her on the couch. She laughed up at her brothers as they set her down. "Guys, I could have walked."

"None of that, remember. Kate said you have to take it easy," Mike grumbled.

Mama and Agatha rushed into the room carrying pillows and a blanket, which they began to attack with great enthusiasm to make them plump and fluffy as they helped Hope get situated. "There you go, Dear," Eavenly breathed. "All comfy, aren't you? Agatha and I have some of your favorites cookies baking in the oven."

Eavenly was interrupted by the sound of falling videos as Ty attempted to carry a stack of DVDs he had rented in the same arm he used to open the front door. He looked down at the dropped movies with disgust, "Damn sling."

"Language, Son," Sam admonished from behind Ty where he was carrying an armload of grocery bags. Hope's eyes widened in delight as she spied several containers of Ben and Jerry's ice cream on top of one of the bags.

"Let me help you, Ty." Eric helped Ty pick up the videos and stack them near the television.

"Oh, I just remembered something." Agatha rushed from the room.

"Agatha and Bob have agreed to stay here, too, Hope. You won't have to lift a finger until you're one hundred percent better." Eavenly beamed with the news.

Hope glanced at Eric, giving him a weak smile. "Uh, that's great Mama."

Sam shoved the groceries into Mike's arms and walked across the room, moving in between the others. He bent down to give Hope a quick kiss on the forehead. "You need anything, Sweetie, and you just let one of us know. Bob and I are working on a project outside. I'll be back in to check on you in just a little while." Hope couldn't blame her dad for retreating to a quieter area.

Agatha ran back into the room carrying a bell, which she was ringing gleefully. She sat it on the table within easy reach of Hope. "See, Hope, you need anything and you just ring this bell." She picked it up once more, ringing it loudly to demonstrate. She then turned to eye Mike who was struggling with the groceries. "Well, Child, come on. Let's put those things up before they melt all over the place."

"Hope, you wanna watch a suspense movie or a comedy?" Ty called from where he was placing DVDs into her DVD player.

Hope started to answer when her words were cut off by the entrance of a cheerful Kate, who was carrying boxes of bandages and all of Hope's pain medication and ointments. "Well, here's all you'll need to make sure she doesn't get infected. I'll take these into the kitchen and write down a schedule for when she should take her medicine and change her bandages and stuff."

"Thanks, Kate." Hope called to the retreating back of her sister.

"Darn, I'm missing a couple of videos." Ty went back out to his car to see if any videos had fallen down behind his seat.

Eric sat down on the couch beside Hope, leaning in to adjust her pillow. "Boy, everyone's being super-helpful."

Mama poked her head over Eric's shoulder. "You sure you're going to be okay in here, Hope? Wouldn't you rather be in your bed?"

"I'm tired of being in bed all of the time. Two weeks in the hospital was enough. At least this way I don't feel like such an invalid," Hope grumbled.

Eavenly turned to Eric. "Hope always has hated hospitals. When she was younger she had pneumonia, you talk about an irritable child. She had her reasons, though, such a sick little thing. That reminds me, have I ever told you how Hope got her name, Eric?"

"No, Mama Rhineholdt, I don't believe you have."

Eavenly began to relate her story, but was interrupted by the doorbell. Hope's face broke into a smile as Joe peeked his head around the corner. "Knock, knock. You up for visitors?"

"Definitely!" Hope squealed.

"Good." Joe stepped back outside opening the front door wide to allow Kyle to carry a bandaged, but otherwise happy-looking Scout into the living room. Kyle set Scout down on the couch beside Hope, where she giggled with delight as Scout began to lick her on the face, his tail thumping enthusiastically against her side. Hope's eyes welled with tears as she gently pulled the dog close to her in a hug. "Thank you for taking care of him, Kyle."

Kyle, looking embarrassed, shuffled his feet. "I, uh, have some toys and things I bought him still in the car. I'll go get them."

Hope shared a quick look with Joe as Kyle walked back outside. "How's he doing?"

Joe shrugged. "Okay. The job you decided to give him working at that community center you're planning has seemed to help."

"I thought the kids would be able to relate to someone who's had a few problems of his own. Besides, I need someone I can trust to help run it, and there's no way Kyle will ever give me a reason to not trust him again."

"Hope's going to name the center in memory of Jimmy. Two weeks in the hospital and she comes up with plans for the center and decides to write a book. She just can't handle being still." Eric smiled proudly at his wife.

"I'm surprised Hope's not finagled you into helping out, Joe. She already has all of her brothers and Kate lined up to teach some kind of course or another. Heck, Sam's going to give gardening advice, and I'm going to lead a book discussion group," Eavenly added.

Joe shuffled on his feet. "Well, Ma'am, Hope did mention something about a self-defense course she wanted me to help out with."

"That's great, Joe!" Eric clapped him on the back.

Joe, still reserved around others, tried to move the attention away from himself. "So, what's your book going to be about?"

Hope smiled at Joe, knowing full well that he was trying to change the topic. "I'm thinking of a book about family and maybe beagles."

Joe laughed. "You going to have any terrorists in this book?"

"Nope. It's going to be pretty tame in comparison. I'm thinking along the lines of a children's book," Hope admitted.

"Well, I'm sure it will be a best seller," Joe added, both Eavenly and Eric nodding their heads in agreement.

"Now, Joe, how can you possibly know that?" Hope argued, as her face reddened in modesty.

Joe grinned, "Easy. It would have to be because it's going to begin and end with Hope."

Eric laughed with the others. "Speaking of the book. I'm going to get you my old laptop and bring it in here. That way, anytime an idea hits, you'll be able to work on it right away."

"So, Joe. I hear you and my Aunt Sherlock spent some time together avoiding everyone else at the hospital." Hope regretted her timing of mentioning the pair's interest in each other as Ty walked back inside carrying a couple of DVDs while he held the door for Kyle who was carrying a dog bed full of rawhides, balls, and treats. Agatha, using some form of sonic-hearing poked her head around the corner, followed quickly by Mike and Kate. Joe shuffled his feet back and forth nervously, looking up hopefully at Sam and Bob's entrance, needing some kind of distraction. He cleared his throat, his eyes connecting with Hope's apologetic ones. He started to speak, but before he could, Eric's shaky voice interrupted from the hallway.

"Hope?" All eyes turned to stare at an ashen-faced Eric. He took wobbly steps forward until he was standing beside his wife. "Hope, why is the guest room across from our room now a nursery? The walls are covered with duckies and bunnies, and there's a crib."

Hope's startled eyes linked with her husband's, before she glared suspiciously at the rest of her family.

Eight accusing fingers flew through the air pointing at each other as their voices simultaneously cried out, "I thought *you* told them!"

"Mama?" Hope's voice was choked with emotion.

Eavenly smiled down at her youngest child. "My baby's going to have a baby. You're going to have a little girl, Hope."

"A baby?" Eric knelt shakily beside Hope, his eyes moving from her face to her belly where he gently placed his hand, stretching out his fingers to span her skin. "A baby." They shared a smile filled with joy.

Agatha interrupted, "Eavenly thinks you should name her Faith."

"As long as it's not Claire," A newly arrived Sherlock added from the doorway. Agatha, Eavenly, and Sherlock shared a look and shivered at the thought of such a possibility.

Hope raised moist eyes to stare into her husband's. "Faith?"

Eric felt his chest ache with the joy that flowed through him. He felt that any more happiness would make him explode. He took his other hand and reached around a now sleeping Scout to brush a lock of hair from his wife's face. "I think…" He took a deep breath to get the words out past the tears of happiness flooding his throat. He looked around at the loving faces of Hope's family…his family. Everyone leaned forward to hear his answer. He turned love-filled eyes back to his wife. "I think I could spend the rest of my life with Hope and Faith."

Agatha cooed, "If this was one of my romances, I would end it right there!"

Mama opened her mouth as if to argue, but for once the two were in agreement.

D. L. Roberts lives in Kentucky where she teaches reading. She has been a reading specialist for high school and middle school students and has worked diligently to pass along her love of books to the young. She spends much of her time traveling with her husband Estill and hanging out with her three beagles: Ace, Radar, and Scout. She is the youngest in a large family and has many nephews and nieces on whom she first tried out her story-telling prowess as fairy tales and bedtime stories. This book is the first in a series of novels that focuses on the fictional exploits of Hope Rhineholdt Jamison and her family. They are the "Little" series.

You can visit her website at:
http://dlroberts.org

LITTLE HOPE

www.ingramcontent.com/pod-product-compliance
Lightning Source LLC
Chambersburg PA
CBHW031217020726
47499CB00002B/619